THE KING'S BROTHER

THE EARLS OF MERCIA
BOOK ELEVEN

MJ PORTER

MJ PUBLISHING

Porter, M J
The King's Brother (The Earls of Mercia Book XI)

ISBN: 9781914332142 (ebook edition)
ISBN: 9781914332340 (paperback edition)
Cover image dreamstime_l_165741499
Cover design by MJ Porter

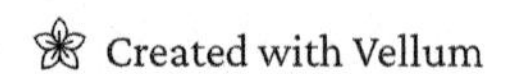

For all those who enjoy my tales of Mercia

CONTENTS

1

AD1045, SPRING, OXFORD, LEOFRIC

'The king has gifted more land to his wife,' Lady Godgifu hissed to Earl Leofric as she strode from one end of their private quarters to another. He winced to hear the fury in her words.

'She is his wife. It's to be expected. He does no more than gift her the lands his mother held when she was queen.'

'Is that right?' his wife rounded on him, coming to an abrupt halt and rearing up before him. 'It is merely the lands due to the queen, is it, just as the earls have lands due to them?' Once more, Leofric grimaced to hear the fury in his wife's words.

'It is right, yes, and I've told you of the king's reasons for making this marriage.'

'Yes, you did, and with them, you implied that it would be a union worth nothing to the bloody Godwine family, and yet now, they have more landed possessions to laud over us and the other earls and their families.'

Leofric watched his wife, noting her flushed cheeks and how her lips were pursed as she once more paced from one end of the room to the other. All could hear the sound of her shoes over the wooden floorboards. All would hear, but whether they knew what it meant remained to be seen.

'The king does us no disservice.'

'And neither does he reward us for our loyalty,' and here, his wife stabbed her chest forcefully with her finger. 'Our loyalty and our desire to keep England united.'

'The king must be seen to be caring towards his wife and any future children she must think to bear for him.'

'But there are to be no children,' Lady Godgifu all but shrieked, and now her face had bleached of all colour. 'You've assured me,' she almost spat.

'And the king assured me. My dear, really, you must understand that this game the king is playing isn't going to be concluded in a matter of months. He must be shown to be thinking of his wife's future.'

'Then he needs to do something to rein in that fat old Lady Gytha.'

Leofric recoiled at his wife's harsh words, yet they were true. No one would deny them. Lady Gytha and her many, many years of childbearing had ensured the Godwine clan was huge. The House of Leofric was the very opposite, although his son, Ælfgar, was doing his best, alongside his wife, to ensure that the lack of children born to his father and mother was rectified in the next generation. Already they were the parents to three sons and a daughter.

'What would you have me do?' Earl Leofric capitulated. 'The king can't cast his wife aside so soon after the marriage. Neither can he purposefully withhold lands normally in the possession of the woman who is queen. Should he even attempt to do so, Earl Godwine will raise a stink at the witan.'

'The king shouldn't be fearful of that man,' Godgifu sneered.

'I don't for one moment think he's fearful of Earl Godwine. As I said, to ensure the earl and his family don't suspect the king, he must do everything as he would, as though he knew there would be an heir at some point in the future.'

'I don't like it,' Lady Godgifu finally swept onto the chair beside Leofric's. 'I don't like it at all.'

'And why, this morning, of them all, has it riled so much?' Earl Leofric risked her wrath but knew the question needed asking.

'Lady Gytha,' Lady Godgifu began.

'What of Lady Gytha?' Leofric prodded when nothing further was forthcoming.

'She, she,' and here Lady Godgifu took a steadying breath and actually looked at her husband without the fury in her eyes. 'She's determined I'm only too aware of what her daughter has accomplished. She's ensured word reached me of the queen's latest acquisitions at Wantage and Lambourn.'

'And they came as a surprise to you?' Leofric felt safer now that Godgifu's flash of fury had dissipated.

'No, not really. I knew it would happen. It's just the way that terrible woman has of making sure all know about her family and its wealth. She has no shame.'

Leofric found a grin on his face and chuckled gently.

'Why should she be any different to her husband? He's shameless in his grasping ways. He shows no remorse for those he tramples along the way. He's almost without morals.'

'It's unseemly in a woman,' Godgifu harrumphed unhappily, and Leofric laughed all the more.

'So you wouldn't do it given half a chance?'

'I most certainly would not. There's no need to gloat about my landed interests to anyone. I'm the earl of Mercia's wife. I must have landed wealth, but I don't need to vaunt about it.' Godgifu settled herself, perching, Leofric couldn't help thinking, like a hen over her egg. Not that he dared say that out loud.

'She's proud of her daughter. Think how foolish she'll look when there's no child and her grandson isn't the next king of England.'

Lady Godgifu lapsed to silence, and then a slow grin spread over her face, returning to its normal pale colour. 'It'll be interesting to hear the excuses when they start in September,' she murmured. 'Provided the king hasn't played us for fools. I don't wish to have to contend with that family having a queen amongst them as well as a future king.'

Leofric nodded, pleased to have placated his wife, for all worry ran through his chest. The king had assured him that it was a means of curtailing the growing power of the House of Godwine, but Leofric couldn't help thinking that his king was a wily man. Maybe he was merely placating the House of Leofwine for now. He gnawed on his lip and worked to restore his composure. Only then he heard the loud pounding of approaching horses. He listened, tense, and then recognised the sound of his son calling a greeting to the men and women who'd known him since he was a child. For all Ælfgar's words sounded even, Leofric thought he could detect a thinly held thread of fury in his son's voice. What had happened now?

He wasn't alone with his worries either.

'What's riled our son?' his wife asked briskly. 'He's not himself. A mother knows.' Lady Godgifu spoke with satisfaction, and Leofric might have chuckled had he not been worried that his son's complaints would be the same as those of his wife.

Not that he had long to wait.

'Father. Mother,' his son strode into the great hall, his eyes raking in all around him, his cloak flung over his right shoulder, his hair wild from the speed of his passage on horseback.

'Son,' Lady Godgifu spoke first, her tone lighter than when she'd talked to Leofric.

'Son,' Leofric's response was a little sharper.

'Have you heard?' Ælfgar demanded, stomping to a stop in front of them both. His eyes flashed with fury, and Leofric could tell his son had been on the road for longer than a day, his face grizzled with fuzz that needed taming.

'What is it that we should have heard?' his wife asked quickly, her tone matching that of her son. Leofric looked between the pair of them. He'd like to think they were both doom-laden in their attitude, but he felt the same.

'Earl Sweyn.'

'What of him?'

'He has done more than just lay claim to his earldom. He's incited all against him within his earldom and worse against the damn Welsh. I fear there'll be war again.'

'He's a bloody fool,' Lady Godgifu was quick to expel. 'A hot-headed fool such as him should never have been trusted with such a delicately balanced earldom.' And yet, for all Leofric would have liked to argue with his wife, he found himself nodding along. She was right. For a very long time, Earl Hrani had held the southern midland shires with a careful hand. His death had left a hole, and Sweyn wasn't the man to fill it.

'And that's not all. While he incites war against some of the Welsh, I've also heard, and I believe the messenger who told me, that Sweyn has suggested an alliance with that bastard Gruffydd ap Llewelyn who killed my uncle, Eadwine.'

Leofric felt his air whistle through his tight lips at such a suggestion. He was aware there had been rumours that Sweyn Godwinesson might attack Gruffydd ap Rhydderch of Gwent , but to actually ally with Gruffydd ap Llewelyn of Powys. That was something else entirely.

'He would do no such thing?' Leofric bellowed, recalled to the horror of his brother's death all over again.

'He would, and I believe he has. He intends to cause constant warfare with the Welsh kingdoms.'

Ælfgar's face was white with fury as he paced. Leofric noted with no amusement how his actions so closely mirrored those of his mother's only moments ago.

'Peace with the Welsh kingdoms has been hard fought. We can't allow it to be dismantled on a child's whim,' Ælfgar's voice was mocking. Leofric felt his eyebrows rise. There was little to no difference in age between the two oldest sons of the Earl of Mercia and Wessex. It said a great deal for Ælfgar's current state of mind that he cast doubts on Sweyn's abilities. Not that he was wrong to do so.

Sweyn would not do his brother by marriage, the king, any great favours with his current actions.

'Not just hard fought but bought with the blood of Mercians,' Lady Godgifu ranted. Leofric shook his head. He couldn't help thinking that his remaining brother might arrive at any moment; Godwine Leofwinesson would be even more furious than Ælfgar.

'You're sure of this?' Leofric thought to check.

'I'm not sure, but I trust the man who told me the information. He's nothing to gain from lying about it. Nothing at all.'

'We must ensure this doesn't descend into full-blown war. We can't allow more Mercians to die because of the whim of the Wessex whelp,' venom burst from Ælfgar's lips, but Lady Godgifu looked no less furious.

'We'll send word to the king,' Ælfgar remonstrated.

'No, first we must know what you've been told is correct. I won't go running to the king on rumours and whispers. I won't allow Earl Sweyn to make a fool out of us. He's capable of doing that on his own, as he's shown more than once, especially during the mustering of the ship army last year. No, we must ride towards the borderlands and see if we can determine the truth of the rumours.'

'You think I lie?' Ælfgar hissed.

'I think no such thing. I believe the words, but I wish to see it with my own eyes. I need to know exactly what we must report to the king. I won't have Earl Godwine making light of his son's actions.'

'Do you believe he acts with his father's blessing?'

'I wouldn't be surprised,' Lady Godgifu announced firmly, her mind already made up.

'Did you come alone?' Leofric asked his son.

'Of course not. I have half of my household warriors with me.'

'Good, we can ride with them and take some of my men as well.'

So spoken, Leofric stood, ready to leave immediately.

'And what? I'm just to wait here for you to send me news?' his wife asked cattily.

'Do you wish to ride with us?' Leofric queried.

'Of course not,' his wife countered, affronted at the suggestion.

'Then, alas, you must wait here, and we'll return as soon as possible.'

'I don't like it,' Lady Godgifu continued.

'Then you could travel to visit with my wife in Oxford?' Ælfgar suggested.

'It will only take news longer to reach me then,' Godgifu harrumphed again. 'I'll wait here and hope we don't get overrun by whatever game Earl Sweyn is playing.'

'Either that, or you could travel to intersect the king? It would be good to know where he is should we need to contact him quickly.'

Lady Godgifu's expression darkened at the words, but then she nodded.

'Yes, I'll do that. If I'm with the king and his upstart wife, I'll be in the best position once we know the truth. And, it'll please me to watch Earl Godwine attempt to explain his son's actions to the king. I haven't witnessed that yet.' Leofric nodded, although he was unsure his wife should look quite so pleased with that prospect.

'Then, we're agreed. You'll travel towards Wessex with a quarter of our household warriors. I will take half with our son and me, and the remainder will be here should we need reinforcements. I hope we can avert war, but I'm far from convinced. We all know that Gruffydd ap Llewelyn is a tricky man. He might even be moving against my brother and nephews now.'

Silence fell amongst them momentarily, and claustrophobic worry settled over Leofric. Yet, he'd been to war many times before. He'd kept his earldom safe from the ravages of the Welsh and the Danish king's allies and King Harthacnut's over-zealous tax collectors.

'Then travel safely,' Leofric stood to embrace his wife. She was stoic beneath his hands, and when he stepped back, a glint of combined fear and delight was evident in the tightness of her lips.

'Should Earl Sweyn embarrass his father and king for a third time, he'll be unable to hold onto his position. And then, we can claim back the land that Sweyn took, and Ælfgar can govern it for the king, as he should be doing, anyway.'

'Let's not get ahead of ourselves,' Leofric cautioned, but he couldn't deny that he looked forward to the same. It was beyond time that something untimely befell the House of Godwine. How Earl Godwine had endured after the murder of King Edward's brother, Alfred, Leofric didn't know. Edward held his mother, Lady Emma, personally accountable and had banished her from court nearly two years ago. How, then, did Earl Godwine not only survive but also thrive? It made no sense. None at all, even if the king assured Leofric he was playing the grasping family for fools with his marriage to Queen Edith.

Striding towards the door, the sound of Ælfgar and his men outside, Leofric couldn't help but hope that whatever fighting there might be would be little more than skirmishes, and yet dangerous enough that the king would finally punish Earl Sweyn. Leofric knew that Sweyn's brother, Harold Godwinesson, had no love for Sweyn. If the queen also thought the same, then she must surely be able to convince her husband of his unsuitability. But then, there was also her father and mother to bolster Queen Edith's resolve.

Family before her husband, he could imagine the conversation even now.

2

LONDON, LADY GODGIFU

'My lady,' Lady Godgifu cursed softly under her breath but turned, adding a smile to her lips to face Queen Edith.

'My lady,' she curtseyed low, eyes lowered, not looking at the fresh-faced beauty of Edward's queen. There was no denying that Edith was a pretty thing. But, Godgifu thought there was a lot more to being a queen than being beautiful.

'Please rise,' the woman's voice was soft but firm. Lady Godgifu had heard that Edith was rapidly growing into her position as queen. Now, as she inclined her head in greeting and met Edith's eyes, Godgifu appreciated that those who told her as such didn't lie. The young woman was calm and collected, although, Godgifu noted gleefully that her waist showed no sign of swelling. Once more, she offered a soft prayer that the situation would continue.

'Is Lord Leofric with you, my lady?' Queen Edith asked, not coming any closer. Godgifu had disturbed her on the way into the king's great hall. She'd hoped to slip in unnoticed or as unnoticed as one of the earl's wives could be. The hum of conversation from inside the hall was audible and ideally, she wished to be there, listening to it, and not here, conversing with the queen, who would likely know nothing of her brother's current diversion into Wales.

'No, he has business in the earldom. I came to seek out the king and, of course, to purchase some goods from the market. I hear that there are spices here from beyond the kingdom of the Rus.'

Edith's lips pulled upwards at the words, and now she strode forward and spoke more conspiratorially to Godgifu. 'Indeed there are, and they taste most strange. Not even my husband's cooks have perfected the art of using them yet,' Edith offered as a caution. 'Come, sit with me in the king's hall. We'll shelter beside the fire. There's a chill from the River Thames today, and despite my thickest clothes, I've cold legs and feet.'

Lady Godgifu smiled at the invitation, for all it was the exact opposite of what she wanted. She did cast an eye over the young queen's clothes and realised she was dressed as though riding during a snowstorm. Lady Godgifu felt no cold, but then, she'd heard the same from other women her age. If anything, she felt too hot and would have welcomed removing her cloak and perhaps changing into a lighter dress. But she wasn't to have the opportunity.

'Your mother and father are well?' Lady Godgifu forced herself to make small talk with the queen as they settled before the blazing fire. Already, Godgifu could feel sweat beading down her back and shuffled slightly to move away from the direct blaze of the hearth.

'Yes, thank you for asking. I understand they're both very well, although I've not seen them for some time now.' Lady Godgifu was surprised to hear that. She would have expected Earl Godwine and his wife, Lady Gytha, never to be far from their daughter's side. Now that they had the bed of the king and not just his ear, Godgifu couldn't see why they'd suddenly be so distant.

'But, my brother, Harold, has spent much of that time with me, and when he's not here, he's been returning to Wessex and sending messengers between my parents and me.'

'Then he's a good brother to you,' Lady Godgifu murmured, her eyes raking in all those in attendance at the king's court. 'Where's the king?' she realised that should have been the first question.

'He's hunting or praying, one or the other. He's determined to take a day away from the court's business. And tomorrow, we'll both be attending the market. The king's keen to see what exotic gems and spices are to be found now that trade is so well established in London.'

'Then I'll see him tomorrow,' Lady Godgifu demurred, accepting a glass of warm wine from one of the queen's many attendants. Again, Lady Godgifu realised her family felt the absence of young women suited to keep the queen company. While she would sooner not blame herself for any lack of producing children, there were occasions when she was keenly aware of it, and now was one of those. A chattering horde of young women surrounded the queen, bright-eyed and hopeful, while Lady Godgifu's only son was already wed. Ælfgar's children, so far, three sons and only one daughter, were too young to begin the game of politics. Little Eadgyth was no more than a toddling baby. No, Lady Godgifu realised once more that her family was playing the waiting game. And they'd have to be patient unless Earl Sweyn entirely mistook his ambitions with the Welsh king and his own king.

'Why do you seek out the king? Is there some matter that concerns you in Mercia?' Queen Edith asked when she'd drunk her warmed wine and called for more. She did look cold, Lady Godgifu appreciated. Surely she should be busy making new wall tapestries to keep the wind at bay if she was so chilled. Perhaps she might even suggest it to the young woman. She remembered how difficult it was to learn to keep a house as a married woman. The problem would only intensify when the home to be furnished and maintained was that of the king. And if her mother wasn't in attendance, Queen Edith couldn't rely on her for assistance. Lady Godgifu shook her head in answer to the queen's question, even as she wondered why she felt sympathy for the young woman. That hadn't been her intention. Not at all.

'I'm unaware of problems in Mercia, my lady. Why, have you heard of something? I could have one of my men ride to inform my husband.' For the briefest moment, Queen Edith's face showed a flicker of unease, and Godgifu realised that whether or not Edith knew what her brother was up to, she was uneasy beneath her pleasant façade. She probably had every right to be.

'No, no, my lady,' Queen Edith countered too quickly, and Lady Godgifu narrowed her gaze as she eyed the younger woman. Someone so young and inexperienced wouldn't make a fool of her. If she had the guile of her father, and Godgifu couldn't see why the queen wouldn't, then she was right to be on her guard. All thoughts of sympathy immediately evaporated.

Only then Queen Edith leaned towards her, just at the moment that most of her young women friends were tittering as some of the sweaty household warriors marched into the hall from where they must have been exercising.

'My lady. It pains me to say this, but I don't trust my brother, Sweyn. He might be the oldest, but we all know he thinks himself a son of King Cnut and that my mother was little more than the Danish king's whore. I fear for Mercia under his command. He'll cause more problems. I don't know what they are yet.' Queen Edith's face flushed with unhappiness as she spoke, her cheeks attaining more colour than Lady Godgifu had seen in them since meeting the queen outside.

'I'm fearful as well,' Lady Godgifu conceded conspiratorially. 'He failed to take the estates my nephew held close to the borderlands with the Welsh, but now there are reports that he means to make war on Gruffydd ap Rhydderch. If that's not bad enough, he also means to ally with the Welsh king responsible for my brother by marriage's murder, Gruffydd ap Llewelyn.'

Queen Edith's eyes narrowed at the words, her thin lips trembling. Lady Godgifu berated herself. She hadn't meant to share such confidence with the queen.

'We must send word to the king,' the queen announced, a look of determination on her face.

'I'll seek him out if you inform me of where he is,' Lady Godgifu once more found herself taking pity on the young queen. It would be better if such intelligence came from the Mercian earl's wife rather than the king's wife and brother of the man accused of meddling in Mercia.

'I think I should speak to him,' the queen countered.

'You're wise to think as such, but perhaps it would be more politic for it to come from my lips. Surely, you'd rather I complained about your brother.' Lady Godgifu thought the queen might defiantly deny that logic, but Queen Edith thought for a while and then nodded. Before her women returned to inform her of the antics of the men, she gripped Lady Godgifu's hands.

'The king is at St Peter's, and then he means to hunt to the west of London. Take your household warriors and find him. If I hear of anything else in the meantime, I'll send the intelligence onward. The king will be displeased,' she continued an unhappy and furious expression on her face.

'He's fought worse than your brother,' Lady Godgifu felt compelled to console, only for the queen's face to bleach white again. Hastily, Lady Godgifu corrected her words. 'I didn't mean fight. I meant countered. The king is a wise man. He'll know how to contain your brother,' but that didn't assure the queen either, Godgifu could tell.

'The king's a wise man. But he's shown his weakness in granting Sweyn an earldom. It should have gone to Harold,' the queen countered; only then her women were back, and they both lapsed to silence. A short while later, Lady Godgifu stood, apologising for needing to leave. As she left the king's hall, Lady Godgifu looked back at the queen. She looked far from happy. In fact, and Lady Godgifu fought the urge to turn around and offer some more reassurance, Edith looked like her granddaughter, sitting on the wooden floor, wanting only to play with her toys while marooned in a world of men and weapons.

3
LEOFRIC

His horse powered over the road beneath his feet. He considered the number of occasions he'd ridden to England's western borders or, rather, those of Mercia and the Welsh kingdoms. It was many and often, and last time, it had been to remove Earl Sweyn from trying to claim his dead brother's holdings, now restored to the hands of his nephew. The time before that, it had been to counter the murder of his brother at the hands of the Welsh king. Now, he felt a similar rage, but not directed at the Welsh. Well, not wholly directed at the Welsh. There was room for the Welsh alongside his ire at Earl Sweyn's actions. The boy was childish and rash. He still couldn't understand why the king had acted in such a way. It was almost as though King Edward wanted discord between the Welsh, Earl Sweyn and the House of Leofwine.

The king was beyond half-witted if he thought it good to stir up more unrest and unease. Not for the first time, Leofric despaired of the new king's actions. It had been difficult when Harald had been king and doubly so when Harthacnut had claimed England's crown. Leofric had believed that Edward would bring some much-needed stability. And yet, the advancement of the House of Godwine was not in the best interests of anyone. Earl Godwine had long thought himself beyond reproach. Now, it seemed, his son felt the same. Not content with being chastised for problems during the first year of holding his earldom, or his thoughtless behaviour with the ship army, he was now misbehaving again. If the rumours were to be believed, and Leofric didn't doubt them.

'My lord,' Leofric turned and caught the eye of Ælfwine, his nephew. He'd not realised Ælfwine had joined their collection of warriors riding westwards. They'd travelled from Oxford to Akeman Street and then toward Gloucester, although they'd stopped for the night. Now, as they drew ever closer to Deerhurst, Leofric felt as though the path was one too well travelled throughout his life.

'Ælfwine, you're well?' Leofric demanded.

'Aye, my lord, thank you. I would feel less apprehensive if we could dismiss these rumours about Earl Sweyn.'

'We'll only know when we get to Hereford,' Leofric countered quickly. He could sense the dismay running amongst his household warriors and those of his son. None of these men wanted to believe the impossible that an alliance had been forged with the bastard King Gruffydd ap Llewelyn, but equally, none of them had any faith in Earl Sweyn that he wouldn't have done so.

'Perhaps there'll be news at Gloucester?' Ælfwine argued, 'Maybe we won't need to travel as far as Hereford.'

Leofric conceded the point with a wry smirk but believed it as little as the other mounted men. There were ten of them all together, including disloyal warriors, Godwulf, Winhus, Scirwold, Cena and Æthelheard. Leofric counted them now, aware that while his nephew Ælfwine was with them, his other nephew, Wulfstan, was not. He hoped the young man, or rather, not so young anymore, wasn't already embroiled in whatever was happening between Earl Sweyn and Gruffydd ap Llewelyn. Wulfstan had already been tested by Earl Sweyn once when Sweyn had tried to take his landholdings. He doubted Wulfstan would be so calm if Sweyn were meddling once more. Leofric resisted the urge to double the speed of his horse. He wanted answers, needed them. But he must be patient. They wouldn't arrive before he did, and killing his favourite horse, Oswald, in the process would do no one any favours.

'We'll arrive at Gloucester before nightfall,' Ælfgar called over his shoulder, where he led the collection of men. 'After we cross the bridge over the River Severn, we should arrive in Hereford the following day.' His words fluctuated with their passage, coming in fits and bursts, but Leofric understood them all the same.

'Tell me, Ælfwine, how's your mother?' Leofric had realised he'd not seen Lady Mildryth since the king's marriage to his young wife, Edith Godwinessdottir at the beginning of the year.

'She's still determined I should marry,' Ælfwine sounded martyred.

'Then you should just do it,' Leofric urged his nephew. 'Surely it would be better for you than all this constant complaining?'

'I don't like to give her the satisfaction,' Ælfwine grinned, but the smile slid from his face quickly. 'I fear she ails,' he admitted, the words seeming to wound him. 'I fear she's not as strong as she pretends to be.'

'Then a grandchild is what she needs,' Leofric quickly countered. He didn't like to think of Mildryth and her long years of loneliness since his brother's death. He wished she'd remarried and allowed herself to love again.

'That's what bloody Ælfgar advises,' Ælfwine muttered darkly, occasioning laughter from Leofric.

'Well, if that's what my son says, then you would do well to heed such advice. He's wise beyond his years.'

'Now you sound like my brother,' Ælfwine argued, but his voice was lighter.

'Just something to consider,' Leofric offered, his eyes on the road ahead as he took in the view surrounding them. The warmer weather was on the way. The winter had been long and cold once more, but now that Easter had been celebrated, there was the promise of good times ahead. They needed a good harvest this year.

They needed to be blessed with abundant crops and spring lambs, not the spectre of war with the Welsh. There had been too much hardship of late: poor harvests, bitter weather. Many had died.

Not that he wouldn't welcome the opportunity to exact more revenge for his brother's murder against the Welsh. And yet, good men had already lost their lives. No more needed to die. In fact, the exact opposite needed to happen. Perhaps, Leofric considered, his wife might be able to encourage the king to visit Gloucester once more. If he did so, the king would surely be able to control events so they didn't spiral out of control.

Unless, of course, this was what the king had intended all along? Or if not the king, then Earl Godwine? Did he mean to exact the most leverage possible over the king by causing a war with the Welsh that the House of Leofwine would be compelled to participate in, perhaps decimating their numbers in the process? Earl Godwine was a man who knew there was always more than one way to achieve an objective. His son was as devious as his father. Well, when he was prepared to admit that Godwine was his father, not King Cnut. Earl Sweyn had tried to force an admission from Lady Emma to that effect, but she'd been staunch in defence of her second husband.

Ahead, the settlement at Deerhurst came into view, and Leofric longed to enter it to find his father and seek his advice on what he should now do. But his father had been dead for many long years, and he was now responsible for his family's fortunes. Whatever happened, he would be accountable. If Earl Sweyn's imposition over the area hadn't been bad enough, to know that he could cause all of the delicate alliances, so long held, to fall was an unpalatable thought. No, he needed to find his resolve and contend with whatever issues there were, happy to know that he could do no more.

'Shall we stop?' his son called to him.

'No, continue to Gloucester. We'll stop there tonight and then move towards Hereford in the morning.' His son had no problem with the command, and Leofric felt a twinge of unhappiness that he didn't share his attachment to Deerhurst, but perhaps that was a good thing.

Having sought shelter with the portreeve of Gloucester and paid his respects at the mausoleum for the lady of Mercia, Æthelflæd, and her husband, the following day, they crested the wooden bridge that spanned the river at Gloucester. Leofric felt the vibrations of his horse's hooves over the wooden struts and tightened his hold on his horse's rein. They were still in Mercia but not the part of Mercia that owed its allegiance to the House of Leofwine. No, on this side of the River Severn, the House of Godwine held sway, which didn't feel right. Admittedly, he'd grown to accept the Danish earl who'd governed Hereford on behalf of King Cnut, but that was completely different. Earl Hrani had been a good Danish man. Earl Sweyn was not Danish or English. He was a mixture of the two, which meant he was unpredictable.

'Ride alert,' Leofric cautioned his fellow horsemen. 'We don't want to be ambushed or set upon by a rampaging group of the Welsh. If Earl Sweyn has riled them, they might just do so.'

His words occasioned a rustle of iron and metal. That no one assured him it was an overreaction was little consolation. They all feared war would come. They all knew that Earl Sweyn was capable of it. And certainly, the bloody Welsh were always keen for a battle.

And yet, the day continued calm, the sun offering a pleasant warmth through thick cloaks and black boots. Even the horses seemed to be enjoying the unexpected heat. But Leofric couldn't help but think it was all too pleasant. He feared being lulled into a false sense of safety, only to be overwhelmed by Earl Sweyn's men or even the Welsh. All the same, they arrived at Hereford without incident and were given admittance by those manning the gates as they prepared to close them at the end of another day.

'Where's the earl?' Ælfgar called to the guards.

The three men looked from one to another, only to shrug.

'He's not within, my lord,' the older of the men, white hair and a thick beard covering his lined face, directed this to Leofric. He inclined his head in thanks.

'When was he last here?'

'Two weeks ago, with a contingent of mounted warriors. They rode off into the hills, but we've received no word from them since.'

'You show no fear?'

'No, my lord, we don't. Our job is to guard the people of Hereford, whether the earl is in residence or not. As he's not here, we must perform our duties to even higher standards. Not that the earl would inform us of his intentions. The bishop might know. He can be found in his residence.'

'My thanks,' Leofric called to the men, riding on as he listened to the sound of the gates closing against the night. Hereford was too close to the Welsh borderlands to countenance allowing the gates to remain open all night. Not that the knowledge they were enclosed gave him any comfort. While they were inside Hereford, Earl Sweyn might be doing anything. They could even wake to find the Welsh king of Powts, Gruffydd ap Llewelyn, demanding entry on pain of death.

'This way,' he directed his horse along the roadway. Leofric was no stranger to Hereford. None of them was. Yet, they came without an invitation from the earl. People were hurrying about their business as the spring night drew in. The smell of meat cooking, the stink of horse shit, and the smoke from hearth fires filled the air.

'We know,' Ælfgar chuckled, but the sound was off, and Leofric noted how his son clamped his hand around the reins of his horse. He might have replaced his seax on his weapons belt, but the danger wasn't entirely past. Ælfgar wasn't the only one to feel it either. Leofric could sense menace in the air. Perhaps, he tried to console himself, the bishop would be able to allay his fears.

4

LADY GODGIFU

'My lord king,' she swept into a deep curtsey before the king as he emerged from inside St Peter's Church. The king, she noticed before dipping her head, looked in fine form, a healthy glow to his cheeks. As he bid her rise, she noticed that Edward wore a faint smile on his lips.

'Is your husband with you? Or your son?' Such warmth from the king made her question whether he could genuinely be complicit in what Earl Sweyn was attempting.

'No, my lord king, alas, he's not here with me but attending to urgent matters in Mercia.' A brief frown crossed the king's face, but he bid her walk beside him.

'I'm going hunting, and I imagine you don't wish to take part, but there must be something on your mind to bring you from the fastness of Mercia.'

'Indeed, my lord king,' she hastened to follow him as he strode towards where the horses were waiting. The smell of manure was ripe in the air, and she wrinkled her nose.

'For now, my lord king,' she spoke softly as soon as they were beside the king's horse. 'It's little more than rumours, but it concerns

Earl Sweyn.' This time, there was no denying the frown on the king's face, and it settled there, his attention now firmly on her.

'Rumours of what?'

'Of war with the Welsh and equally, an alliance with Gruffydd ap Llewelyn of the kingdom of Powys. I take it you were unaware.'

Lips suppressed in a tight line, the king shook his head. 'It seems that such reports are yet to make their way to my ears.' Lady Godgifu noted those in attendance on the king. Young Ralph was here, his nephew, as so often the case. And indeed, so was Beorn Estridsson. Both men were firmly in the king's good favour. And yet, other members of his extended family were more problematic, even when gifted with huge responsibility, as Earl Sweyn was.

'Are you sure of this?' the king pressed.

'No, but my husband and son are now riding to the borderlands. They mean to determine the truth.'

'Then, once they know what my earl is up to, ensure I'm made aware. I won't take kindly if this is little and nothing, but I'm sure you wouldn't come running to my side if you or your husband thought there was no truth to the rumours. Now, my lady, return to London, and my wife and I will speak with you again as soon as you know more.'

Lady Godgifu curtseyed again, ensuring her skirts were held away from the steaming pile of horse manure, biting her tongue to hold back her unhappy response. The king seemed to think this was an attempt to besmirch Earl Sweyn's name, despite the fact that Earl Sweyn had already gained himself a reputation for interfering in matters that didn't concern him, and the king had taken steps to bring him to heel.

King Edward's thoughts couldn't be further from the truth. Yes, they didn't want Sweyn in Hereford, but if he could learn to govern as an earl should, then they would be able to get along. Despite the fact the earldom should have passed to her son.

'And my lady,' the king called to her just before she turned aside.

'You have my sincere thanks for doing the honourable thing in coming to me first. Thank your husband.'

Now she stood a little taller, watching the king and his favoured allies as they rode towards the west. For a moment, she considered the wisdom of such an act. It was not truly that far to the Welsh borderland from London, not on a good day and with pleasant weather. If the Welsh had decided to rise up and attack the English king, they might be able to capture the king unawares. But no, she dismissed the notion. Earl Sweyn's urge for the kingship had been dealt with. Or at least, she hoped it had. Whether his father was Earl Godwine, or King Cnut, England needed the continuity of the ancient House of Wessex, not that of some upstart dynasty. The ravages of King Swein, his son, King Cnut, and his sons, Kings Harald and Harthacnut, had done more than enough damage to England. And yet, she couldn't deny the prospect of King Edward having no direct male heir to leave the kingdom to might just be storing problems for one day in the future. And on that day, it would impact her son and his children, for she believed she'd be long dead by then.

'My lady,' Lady Godgifu returned to the king's hall as dusk fell. She yawned and then closed her eyes briefly. She'd welcome somewhere to rest that wasn't the king's hall, but the king had commanded her to return to his wife, so she had little choice. She dipped her head to the guardsman and dismounted in the quiet courtyard. From close by, she could hear the chanting of the monks and knew she might have missed the chance to sate her rumbling stomach. As she left her horse with a stableboy, her eyes alighted on another party entering the king's palace, and her heart sank a little. Queen Edith had said her mother and father were in Wessex, but certainly, someone bearing the Wessex lord's insignia had been granted entry into the palace.

She hastened her steps, not wanting to be caught by the increasingly corpulent Earl Godwine or his wife, only for a much younger voice to call out to her.

'Lady Godgifu, good day to you.' She turned and affixed a smile to her face. Young Harold was a pleasant enough character. It was a pity he had such brothers and such a father as he did. Her son liked Harold. She trusted his judgement.

'Lord Harold, good day,' she greeted him, pausing in the act of trying to enter the king's hall.

'I've come to visit with my sister,' the younger man offered conversationally.

'I've been to speak with the king,' she countered quickly, hoping Harold wouldn't ask what it was all about. She detected no guile in him, and yet, it seemed impossible that Earl Sweyn could be acting without the implied support of his family.

'The king is here?'

'No, he's hunting to the west.'

'So, you've been hunting as well?' Harold asked, hand raised to indicate the encroaching night, as they gained entry into the long wooden hall adorned in tapestries, which Lady Godgifu noted, did seem to bellow with stray gusts of wind from all around. Perhaps Queen Edith was correct to complain about the cold.

'No, I've only been hunting the king,' Lady Godgifu demurred, shrugging her riding cloak free from her shoulders and allowing one of the servants to take it to be warmed. She shivered and strode towards the hearth fire, where Queen Edith already sat.

'Brother,' the young woman exclaimed, standing and knocking her embroidery to the ground excitedly. The queen ran to Harold Godwinesson and embraced him. Lady Godgifu could see the brother and sister were close. Certainly, Queen Edith had shown no such regard for Earl Sweyn.

'My queen,' Harold piped up with a wry smirk. Queen Edith gripped his hands and dragged Harold closer to the hearth, where one of her women had collected the abandoned embroidery and moved it to safety. Only then did Queen Edith seem to notice Lady Godgifu.

'My lady, you spoke to the king?' she enquired, her words deceptively light.

'I did, my lady. And he has bid me stay here until we know more.'

'Then we shall have entertainment, and I'll arrange a small feast while we're all together.'

'My lady, there's no need.'

'Of course, there is. I'm delighted that my brother is here and that you're here as well. It has been many months since I last spoke in person with my mother. I've missed her sage guidance, and you can stand in her stead for now.'

Lady Godgifu knew there was little point in arguing with the queen, so she gratefully took a seat close to the fire and peered into the recesses of the room. Few were attending upon the queen. She knew many of the king's favoured friends and allies had been accompanying the king on his hunt. There were just enough women present with the queen to make it seem like she'd not been abandoned by the king.

A giggle erupted amongst the young women assisting the queen as Edith bid her brother to sit beside her. With the jaundice of age, Lady Godgifu appraised the queen's brother. It couldn't be denied that he was a handsome man. She could see little of his father in him. Perhaps, then, Harold took after his mother's side of the family.

'I expected you last week,' the queen chastised her brother.

'I meant to come, but Father bid me stay by his side and assist him with some matters in Wessex.'

'And Mother and Father are well?' the queen queried, although her tone implied she expected no problems with them.

'Of course, as hale and hearty as ever. And you? You look well,' Harold teased her, and Lady Godgifu didn't miss his pointed look at her flat stomach.

'Very well, thank you,' Queen Edith's voice broke a little at that, a slight shake of her head to indicate she wasn't yet with child.

'Then,' and her brother adopted a carefree tone. 'We shall eat and drink liberally tonight and listen to the tales of the scops. It will be good to be away from Father and all his politicking.' Queen Edith chuckled at her brother's words, but the sound was forced. It seemed the queen longed to be carrying the king's child, and once more, Lady Godgifu found herself wondering why she felt any sympathy for the young woman, who, if the king's words to her husband were correct, would never carry the king's child.

Lady Godgifu knew what it was like to yearn for a child, and she, at least, had one son and now four grandchildren, to make up for her perceived lack. Queen Edith would never have that. Not for the first time, Lady Godgifu considered how her political requirements often contradicted what she hoped for the individuals involved. Perhaps the king was cruel for countenancing this marriage to Queen Edith. Maybe he was even more calculating than those who'd ruled before him.

5

HEREFORD, LEOFRIC

'My lord Leofric,' Bishop Æthelstan called as Leofric neared him, close to the hearth fire. He shivered inside his cloak and cast his gaze over the blind bishop. Æthelstan had lived through much. The loss of sight had led to him having another to assist him, but it seemed that Tremerig wasn't in attendance upon the bishop that day.

'My lord Æthelstan,' Leofric approached the bishop and bowed low, for all the blind man couldn't see it. Still, there was much to be said for being respectful. A monk stood to the bishop's right shoulder and bent to whisper into the man's ear.

'So, it seems you come seeking the truth of rumours regarding the erstwhile young earl?' For all Æthelstan couldn't see, he knew much, and Leofric felt a smirk playing on his lips. The lack of vision hadn't stopped Bishop Æthelstan from knowing everything about his diocese.

'Indeed, we have, my lord. My son and a handful of my household warriors. We don't ride to seek war, but only the truth.'

'Indeed, then sit, and we'll talk. Food will be served to your men, and you may spend the night within these walls. I can't see that Earl Sweyn will object to such common courtesy.' The bishop spoke with the assurance of his years in the post. Bishop Æthelstan had been bishop since long before Sweyn had even been born.

'My thanks,' Leofric said, gesturing for Ælfgar to join him as he settled close to the bishop. Leofric eyed the monk. He was an older man. His tonsure was almost irrelevant now, with only a wisp of hair here and there visible. No doubt, it was easier for him now that his hair had mostly all fallen out. The bishop was the exact opposite, with a full head of snowy-white hair. Leofric could see where he must have recently been shaved, a small thicket of hair stubbornly clinging on close to his left ear.

'Tell me, what does the king make of Earl Sweyn's statement that he's the son of Cnut?'

Leofric shook his head, even as he took the offered cup of warmed wine from one of the servants with a smile of thanks.

'The king pays no attention to Earl Sweyn's assertion. It would, of necessity, embarrass his wife and her family should it prove true. Lady Emma has tried to discourage him.'

'Indeed, yes. Lady Gytha was an attractive woman when she was younger. I remember that well from before I lost my sight. Perhaps she did open her legs to the young Cnut. Perhaps she didn't. Only our Lord God knows, and he isn't revealing that truth anytime soon, and neither, it seems, is Lady Gytha or her possibly cuckolded husband.'

Leofric opened his mouth to reply but then snapped it shut again. Earl Sweyn was making no friends in Hereford if even the bishop was prepared to discuss the scurrilous rumours so openly.

'I do hope the king pays more attention to Earl Sweyn's activities with the Welsh than he does to the boy's parentage.' The disdain with which Bishop Æthelstan spoke surprised Leofric. Earl Sweyn had done more than ruffle a few feathers.

'And that is why we're here. To determine the extent of the earl's interactions with the Welsh. Tell me, what do you know of it?'

'As it happens, very little until this morning, and now I know too much. He is determined to ally with that bastard Gruffydd ap Llewelyn. Earl Sweyn has announced that there can only be peace with the

Welsh if an accord is reached. As you can imagine, that's riled many of the people who live hereabouts. I wouldn't be surprised if there were unrest because of this accord. Earl Sweyn might think to win peace with the Welsh, but he'll face nothing but war from the Mercians.'

Leofric nodded, and then remembering the bishop couldn't see, he grunted instead. The news was unwelcome. Very unwelcome. It also revealed once more that Bishop Æthelstan was no fool.

'Many more families than yours lost people in the bloody wars with Gruffydd.'

'Indeed, my lord. I'm very aware of that. And where is he now? Earl Sweyn?'

'That, I don't know. I fear the young half-wit has made an accord with Gruffydd without heeding the instructions of his king. Earl Sweyn has no regard for authority. He does what he wants and when he wants it.'

Leofric grunted again and then sipped his warm wine, welcoming the bloom of heat on his lips. He was only too aware of how problematic Earl Sweyn could be. He cared nothing for law, the written word, or even the ability to fight.

'When was he last at Hereford?' Leofric asked. The monk answered as Bishop Æthelstan was carefully drinking as well, the steam from his wine obscuring his face briefly.

'No more than ten days ago. He didn't tell us where he was going or why he was here. But he had over thirty of his household warriors with him.'

Beside him, Ælfgar shuffled.

'A small force to make war?' he countered, although his tone was bleak.

'To make war, yes, but not to make peace,' the bishop grumbled, cupping his warm beaker between his lined hands. 'Enough to prove he has men that are his to command. Enough to prove that he's held in high regard by the king of England and can ride roughshod over any pre-existing accord between the Mercians and the Welsh of Powys.'

'Do you fear coming war or the coming peace?' Leofric interjected.

'I fear there'll be no peace, no matter what the young fool believes. There's not meant to be peace between the kingdom of England and those of the Welsh kingdoms. There can only ever be an uneasy truce, and Earl Sweyn doesn't understand that. He's acting as though he were the king, and that, more than anything, should worry King Edward enough to send more than just a handful of loyal Mercians to uncover the truth.'

'Have you sent word to the king?'

'And what could I say? Like you, I hear rumours and have my suspicions. But Tremerig is in awe of the young lord. He sees that only good can come from this and hasn't heeded my instructions that the king must be aware of my fears.'

'Then it's good that my son and I have ventured to Hereford. I'll send word to the king. I should like to be able to inform him of something more substantial as well,' Leofric murmured, not wishing to upset the agitated bishop more.

'Then ride to the west in the morning. Ride westward and see what you can determine from the men and women of the borderlands. The Mercians will speak to you. The Welsh might well speak to you as well. Find the damn boy, and then inform the king that this area has seen enough war and destruction. We want no more, and he must bring that boy to account.'

The bitterness of Bishop Æthelstan's words sent a shiver of unease along Leofric's spine. The bishop hated Earl Sweyn, perhaps even more than Leofric and his son did. Not for the first time, he considered the wisdom of the king's actions in appointing Sweyn to the earldom once held by Hrani. Hrani had died more Mercian than Danish. Yet Sweyn was determined to be more Danish than Mercian. It wouldn't end well. Leofric knew that. That the bishop knew it as well reinforced his surety of the matter.

Earl Sweyn would rain death and destruction on the borderlands between the Welsh and the Mercians, and Leofric was sure that as much as he feared what might happen, he wouldn't be alone with his worries. The king had enough battles on his hands. He didn't need another one.

6

LONDON, LADY GODGIFU

'My lady Godgifu,' the pleasant voice interrupted her thoughts as she hurried back towards the king's hall in London. The wind was bitter, and she wanted nothing more than to find a warm hearth and drink to drive away the chill.

'Lord Harold,' she acknowledged him as he hastened to join her.

'I would speak with you,' the young man announced.

'Inside then. It's too cold here.' The night had been bitter. Her journey to hear morning Mass even more bitter, and now she hobbled rather than walked, her toes numbed by the unexpected chill of the day.

'Of course, my lady.' Harold was immediately courteous, and Godgifu allowed herself to consider where Harold had learned his manners from. Not his father. That was a certainty.

Lady Godgifu rushed to the hearth and, finding the king's hall unexpectedly empty, felt no compunction in sitting almost within the burning logs of the fire. She shivered. Edith was right. It was cold inside the king's hall, and then turned to face Harold once more. His face was white with cold, yet his eyes were dancing with the flames of the fire.

Perhaps without even realising, he beckoned a servant close and ordered warmed wine. Lady Godgifu wondered if Lord Harold was aware he was so imperious. He was as comfortable playing the lord as the king was. Perhaps, she mused, more so.

'I've heard some worrying rumours regarding my brother,' Lord Harold began, showing no hesitation in speaking against his older brother. 'I wish you to be assured that my sister, the queen, and myself have no knowledge of Earl Sweyn's intentions. If we knew that he planned to invade the Welsh kingdoms or ally with King Gruffydd ap Llewelyn of Powys, we'd have informed the king and your family. His actions are irresponsible.' Blazing fury swept through Lord Harold's words, so much so that they warmed her more than the hearth flames.

'Then it seems,' and she quirked a smile. 'That he's caught us all unawares.'

'Indeed, my lady. And I can imagine how furious your entire family is.'

'Yes, my lord Harold. Should the rumours be proven correct, it'll be difficult to contain certain members of my family. My brother by marriage, my sister by marriage, and of course, my husband. The Welsh of Powys under Gruffydd ap Llewelyn killed Lord Eadwine. His death is still grievously felt.'

Lord Harold bowed his head low as she spoke, his shoulders sagging like he might sob with grief alongside her husband's family. Only now did she consider his intentions. Did he mean to distance himself from his brother, or was this merely an attempt to win over the support of the House of Leofwine? She'd thought him genuine, but now she wasn't so sure. His act was a little too exaggerated.

'I assure you my sister will do all she can to counter my brother's actions. Our king is most enamoured of my sister. He'll do everything to give her ease and please her.' Harold brought his head upwards and met her gaze evenly. Only then did she notice his flagrant ambitions. Perhaps, she realised, her family weren't alone in decrying Earl Sweyn's advancement. It was evident that Harold thought he should have an earldom as well. His ambition almost took her breath away. Why, then, had King Edward advanced Sweyn and not the brother who seemed closest to his wife? Perhaps the king was playing even more games than she'd realised with the family of Godwine. The marriage was a mockery. Was making Sweyn an earl the same?

King Edward was a man who lacked a firm power base, but of course, one way to gain one was to dismantle those of others and then, by being the one left standing, to be most powerful.

'Then you have my thanks, Lord Harold. I hope to hear from my husband soon, and that information will be shared with the king and the rest of the earls and holy men.'

'My thanks, my lady. I'll leave you.' And so spoken, he departed in a flurry of his fur-lined cloak, and Lady Godgifu found herself almost laughing. There was much more at stake than just Earl Sweyn's actions, yet she had no time to think further, for at that moment, a man she knew only too well strode into the king's hall.

'Aunt,' It was Ælfwine who spoke. His face was flushed from riding and the bitter wind blowing along the River Thames, carrying the bite of salt. She made to stand but then stayed seated. It was too cold to move away from the hearth. Ælfwine moved close to her, his hands extended towards the leaping flames.

'Ælfwine, you're well?' She demanded quickly.

'We're all well, my lady. Well, as well as we can be. Earl Sweyn has disappeared. We went to Hereford, but he's not been sighted. Bishop Æthelstan believes he's gone to make an alliance with that bastard Gruffydd ap Llewelyn. I must inform the king. Is he here?'

Lady Godgifu stood, startled to hear her worst possible imaginings coming to fruition.

'I'll have the king summoned,' she commented quickly, looking for a senior member of the king's serving staff. A bald man approached her as though sensing her need.

'The king and his wife have left London. They've travelled to Kingston upon Thames this morning.'

Lady Godgifu barely let the man finish speaking before she was striding towards the door, Ælfwine scampering after her, the cold forgotten about as he blood ran too hot. He'd not removed his cloak, and she quickly called for hers, hardly even considering how numb she had been.

It wasn't far to Kingston upon Thames, yet she couldn't help feeling frustrated that the king had left London without informing her. He knew of the potential problems in Mercia. Why had he travelled away from the place where the news would be sent? He'd told her to wait, but he hadn't done so. They must have left while she was attending Mass.

Outside, Ælfwine's horse had barely been divested of its saddle before it was replaced. She looked around, noting that her maid had followed her from the hearth, yet she turned to her.

'Remain behind. We won't be long, and you don't need to get benumbed.' Her maid bobbed quickly, yet a look of relief covered her face. The men of the household troop who'd accompanied Ælfwine on his journey tumbled from the king's hall, and Lady Godgifu didn't send them back. They were more used to travelling quickly in the saddle.

While impatience warred inside her, she allowed Ælfwine to lead the way through London, the streets almost deserted with the chill wind, towards the bridge that crested the River Thames. Out on the bridge, the wind was even more bitter. As she licked her cold, chapped lips, she tasted the salt of the distant ocean. She huddled into her cloak, wishing the early spring weather hadn't deserted them so quickly to plunge them back into near winter. She'd been too hot when she'd first arrived. The same could no longer be said.

The sound of the horses' hooves was overly loud, and the shriek of gulls came to her with each gust, as did the smell of the River Thames. It wasn't pleasant on a good day, and today it seemed as though every fish net and crab pot had been brought ashore, and now the stink of the river was everywhere. Almost coughing on the aroma, she was pleased to emerge on the far side of the River Thames and urge her horse towards Kingston upon Thames. There had been a time when the kings of England had undergone their coronation at Kingston upon Thames. But now that the English kings were more English than Wessex, London was often the chosen location.

'Ælfwine, tell me more,' she caught him and called across to him. Ælfwine reined in his mount a little.

'My uncle was eager that you knew all that he did. Bishop Æthelstan is, as you know, blind and reliant on another for much of the day-to-day affairs of the bishopric. But, this Tremerig seems to think more of Earl Sweyn than Bishop Æthelstan.'

'And so Earl Sweyn labours with the tacit acceptance of the bishopric?'

'That's the way the bishop spoke, yes. He was displeased, to say the least.'

'A man lacking his sight doesn't lack his wit,' Lady Godgifu snapped. She felt her anger blazing once more. Earl Sweyn was finding men to support him, making the situation even more complex. She didn't believe the men were loyal Mercians. No. No doubt Earl Sweyn was bringing disaffected men from elsewhere in England, specifically Wessex men, she wouldn't be surprised to find.

'My lady,' the caution in Ælfwine's voice broke through her furious thoughts, and she looked ahead. Another group of riders made haste towards her, and she cringed, recognising Earl Godwine at the head of the horses. It was impossible not to know the man. For decades he'd been at the forefront of English politics, whether under a Danish king or an English one. And yet?

'Why does he head for London if his daughter and the king are at Kingston Upon Thames?'

'It would seem he doesn't know that,' Ælfwine cautioned.

'Then I should like him not to know, although that seems difficult. He knows I'm not often found south of the River Thames.'

'Indeed, my lady. Let's see if he wishes to speak with us.'

'I'm sure that his unfailing curiosity will demand that he stops to ask me the nature of my journey.'

Resolving herself to being forced to speak with Earl Godwine, Lady Godgifu watched him approach almost through narrowed eyes. Would he stop? Wouldn't he stop? Of course, there was never really any doubt that he would.

'My lady Godgifu,' his bluff voice rang out as soon as they were close enough for his words to be heard.

'My lord Godwine. An unpleasant day to see you on the road,' she murmured. She didn't like the man, not at all. He was filled with a sense of his own self-importance. And honestly, she did find it strange to believe he was the father of Queen Edith.

'Indeed, yes, but business is business. And I seek out the king, and the queen, of course.' A self-satisfied smirk touched his lips, but Lady Godgifu held herself firm. As much as she'd like to see that look wiped from his face when he was informed the king and queen weren't to be found in London, she stopped herself.

'Then, I wish you a good day,' she lifted the reins and was just about to knee her horse past the men of Earl Godwine's guards, only the earl spoke.

'And you, my lady? Why are you about on such a biting day?'

'I have business for my husband, the earl.'

'That takes you into my earldom?' This interested the earl too much, and Lady Godgifu realised she should have said something else. Perhaps she could have murmured something about Wilton or Nunnaminster. It was expected that women seeking the solace of the nuns in their nunneries weren't to be too closely questioned.

'Indeed, my lord. But there's nothing to concern yourself about.' This time, she purposefully encouraged her horse to a quick canter, not wanting to discuss anything further with the Earl of Wessex. Unless he was an exceptionally skilled liar, it was evident that Earl Godwine was unaware of his son's current activities in Mercia.

She continued on her journey without waiting for the rest of her entourage to catch up. For a while, she feared that Earl Godwine would consider following her, demanding to know more. But the only horses' hooves that raced to join her were those of Ælfwine and the members of her husband's household warriors.

'What did he make of that?' she called to Ælfwine, having first glanced over her shoulder to ensure that Earl Godwine had sent no one to follow them.

'I don't think he knew what to make of that, my lady,' her nephew chuckled, malice in the sound. He'd enjoyed the little exchange. Lady Godgifu hoped she didn't regret her refusal to inform Earl Godwine of the location of his daughter and her husband. Not that she had any intention of recalling Earl Godwine. No, she needed to seek out the king and his wife quickly. And indeed, it would be better if it was only the king she saw. While Queen Edith professed to have no love for her oldest brother, it was entirely possible that she did.

7

WEST OF HEREFORD, LEOFRIC

It was an uncomfortable reminder of his brother's murder at the hands of the Welsh king, Gruffydd ap Llewelyn of Powys, but Leofric had no intention of reversing his decision to venture into the borderlands. Whatever Earl Sweyn was playing at, someone with a more reasoned head on their shoulders needed to be there to bring it to a close. Not that he wanted to start a war with Gruffydd ap Llewelyn, but he would if there was no other way. The Mercians had no love for the Welsh king, he was far from alone in that respect.

West of Hereford, the landscape quickly climbed to small hills and hillocks. They were far from ideal, but at least atop each hill, it was possible to scout the terrain. Not that anything seemed out of place. As so often the case, the sky was leaden, rain falling in sporadic bursts, visible as the clouds moved across the grey skyline. Never one to think the weather was against him, Leofric hunkered into his cloak and tried to recall the gentle warmth that had coated the land only seven days ago, bringing the promise of a warm summer. Somehow, that heat had been blown away or had arrived too early. Either way, it felt like winter again, and his body wasn't appreciating the cold that attacked him, despite his warm horse and thick cloak.

'My lord, I think we should head this way?' It was Ælfgar who called to him, his finger pointing slightly southwards. Leofric considered if his son had forgotten he spoke to his father or if he just named him as such to be like the rest of the men.

'Lead on, Ælfgar,' he toyed with naming him as his son but chose not to. If his son called him lord, he'd be respectful in return. He imagined the seriousness of the situation they found themselves in was the reason for Ælfgar's formality.

His horse, Oswald, easily took his commands, and the journey down the small hill was easy on the horse's hooves because there was no firm path, only churned horse hooves.

'How many do you think travelled this way before?' Earl Leofric called to the men at large. He had the uncomfortable feeling that they were far too late to prevent whatever Earl Sweyn had planned. These marks could be from the collection of warriors who'd escorted Sweyn. Or they could be from the Welsh contingent who'd met him.

'No more than fifty,' came the less than reassuring reply from the rear of the line. The bishop had said thirty, but it was possible more had joined them.

'That's what I thought,' Earl Leofric countered. It shouldn't matter that Earl Sweyn's force was more significant than his. It really shouldn't come to a fight, yet this was Earl Sweyn. He was far from a reasonable individual.

They rode on. The daylight never seemed to change, no matter how violently it rained or didn't. Not for the first time, Earl Leofric threw back the hood of his cloak, content that the rain had abated for now. He peered all around him from the vantage point of yet another hillside. It was just about impossible to find a single route that would lead them where they wanted to go.

'Anything?' he called to Ælfgar, up ahead.

'Yes, I think so,' Ælfgar's reply was tight, his tension easy to hear. 'I can see a settlement ahead, and an unusually large number of horses nearby. I can't see how one farmer could claim so many, not here, in the disputed borderlands. The Welsh or Earl Sweyn would surely have taken them as their own.'

'So a meeting of some sort. It's just a matter of whether it's our meeting.' But Earl Leofric somehow knew it would be. They were far enough from Hereford now that whether they remained on Mercian or Welsh land would be very much open to debate. He rode to the front of his drenched warriors, encouraging Oswald onward as he carefully picked a path down another muddy slope.

'We need to be careful,' he cautioned his son. One look at Ælfgar's face, and he could see that Ælfgar was furious at having their fears confirmed.

'I know how to behave around the bloody arse,' Ælfgar countered too aggressively. He faced his father and attempted a smile. 'I won't start a war if that's what you mean,' Ælfgar tried in a more even tone.

'Then you have my thanks for that,' Earl Leofric responded, trying to ignore the tightness in his shoulders. Earl Sweyn Godwinesson was a liability. And while it should be nothing to do with him or his family, it couldn't be denied that it just was. Even when the Danish jarls had commanded much of western Mercia, Leofric knew that his father had trusted them much more than he now trusted Earl Sweyn. The man was a hot-headed fool. The king shouldn't have gifted an earldom to him. There was no denying that. Or rather, if he was adamant that Sweyn should become an earl, he should have sent him to somewhere without the potential for war to descend upon Mercia and England as a whole from the western kingdoms of the Welsh kings.

Now they'd have to deal with the consequences.

'Who are you?' An angry cry from inside the settlement, surrounded by a small raised dirt wall, and its accompanying ditch, was far from friendly as they rode close to it.

'I'm Earl Leofric. Where's Earl Sweyn?'

'What?' the cry ended on a squeak, and a furtive glance towards the low-roofed building, smoke streaming through the smoke hole, told Leofric all he needed to know. He sighed and then settled himself in his saddle.

'Go and get Earl Sweyn on the king of England's commands.' Leofric didn't hesitate to use the king's name. Despite it all, he knew that King Edward would want to know just what Earl Sweyn was playing at.

For a long moment, while the scruffy-haired warrior, armed with good iron and an even better byrnie, stood his ground, Leofric thought he'd refuse. Leofric could almost hear the man's thoughts. Who was it better to aggravate, Earl Sweyn, Earl Leofric or King Edward? At last sense prevailed with him, Leofric decided, as the man turned and entered the building.

Leofric pretended not to listen to the outraged cry of Earl Sweyn when summoned outside. He also pretended not to hear the oaths and complaints that burst forth from his mouth and were mirrored by others inside. In fact, by the time Earl Sweyn, rolling from side to side as he walked, struggling to stay upright, made an appearance, Leofric was surprised by the number of things he'd have to forget ever having heard if that was even possible.

Certainly, Earl Sweyn was either a bigger arse than he thought, or he intended to cause as much offence as possible. It was probably both, Leofric admitted.

'My lord Leofric, and his pestilent son, Lord Ælfgar. What brings you to this out-of-the-way place? Seeking some smooth Welsh flesh to ride?' Earl Sweyn spat. His eyes were red-rimmed, his beard untidy and in need of a good shave, and Leofric didn't need to get any closer to know that he stank as well, from ale, mead and wine.

'We seek you, my lord,' Leofric held onto his temper. Behind Sweyn, more and more men had rolled outside to escort their lord. There were more than a few faces that Leofric knew well. He couldn't admit to any surprise that they were with Sweyn.

'And you've found me,' Earl Sweyn attempted to bow low but wobbled so much two of his allies were forced to grab his arms to keep him upright.

'Why are you here?' Leofric ignored his performance while his fellows chuckled at his antics in a way only the very drunk could do. Earl Sweyn seemed to have won these men over by playing to his audience.

'I'm here seeking some soft Welsh flesh,' the young lord countered a hint of heat to his words.

'But I see no Welsh flesh,' Ælfgar retorted. None of his men had dismounted. It gave them a distinct advantage, almost able to see over the roof of the building and certainly able to see into the far distance. There was no sight of others coming to join Earl Sweyn's party, for that was what it seemed to be. Perhaps the rumours of Earl Sweyn and King Gruffydd ap Llewelyn were simply that? Rumours.

'The Welsh flesh will be here by nightfall. Ah, now I see you were after the same. All men seek something a little more exotic in time. Even the most loyal of husbands,' Earl Sweyn leered at Leofric and his son, and Leofric gripped Oswald's reins even tighter. 'If you wait, I'm sure you can have some,' Sweyn continued. Leofric kept his temper, but only just.

'Would it not have been more suitable for you to have your Welsh flesh sent to you at Hereford?' Leofric felt as though he spoke to a small child.

'Ah,' and Sweyn wagged his finger in front of his face, and Leofric sighed unhappily as the half-foxed's focus ended on his finger, causing him to go cross-eyed. 'Then that would have prevented the other part of the Welsh surprise,' Sweyn giggled, and now Leofric reached over and prevented Ælfgar from dismounting.

'What's the rest of the surprise?' This was like pulling teeth.

'The king is coming as well, along with the Welsh flesh. In fact,' and now Sweyn stood abruptly, as though sober, and Leofric tried not to allow his lip to curl. Earl Sweyn was play acting and knew only too well what he was about.

'You need to mount up and take yourself and your allies from this place,' Leofric ordered the earl. Now it was Sweyn who would have benefitted from someone holding him back, for he leapt over the still-closed gateway and thundered towards Leofric. Oswald reared backwards, and Leofric was forced to hold firm with his thighs and hands to prevent falling on his arse in the mud-churned earth.

Sweyn's laughter thundered through his head, the sound discordant and filled with mocking.

'You've no right to order me to anything,' Sweyn croaked. 'I'm the earl of Herefordshire. The king has given me his permission to govern as I deem fit. And I see fit to reach an accord with King Gruffydd ap Llewelyn.'

'The king wants no such thing as peace with the Welsh,' Ælfgar roared.

'The king will accept this once it's done, and I would suggest, Earl Leofric, that you ride from this place before King Gruffydd ap Llewelyn arrives and finishes what he began six years ago. I'm sure he'd like to take a few more lives in recompense for your family's aggression throughout the years.'

This time, it wasn't just Ælfgar who needed restraining. Leofric bent his head low enough to be level with Earl Sweyn's, now that Oswald was once more under control. While he might look sober, he smelled as though he'd been bathing in mead and ale.

'If you consort with an enemy of England, then the king will deem you an enemy, and you'll lose all you have.' Leofric menaced, wanting nothing more than to punch the upstart young man in the face.

'And the king has the military might to do that, does he? That old man will do nothing. When I present it to him as complete, he'll merely accept it.'

'He won't, Earl Sweyn. The king is our ruler. He has an ultimate say. There are no earls who call for peace with the Welsh other than you. And your one voice won't sway the king.'

'My father will speak for me,' Sweyn countered, his red-rimmed eyes furious again. He was like a child who'd been berated. 'The queen will speak for me.'

'My lord,' Winhus called for his attention before he could reply.

Eyes narrowed in a thin stream of bright sunlight, he saw what he didn't want to see. A mounted band of warriors coming towards him.

'The queen will not speak for you. And your father might well lose his earldom as well as punishment for this. Your sister will be a queen with no family.'

'Ah well,' Sweyn shrugged, also alerted to who was coming. 'I never liked the bitch anyway, and Earl Godwine isn't my bloody father.'

8

LONDON, LADY GODGIFU

She watched Earl Sweyn with careful eyes. How she despised the young man. As he evaded the king's increasingly angry questions, she knew he'd be unable to hold onto his position, not this time. It was impossible.

Some seemed to believe King Edward was a lesser man than those who'd gone before. If they meant, by that, that King Edward was unprepared to punish his people for his own mistakes, then yes, the king was weak. But he wasn't. Not since King Cnut had England enjoyed a king who knew his mind so well. And perhaps, not since King Æthelred II, had England had a king whose thoughts were so closely aligned with the people he ruled over. Some thought Æthelred had been weak, and he had been, in some respects, but all he'd wanted was peace, not war. The threat of Viking raiders had undone much of the work of the king who'd ruled for so much of his life and wanted to do nothing more than earn the epitaph of peaceable, as his father had owned.

The king was arrayed in all his military majesty. He didn't wear his crown as he faced the members of the witan called together to discuss Earl Sweyn's attempt to undermine the security of Mercia and England as a whole. Instead, he wore his weapons belt and was armed, whereas all others had been forced to disarm in the king's presence.

'My lord king,' Earl Sweyn wasn't belligerent, but he was far from respectful towards the king. She noticed that he didn't look towards his sister. And she was not staring at him, either. No, Queen Edith sat beside her husband, back rigid, face showing her fury. Lady Godgifu, seated beside her equally tense husband, wanted nothing more than to smirk in triumph. But, of course, Earl Godwine and his host of sons were also in attendance upon the king.

Earl Godwine was dressed as though he wore all of his family's wealth in the gold-threaded embroidery and the heavy belt at his waist, which did little to hide his growing paunch and everything to show how wealthy he was. Lady Gytha was also with her husband. Since she'd allowed Godwine to ride to London in search of his daughter while she went to seek out the king, the earl had done little but cast slanted-eyed looks her way. She bore them easily and ensured she spent as much time as possible with the queen. Queen Edith seemed to appreciate her steadying presence much more than she did that of her mother, who'd arrived at court only the day before.

'I was working to ensure peaceful relations between the kingdom of England and that of King Gruffydd ap Llewelyn proceeded smoothly. The House of Leofwine has caused years and years of damage, and all Gruffydd wishes to do is live in harmony and peace.'

While her husband tried not to fidget beside her, Ælfgar, her son, struggled even more. And yet, King Edward wasn't being swayed.

'The relationship between my kingdom and that of Gruffydd ap Llewelyn, exists in a near-constant warfare. And we'll not ally with him to produce a peace which all know he'll break. King Gruffydd has killed good men, and he's never paid for those crimes. There's to be no peace, and if there were a peace, then it would be under my auspices and not yours.' The king didn't shout or rant. He spoke with a calmness that was ever more lethal.

'You've proven yourself to be unworthy of the position of earl once more.' Lady Godgifu sensed her husband's tension draining away, only for it to return in full force.

'My lord king,' of course, Earl Godwine wasn't likely to accept the inevitable without a fight.

'You interrupt me,' the king turned his blue eyes on the glittering object of Earl Godwine. Whatever his thoughts, Lady Godgifu couldn't deny that the king masked them well enough. No one would think the king hated the earl for his part in murdering his brother, Alfred, near-enough a decade ago. And indeed, Lady Godgifu sometimes considered whether he truly did hate the other man or if it was merely wounded family pride. It was impossible to understand the king fully. Perhaps he didn't blame Earl Godwine at all, but his mother, the disgraced Lady Emma.

'I do, my lord king, and with my heartfelt apologies, but you've not asked for any to speak in support of Earl Sweyn.' Godwine turned to survey the room as he spoke, lifting his hands outwards as though he couldn't help but speak those words. 'It's the way these things are done.'

'It is, yes, unless treason is under discussion.' The king's words could have frozen the River Thames, and yet Earl Godwine didn't seem daunted by the struggle he faced.

'I don't believe the young earl...'

'Who is your son,' the king countered, just to ensure all knew, not that any would doubt it. Whatever Earl Sweyn's assertions about who'd fathered him, the two men were almost mirror images of one another.

'Who is my son, yes, my lord king.' Earl Godwine bowed slightly. His words were unctuous and oiled. 'But, as much as he's my son, I still believe his actions were for the good of England.'

'And how do you suppose that?' the king sat back on his chair, the very image of ease. Lady Godgifu tried not to let her frustration show that Godwine had interrupted what was sure to be a verdict that removed Sweyn from the earldom.

'My lord king, affairs in Mercia have been complex and difficult. For many years, one single family has held great power and authority. As you know, King Cnut, your father, ensured their ambition was countered by placing many of his jarls and earls in places of importance, most notably along the border with the Welsh kingdoms. And for many years, his judicial use of such loyal men worked well. But they're all gone now. And so, one family, a family I might add, whose brother, uncle and father were executed for the very same treason you accuse my young and impetuous son of perpetrating. That one family have had years to counter their loss of power and influence and, of course, to consider their revenge against the English king.'

The audacity of Earl Godwine's words had even Lady Godgifu struggling for composure. All knew that Northman should never have been executed. All knew that King Cnut had repented his hasty actions and spent years rebuilding his relationship with her father by marriage, the half-blind Ealdorman Leofwine. Such words as Earl Godwine spoke were poison, and the fact that no one stood to counter them was telling.

'And of course, this family, my lord king, were heavily involved with the family of Lady Ælfgifu of Northampton, who claimed to be wife to King Cnut, although all knew it was false, even when her son took the English crown which should have been yours to wear by right.'

She felt her husband's hand on her sleeve, and Lady Godgifu could feel the tremor that ran through his entire body. To dismiss what his family had done, for Cnut, for Mercia, for England as a whole, as little more than treason was too much.

'Earl Godwine,' another had finally swept to their feet. She eyed Earl Siward uneasily. He was a man who'd committed terrible acts in the name of Harthacnut. She wasn't sure that any sort of defence from him for the House of Leofwine would be welcome. Earl Siward's voice was loud enough almost to boom. 'Dragging up such matters, which are baseless, and using them to excuse your son's actions, is entirely inappropriate. You make a fool of yourself. This isn't a childhood misdemeanour. This is treason against the kingdom of England. I suggest you shut your mouth and let the king say what must be said. And you, Earl Sweyn,' for the boy had jumped to his feet, his face puce with rage, 'would do well to remember the same.'

Silence roared through the assembly. No one spoke. Few seemed to barely dare breathe. This was a true test of King Edward's kingship. He would know it as much as everyone else.

Did he dare replace Earl Sweyn, his wife's brother? And if he did, with who would it be? Lady Godgifu had heard the rumours that the earldom, should it be rescinded, would fall into the hands of either another of Godwine's children, or even his nephew, Ralph, the son of his sister, Countess Godgifu, who shared her name. No matter what, the House of Leofwine wouldn't reclaim it.

And still, silence rang out.

'Sit, gentlemen,' the king spoke just loud enough that all had to listen carefully. 'This isn't how we conduct business in the witan,' his words rang with conviction. 'We're not misinformed men to shout one to another and lay barbs against each other.' Again, there was silence. Lady Godgifu considered moving to ease her aching back but could do no such thing, for it would draw every eye to her.

'Earl Sweyn,' the king's eyes were colder than ice when he looked at the young man, who stood abruptly to face his king. For this act, King Edward showed some pleasure. Lady Godgifu sensed that what she wanted wouldn't come to fruition.

'You've acted in bad faith and taken my name in vain. Again. Luckily for you and England, Earl Leofric and his son, Lord Ælfgar, prevented anything worse from happening. As such, you'll keep your earldom. For now. My nephew, Ralph, and my cousin, Beorn Estridsson, will be assigned to the earldom alongside you. If you can rule, they will be withdrawn after some undesignated amount of time. If you prove yourself worthy of the honour.'

A collective exhalation seemed to emanate from every person in that room. Lady Godgifu determined to show no external emotion, yet internally, she found the arrangement met with her approval.

The king was allowing Earl Sweyn the rope to hang himself with and imposing nothing short of personal rule. Lords Ralph and Beorn were not likely to be easily swayed by Earl Sweyn's entreaties. The fact that Sweyn Godwinesson and Beorn Estridsson were cousins would have no impact on Beorn. He was a hard man. Rumour had it that he'd come to England to escape from his brother's desires to rule. Beorn was a man only too aware of sibling rivalry, let alone when it extended to cousins.

'My lord king,' Earl Sweyn opened his mouth to squeak a complaint, only for his father to rise and talk over him.

'My lord king, you're most wise,' Earl Godwine ensured his voice carried over that of Sweyn's. 'My son will thank you for such a benevolent response to his... mistake,' still Earl Godwine smiled. Lady Godgifu finally allowed herself to look at her husband. Leofric's face was white with suppressed fury, yet he seemed calm enough. Her son looked fit to burst, and she reached across and gripped his forearm in support. She wouldn't allow her son to humiliate their family like Sweyn had humiliated the Godwines. The House of Leofwine was better than that.

'And now,' the king spoke, ignoring that Sweyn still stood. 'We've other matters to discuss. We will say no more of affairs with the Welsh, but be assured, our only interest in any of the Welsh kings is ensuring they stay behind their borders and harass our border-dwellers as little as possible. We're not at war with the Welsh. Neither are we allies. Remember that, all of you.'

And so, Lady Godgifu turned her mind to other matters and knew that while the king's solution was sensible, it was likely only storing trouble for another day.

9

ÆLFGAR

'THE KING'S DECISION DISPLEASED YOU?' HIS WIFE, ELGIVA, ASKED HIM, lying beside him in their bed. Outside, the weather had finally begun to warm up, and he no longer needed to surround himself in every available fur each night.

'The king's decision was a wise one for him to make. His marriage is still too young for him to offend Earl Godwine and his family. But, it wasn't a good decision for Mercia.'

'But,' his wife countered, 'your father said there was no possibility of you gaining the earldom if Earl Sweyn lost it?' He nodded, staring upwards at the wooden strutted ceiling. A winter's dust was settled up there on the wooden slats, but he felt no desire to urge a thorough cleansing. Not yet.

'It doesn't matter whether I have the earldom or not,' he knew his tone was hot. How he cursed the day Sweyn had been gifted an earldom. Since then, all the boy had done was laud it over his peers, and he little cared whether that included his brothers or his family's longest-held adversary, the House of Leofwine. 'It shouldn't be in Sweyn's hands. And why the king believes Beorn and Ralph can keep him under control, I've no idea. If Earl Godwine can't restrict

Sweyn's activities, then Ralph and Beorn will have no chance. Beorn and Sweyn are of age, Ralph is younger, if age even comes into it.'

'The king has made it clear he'll lose his position if there should be more problems,' Elgiva tried to console him.

'The king will struggle to do anything now he's allowed this treason to go virtually unpunished. King Edward should have removed Earl Sweyn from the earldom and banished him from the kingdom. That's the only way to ensure there's no opportunity for him to repeat his actions. We've seen Sweyn for what he is. He was incompetent with the ship army last summer. He just causes problems wherever he goes.'

Elgiva lapsed into silence, and he reached over to grip her hand. There were no solutions and no answers to what had happened. Not yet. But Ælfgar and his father agreed with one another. They felt it was merely a matter of time.

'The king will act next time if there is a next time. If he doesn't do so, there'll be an outcry. No one wants any more war. All we've endured for years is war after war after war.' Her words ended on a croak. War and treachery. For too many years, that had defined Ælfgar's life. He was heartily sick of it, yet he could see how some thrived on it.

'I hope you're right,' he answered dolefully. He'd spoken at length with his mother after the king's pronouncement. She shared his feelings regarding the king. And yet, she had an entirely different viewpoint to the one he held.

'The king,' Lady Godgifu had told her son. 'Must be seen to give his brother by marriage the opportunity to correct his ways. We all know he won't do it. The king realises Sweyn is beyond redemption. The only hope is that Sweyn gets himself killed fighting against the Welsh. If he doesn't, then the king will remove him. He'll have no choice. But what Sweyn does after that might prove even more problematic. The king continues to build his power base. When he knows the firm loyalty of his supporters is assured, he'll stand against the House of Godwine. It might be that Earl Godwine loses his prominence. We'll have to see.' He'd pushed his mother, desperate to know what the king would do with his wife, the daughter of Godwine.

'The king will get rid of her, as well. Send her to a nunnery or some such. That's what England's kings have always done with a pesky wife they want to be rid of.' Ælfgar wished he could be as sure as his mother was.

'Well, husband dearest, there's little point in being maudlin. We've tasks to accomplish this day.'

He sighed heavily and rolled over to face her. He'd like nothing better than to linger in bed all day, but already he could hear the boisterous cries of his children and the servants busy about their tasks. Elgiva was right to encourage him. If not, then his bed would soon contain all of his children. Better to face them when he was dressed and prepared for their antics. He smiled and ran his hand over her cheek.

'As you wish, my lady,' he kissed her gently, pulled back the furs, and grabbed his tunic and trews. Then, he looked for his boots, but as so often the case, found one missing from where he'd left it the night before. No doubt the dog had stolen it and was chewing on the hard leather and leaving bite marks.

'Your boots?' Elgiva chuckled at his groan.

'My boots, indeed,' he replied, striding towards the door. Opening it wide, he called into the room.

'Three silver coins for whoever brings me my boot.' His older children would do anything for coins to spend at the fairs and religious festivals that happened with such regular occurrence. And, as they were often found rolling on the floor with the hound, they'd most likely know where it was.

'Here you are, father,' he peered at a breathless Burgheard as he abruptly stopped before his father. The boy was tall for his age, a mop of dark brown hair covering his forehead. He really did need it cutting, but that was Elgiva's duty to arrange, not his.

'My thanks, lad,' Ælfgar pulled the coins from his money sack and held them out towards Burgheard only for Eadwine to screech to a halt, his face furious.

'I found it, you bully,' he roared at his brother. 'I found it, and you took it, and now I'll need the coins, Father.' Eadwine was stout at demanding what he felt was owed, whether it was coins for a boot or coins for something else. Or even a weapon or a piece of honeycomb.

'Now boys, don't fight,' Ælfgar cautioned them both, reaching for yet more coins to placate the pair of them. He wasn't always sure how to counter the two exuberant children. He'd had his cousins as friends as a child, but they'd always been his cousins, not his brothers. And yes, he'd watched them interact with one another, but that hadn't prepared him for the rivalry and jealousies between his children.

'Now, Burgheard, Eadwine,' Elgiva appeared at his shoulder, her voice sharp. 'Who truly found the boot? I'll have no lying about this. Who found the boot?' Ælfgar almost felt sorry for his children then, but Elgiva was strict with the boys.

'Eadwine,' Burgheard admitted with a shrug of his shoulders and a cheeky grin. 'Sorry, Eadwine,' he continued, almost sounding contrite.

'Burgheard, you can go and aid the stable hands as punishment,' Elgiva continued. 'While you, Eadwine, can have the coins, but can also go and ask one of the warriors to help you with your weapons practice. Men can't be relied on to tell the truth where money's concerned; therefore, you need to know how to defend yourself. Now go. And no fighting or arguing. That's enough for today.' The two boys hardly seemed cowed by the telling-off, and with fondness, Ælfgar watched Burgheard fling his arm over Eadwine's shoulder so that they walked together.

'Those children,' his wife shook her head. 'Although none of it would be a problem if the bloody hound could be relied upon to leave your boots alone.'

Ælfgar felt a tug on his arm and looked down to see sweet Ealdgyth sucking her thumb and looking at him with wild eyes. She was a beguiling four-year-old. She already had her mother's beauty, and Ælfgar felt a stab of worry for her. There were many men who'd want to marry such a beautiful woman when she was older. He couldn't countenance the thought that her life would be in the hands of someone who wasn't her mother or father.

'What is it?' he asked, bending low and running his hand through her ragged hair. Ealdgyth spoke with a childish lisp that only endeared her to everyone within their home all the more.

'It's Morcar,' she enunciated clearly for once.

'What about him?'

'He might be stuck.'

'Stuck where?' Ælfgar felt his forehead furrow as he looked around the room, trying to find his youngest son. Morcar was a year younger than Ealdgyth and was just truly starting to explore. Everyone needed wide eyes to ensure he didn't get into trouble. He could hear his wife speaking to some of the servants. She wasn't yet aware that Morcar was missing. He bent even lower when Ealdgyth offered nothing further.

'Where's Morcar?' he demanded to know and then became aware of a small voice shouting for help. He turned to stride into the room the children shared and marched straight to the wooden chest at the bottom of Morcar's bed. Lifting the lid, he faced his red-faced and furious youngest son.

'How did you get in there?' he consoled his son, lifting him free and trying not to wrinkle his nose at the smell of piss that showed his son had been very scared and caught out while enclosed in the wooden chest. The clothes and blankets would need to be freshly washed and aired. It was far from a small task.

'Eadwine,' Ealdgyth was still behind him, Ælfgar hadn't realised.

'Eadwine what? Put Morcar in there?' he could feel his temper building.

'He told him to play hide and seek, but then you offered coin for your boot.'

'So Eadwine forgot?' Ealdgyth nodded solemnly, and Ælfgar almost smiled.

'Then, young man, I would suggest that in future, you shouldn't hide anywhere you can't escape from on your own.' Morcar's cheeks were damp with tears, and snot marred his upper lip. Ælfgar took one of the soiled linens to wipe his son's face.

'We need to change your clothes,' he told the boy. Ealdgyth hastened to find some clean clothes for her brother, and in no time, they emerged back into the main hall, Ealdgyth's tiny hand in one of his, and Morcar's in the other. Ælfgar felt a sense of great pride in his children, despite their problems that morning. He also couldn't deny the wild stab of fear that filled his stomach. How would his children ever fend for themselves when it took their mother to determine the truth of the oldest two's actions, and the youngest had trapped himself inside a wooden chest? And Ealdgyth? Well, as his only daughter, unless he and Elgiva were blessed with more children, was going to be highly sought after, and quite possibly, not for the best of reasons.

'Go and play,' he encouraged his children and took himself outside to find Elgiva. Along the way, he called one of the servants to him and explained what had happened. The matronly figure rolled her eyes but smiled all the same.

'I'll see it taken care of, my lord, don't fear. Poor mite.'

'Yes, but he's recovered now,' Morcar had found himself some leftover breakfast and eagerly spooned huge quantities into his mouth.

'Aye, a bit of food will settle all small children,' the woman smiled and then hastened on her way. Yawning wildly, Ælfgar emerged into the busy forecourt of his home. He could hear Burgheard singing something he really shouldn't from the stables while Eadwine and Otryggr Orkningsson were busy with wooden blades, his son doing all he could to overpower Otryggr, although he stood no chance against the older boy and grandson of Horic, who had been such a firm ally of his grandfather.

'Elgiva,' he found his wife in the food store, raised just above the ground to stop rats and other pests from infecting it all.

'The ale's sprung a leak, and it's nearly all gone,' she complained loudly, on her hands and knees, trying to find the cause of the problem.

'We'll just order a replacement,' he consoled. It was a waste, but sometimes, these things couldn't be helped.

'Morcar was stuck in his clothing chest,' he offered, watching his wife with a smile. Sunlight came through the open doorway, but other than that, there was no other light inside the store. It was ripe with the smell of all the herbs and spices they stored inside and the scent of dried meats.

'That boy will do himself some serious injury one day,' Elgiva complained, still on her hands and knees.

'Yes, but it would have helped if his older brother had remembered he was supposed to be playing seek in a game of hide and seek. Luckily Eadgyth told me.'

'She's far too sensible for her age, that one,' but Elgiva spoke with pride as she finally stood, still shaking her head. Only then did Ælfgar realise their steward was also in the room. The two of them were busy assessing their supplies.

'Thank goodness she told us,' Ælfgar reaffirmed, his thoughts still tangled with his worries for his children's future.

'I'm sure that one day your sons will learn to be more responsible,' Elgiva added with an arch of her eyebrows. 'After all, your mother says you were just like them, and look at you now, worrying about your children and the future of the kingdom,' her words were soft.

'Hopefully, the boys will one day care for their sister as she does for them.' And yet, Ælfgar feared that he might be wishing for too much. What he needed was a ride to clear his mind of all his myriad thoughts. He shook his head, kissed his wife, and strode to the stable.

10

DEERHURST, LEOFRIC

He glanced at the building before him before ducking inside and bowing his head respectfully. It wasn't like him to seek solace in the church, yet today, he felt the need to pray for his dead parents and two lost brothers. Grief, he pondered, could be a vicious bitch. He could go for months, sometimes years, without it worrying him, only for it to reappear and almost slap him with its force.

The journey to Hereford seeking out Earl Sweyn had been bad enough, but hearing Earl Godwine speak of his long-dead brother, Northman, in such a disparaging tone was too much. Not for the first time, he wished he and his brother had known each other better. But Northman had been deeply involved in the intrigue surrounding Ealdorman Eadric Streona, whereas he'd been close to their father. He still vividly remembered watching his father's dignity as he'd been told of Northman's execution on the orders of King Cnut. He still recalled returning home, broken and aware that their mother would never recover from what had befallen her oldest child. He was grateful that his father and mother had long been dead when the Welsh had murdered Eadwine. He couldn't have faced witnessing their sorrow twice.

Running his hands over the familiar carvings adorning the sculptures in the church at Deerhurst he considered how many times he'd performed the same action in the past. It was probably innumerable, and yet one day, in the not-too-distant future, he'd be buried somewhere different to his brothers and parents. He didn't welcome that, and yet it was imperative that he do so in this era of ostentatious church patronage. The churches he and Godgifu had endowed would perhaps fight over their bones if he didn't make those wishes clear for all to know.

He took himself to the front of the church, peering upwards at the emblems of his faith and sank to his knees. He would pray. It never came particularly naturally to him. There were some who seemed to be able to spout prayers that sounded filled with respect to their Lord God with ease. He always found his thoughts and words faltering. What, after all, did he desire? Yes, he wanted the reassurance that his parents were safe in their afterlife, but other than through rich endowments and ensuring there were monks to sing Masses for their souls, what part did he truly pay in it all?

All the same, he held his palms together, on his knees, and closed his eyes. He was here, it was apparent, to seek solace. And some idea of what the future might hold for his family.

His son was a fine man, and his nephews were good men, his niece a good woman, and yet, no matter the king's assurances to the contrary, he felt as though the House of Leofwine was struggling. They couldn't counter the huge threat of the House of Godwine. There were just too many Godwine children. They could encircle his earldom, and he could do nothing to counter it. Not unless the king took action against his wife's family.

The future the king had promised him, where there would be no son born to the union, seemed far in the past and far in the future. Queen Edith was a young woman. There were years ahead of her yet when she could produce a child for the king, and while that possibility existed, everyone would look to Earl Godwine and his hoard of children. They were the perceived future. They were the ones who would one day be uncles and aunts to the future king.

He shook his head, attempting to clear his mind of such worldly thoughts, but it was impossible. That was what consumed him. The knowledge that Earl Godwine had been implicated in Northman's death, and that he sought to use that against himself and the rest of his family was a clear indication of what the future would hold.

Leofric knew one thing. He needed to grow his family links. Now that Lady Ælfgifu of Northampton was no longer a powerful force in the Mercian earldom, one of his family's most powerful adherents was gone and never likely to return. Indeed, if he thought about it, he and his family had done all they could to develop links with every influential family in Mercia. Lady Ælfgifu, the Danish jarls while they lived, Lady Gunnhild, now banished, and even Ælfgar had married the daughter of Morcar, another man to die at the hands of the disgraced Ealdorman Eadric. And yet, the family of Earl Godwine was still in the ascendant and was, more importantly, perceived to be in the ascendant.

As he knelt, thinking to pray, Leofric began formulating plans for the future. It was important not to feel defeated by what was happening. King Edward held more control than any might think and indeed, more than any might truly understand. Many thought Edward was only king with the support of the House of Godwine. That wasn't true.

The more Leofric considered it, the more the tension eased from his shoulders, and he felt able to take a deep breath. Yes, Earl Sweyn was an annoyance and quite likely to prove deadly, but he had made many enemies already and would continue to accumulate more. And while he acknowledged that Queen Edith was close to her brother, Harold, he wasn't convinced that the entire family was as united as some might think. Both families were as marked as the other. And while King Cnut had executed Northman, Lady Gytha's brother, the little lamented husband of Lady Estrid, Cnut's sister, had endured the same fate. It was time for Leofric to begin to claw back some of his control and influence. And he knew exactly where to start.

Standing abruptly, he bowed his head and all but marched from the church. He paused to pay his respects to his mother, father, brothers, and indeed, the grandfather he'd never known, but then he was keen to be mounted and on his way. This time, the thought of a repeat journey to Hereford filled him with less fear. He'd seek out Lord Ralph and Beorn Estridsson. They would be powerful allies worth cultivating, and it helped that he already had connections to both men, unlike with Earl Sweyn.

Calling to his men who escorted him, Godwulf, Winhus, Cena, Æthelheard and Scirwold, Leofric rode onwards, filled with resolve. Earl Sweyn was only one obstacle and was not insurmountable, no matter what he thought. In time, Sweyn would make a monumental mistake, and when that happened, Leofric would be sure to profit from it and the damage it would do to the queen and the House of Godwine. All he needed to do was be patient for a little while longer. Leofric knew he could do that. He'd always been a patient man. After all, he'd learned from an expert, his father, Ealdormen Leofwine, a man who'd survived his half-blinding, the enmity of the Danish king, Swein, and the ravages of the wars between the Danes and the English. Leofric realised that he needed to take strength from what his family had survived instead of fearing a repeat of it.

The House of Leofwine were survivors who'd endure for far longer than Earl Sweyn held Herefordshire.

'Bishop Æthelstan,' Leofric greeted the blind bishop respectfully. The old man nodded in acknowledgement.

'I thought you'd be back,' he croaked, and Leofric allowed himself to smile.

'It didn't perhaps happen as we might have liked,' Leofric confirmed. It was a much warmer day in Hereford. Winter had finally been entirely banished. The promise of summer stretched into the future.

'No, it didn't,' Bishop Æthelstan confirmed. 'But Earl Sweyn won't survive for long without making another mistake.'

'I quite agree,' he confirmed to the bishop.

'And so, we must make plans,' the bishop's lips lifted in a smile of anticipation. 'I already like young Lord Ralph. He's respectful and well educated.'

'He is, yes. It's easy to name him as King Edward's nephew.'

'It is, and he's as keen as we are to see the back of Earl Sweyn. And Lord Beorn? Well, he too has his uses.'

'It's good to see you've already met Earl Sweyn's replacements.'

'It's always best to be well-prepared for all eventualities. I'd add a word of caution, though. Earl Sweyn little cares that his time is limited. He still intends to pursue his alliance with the Welsh king, Gruffydd ap Llewelyn. He means to make a name for himself fighting, just as his alleged father did before him.'

'Why he persists with such an obvious fraud is beyond me,' Leofric commented sourly.

'Because he's a fool and likes embarrassing his mother and father.

'He might be a Godwine, but he detests his mother and father. The boy is cursed by his parentage and by his belief in himself. He hates his family, for all he owes them everything.'

'You almost sound sorry for him.' Bishop Æthelstan shook his head.

'Not sorry, far from that. I'm grateful he's such an easy character to understand. If he'd been born during the true Viking Age, then he'd have accomplished a great deal, but we live in more settled times. His sort of aggression is no longer needed. And he hardly made a name for himself when King Magnus was encountered last summer with the king's fleet. If anything, he damaged his reputation.'

'Still, we need to guard against what he might do next,' the bishop persisted.

'He'll bide his time for a while, and then believing we all have memories as short as his, he'll resume negotiations with Gruffydd ap Llewelyn. I would ensure your border holdings are well prepared for any coming war, and at the same time, distance yourself from everything Earl Sweyn does, even as you court Lords Ralph and Beorn.'

'You've given this a great deal of time,' Leofric spoke approvingly.

'A blind man can see only with his mind. I have enough time to see how every future might develop and then determine how to stop it if I don't want that to happen. I see every piece on this *tafl* board, and I can move them at will and do all I can to ensure they follow my wishes.'

Leofric was startled by such a statement. 'And that includes me?' he asked just to be sure, but he didn't need Bishop Æthelstan to answer that. He understood the answer well enough.

11

LONDON, LEOFRIC

Once more, he rode into London, seeing the ships arranged along the River Thames. The king's fleet. The work of the previous winter and throughout the bitter spring had been successful. The king now had the ships to his name that he wanted. Leofric looked forward to seeing Eowa again, the commander of his father's ship. It was to be hoped that the king's new ship army wasn't forced to confront King Magnus of Norway this year. Although, if they did, they would be ready for it, Leofric was sure of that.

'A fine view,' Olaf offered him, smiling broadly. His sister had begged him to take Olaf away with him during his visit when returning from Hereford. In his advancing years, it seemed that Olaf was cantankerous and needed some activity to fill his mind. Leofric knew a great deal of sympathy for that.

For now, much seemed tightly suspended, as though waiting for something to give before events were set in motion. In the meantime, travelling to London, and then to Sandwich, would be good for both of them. Even Lady Godgifu was not beyond being exasperated with him when one of his moods took him.

'It always is, yes.' Leofric kneed Oswald on, and they descended towards London side by side. Leofric was accompanied by men of his household warriors, but not by Ælfgar. Ælfgar had other tasks to carry out, and it would be foolish for every male family member to be absent from Mercia when Earl Sweyn was still causing problems from Herefordshire. Ælfwine and Wulfstan remained behind, seeing to their landholdings, as did Godwine Leofwinesson, his brother. Once more, Leofric knew a moment of worry. The king wasn't treating his brother by marriage quite as harshly as he should. Indeed, Leofric feared that King Edward had almost forgotten Sweyn's mistakes. No doubt, the king was more focused on external threats than internal ones. King Magnus and his war on Denmark was part of that concern. That and Magnus' assertion, reinforced the previous year, that his claim to rule England was based on an agreement forged between him and King Harthacnut.

Quickly, Leofric directed Oswald towards the quayside, keen to see Eowa and ensure everything was as it should be. He was reminded of Earl Sweyn's disastrous attempts at docking last year, and a smile played around his lips until he was recalled to the fact that Sweyn still owed him a great deal of money. And Leofric didn't believe he was alone in this, either. For all the wealth of his earldom, Sweyn managed to overspend wherever he went. Or rather, managed to ensure that everyone else overspent on his behalf.

'My lord,' the coarse cry of his ship's commander recalled him to the here and now, and Leofric dismounted, urging Cena to hold Oswald's reins, and strode towards Eowa.

The other man never seemed to change. Leofric was convinced he'd looked the same age for at least twenty winters. That thought also brought a smile to his face.

'Eowa, you're well?'

'Aye, my lord, but no thanks to these useless half-wits who call themselves shipmen. Only yesterday one of them all but lost the anchor in the reed beds, and it was a damn mess when we finally retrieved it.' As Eowa spoke, he lifted his voice to ensure everyone could hear what he was saying. Leofric didn't miss that a number of fury-filled eyes were fixed on one figure, pretending not to notice as he coiled thick rope around his arm. Olaf moved away, his voice rising and falling as he spoke to the men.

'And the ship is in sea-worthy condition?'

'Always, my lord, always, apart from during the winter, when she must be removed from the water and made watertight once more.'

'And the king's ships?'

And here Eowa did smile, the sight unexpected.

'He's built fine ships for his men. I can't deny that. The wood, good Mercian wood, has been used to construct them. I've never seen a finer sight, not even when King Cnut had his ship army.'

The news cheered Leofric. It was good to know the king had employed good craftsmen. He wouldn't have wanted the funds they'd been given to have been wasted, as might have happened in the past, most notably when they had to pay King Harthacnut for his fleet of ships, even though, in the end, he'd arrived in England in peacetime and as the acknowledged king of the English.

'None of the youngsters with you?' Eowa questioned.

'Ælfgar has remained in Mercia. One of us should always be there. Olaf has his nephew with him, Otryggr, grandson of Horic.'

'And he'll be one of my shipmen?' Leofric knew the mention of Horic would ease Otryggr's passage on the ship.

'I imagine so, but try not to allow Olaf on board. He'll merely cause you more problems.'

Eowa chuckled, but the sound was low and ominous. 'I'd like to see him try.'

Just as Leofric was beginning to relax, pleased for perhaps the first time in his life, to be away from Mercia's problems, a sight made the smile waver. Lord Harold and his younger brother, Tostig, were also examining the ships. Leofric supposed he had to be pleased that Lord Sweyn wasn't with them, but he never liked to be reminded of the huge number of sons Godwine had fathered. Tostig, really no more than a lad, bore his father's cast, like all of his sons. He was also loud, and Leofric could hear him even above the sound of the screeching gulls and pigeons that flocked to the quayside. He was almost pleased to see that Harold had the unwelcome task of trying to keep his brother's voice down and his behaviour acceptable. Not for the first time, Leofric thought it was a shame that Harold wasn't the older son. With Harold as earl in Herefordshire, life would have been much easier.

'My lord,' Harold bowed before him, and Leofric offered the same while Eowa looked on, and Tostig spoke to the shipmen, Olaf keeping a watchful eye on them.

'Are you in command of a ship this time?' Leofric asked Harold.

'Yes, I command my father's ship, in place of Sweyn. Tostig is to accompany me.' Leofric wished him luck with that.

'When do the ships leave for Sandwich?' Leofric thought to ask.

'Two days, my lord,' Eowa was quick to reply. 'The king is keen for us to assemble before midsummer.'

'And his intentions are still to put on a show of strength and defiance.'

'Yes, my lord. That's what I've heard.' Leofric admired his ship's commander, talking when really the question was directed to Harold. Leofric was sure that Harold knew the king's mind as well as his wife. He was aware that the brother and sister were close. His son had informed him of that.

'Reports from Denmark suggest that there'll be no attempt by King Magnus this year. He's deeply embroiled in a battle against Svein Estridsson for the kingdom, but all the same, the fleet have been assembled, and the king means to test it.' Leofric nodded, amused that Eowa had been forced to silence by Harold's greater knowledge.

'Excuse me, my lord, Eowa,' Harold dashed away from them, and Leofric watched them go, shaking his head, for Tostig, despite the ship's men, and Olaf had still somehow managed to entangle himself in the ropes surrounding the ship. Any moment now, he threatened to slip into the water, the ropes falling backwards towards the water.

'Well, I don't want that damn arse on my ship,' Eowa huffed.

'He's only young,' Leofric tried to counter, but all the same, he thought that Tostig should know much better. Godwine and his wife didn't seem to have been blessed with children who gave much forethought to their actions. If Tostig was to be involved in the ship army, King Edward might need to be careful that his wife didn't lose one of her brothers to the icy depths of the sea.

12

MATHAN, HEREFORDSHIRE, ÆLFGAR

'My lord.' He and Beorn Estridsson hand-clasped in friendship and then stood, looking one to another, suddenly uncomfortable in the presence of one another. Ælfgar found a smile on his lips, one that Beorn echoed.

'Wine?' he asked Beorn.

'Water, please,' Beorn quickly countered.

'It's too damn hot for wine,' Ælfgar confirmed. He wasn't at home with the noise of his boisterous family adding a counterpart to their stilted conversation, but still, they'd decided to meet in one of Ælfgar's properties in Herefordshire. It had been his father's idea, and he still felt uncomfortable with it all, but it was better to do something rather than wait for Earl Sweyn to put a foot wrong. He didn't miss that Mathan had been gifted to his grandfather by King Æthelred, the second of his name. It was a long-held possession of the House of Leofwine.

'A fine house,' Beorn offered, having taken his fill of water. Ælfgar wiped sweat from his forehead with a linen as he nodded. Outside, the summer weather was blisteringly hot.

'It requires a few repairs, but on the whole, it's structurally sound,' he offered. 'And you, where do you spend most of your time? With the king?' But Beorn was shaking his head. Ælfgar eyed the other man. They were similar in age, really. Beorn was the son of Lady Estrid, King Cnut's sister, and the disgraced and then executed Ulfr Ulfrsson, and he'd come to England alongside King Harthacnut from Denmark. Somehow, he'd made himself a firm ally of King Edward. Such tenacity was worth admiring.

'I split my time between the king, wherever he may be, and of course, Earl Sweyn's earldom.' A faint smile played around Bjorn's lips as he spoke. Ælfgar would have liked to know what so amused the Danish-born man. But it seemed he wasn't to offer the details.

'And Lord Ralph does the same?'

'I rarely see Lord Ralph. Between us, we ensure that Earl Sweyn is either always accompanied or that one of us can always be found within the earldom. It's for the best,' Beorn commented. His words were tinged with the Danish tongue, but he spoke English well.

'And the earldom is settled, now?' This really was like pulling teeth. Really, Ælfgar thought, his father should have conducted this conversation. Leofric knew Lady Estrid. They shared something in common.

'All is well for the time being. Bishop Æthelstan has eyes everywhere, for all he lacks his own.' Ælfgar just managed not to wince at such a description of the blind bishop. But, on balance, Beorn was correct. Bishop Æthelstan had ensured he knew everything that Earl Sweyn planned.

'Then that pleases me. It's always good when there's peace,' Ælfgar offered, once more wiping sweat from his forehead. Beorn was doing no better. He too, sweated profusely. The thought of having to don byrnies and ride to war was unwelcome. As much as Ælfgar hungered for Earl Sweyn to misstep, he wouldn't welcome it anytime soon. The summer had been slow to warm, but now it was almost unbearable. He would have welcomed the opportunity to sail with the king's ship army. At least out at sea, there would have been a breeze.

'It is, yes, but it won't last. I assure you. I've informed the king as much as well. I confess,' and Beorn lent forward, the scent of his sweat and the aroma of horse enveloping him, 'the king seems keen for Earl Sweyn to make another mistake. Men and women think the king's weak, but he's happy to provide Earl Sweyn with the opportunity to cock up again. He's a despicable man, and I say that with all the familiarity of our cousinship.'

Ælfgar nodded. This was more the type of information he was after.

'Is he still determined on an alliance with the Welsh king?'

'Yes, Earl Sweyn is obsessed with the idea of an alliance with King Gruffydd ap Llewelyn. But the king is adamant there'll be no alliance, as he announced before the witan.'

'And Earl Sweyn knows the king won't be swayed?'

'Of course, he does. But Earl Sweyn thinks with his sword and little else. He dreams of great military victories. Perhaps,' Beorn continued. 'The king would do better to send Earl Sweyn to my Danish home. There's war there, and King Magnus is a clever individual. Magnus will find a way to kill Sweyn, as I understand his shipmen nearly did last year. Then King Edward will have one less problem to think about.'

'What intelligence is there from Denmark?' Ælfgar queried. They still received news from Olaf's family and their descendants, but it was always good to obtain another viewpoint.

'My brother will prevail at some point,' Beorn offered, a strained expression on his face. 'He's another one who thinks with his cock and little else. He has children all over the place. But he also has an enemy to fight without looking for one. I'm sure my brother, Svein, will be king of Denmark someday. That will please my mother, for all I'm content to be far from the war.'

'It's a little ironic that the two men share the same name.'

'It's perhaps a curse of that name,' Beorn chuckled darkly. 'My grandfather, I'm told, was a hot-headed arsehole as well.' Now Ælfgar chuckled.

'My father would tell you stories of your grandfather.'

'I'm sure he would. But would I want to hear them?' Beorn relaxed now, sitting back in his wooden-backed chair, his eyes focused on Ælfgar. 'Our families have been interwoven for many years, despite the fact there has never been a marriage union between us. Some might even say we've gone out of our way to avoid such a union.' Beorn laughed again, reaching for the jug and pouring more water into his cup.

'Perhaps. Others might say we've shown some constraint there. But, alas, I have no eligible daughters, if you're seeking a wife. She is still too small for such a thought.'

Beorn shook his head once more. 'The thought of a marriage doesn't yet appeal. Being beholden to another family when I must still contend with my own would be asking too much from me.'

'And Earl Sweyn?'

'As far as I can tell, he has no intention of marrying. He's a man who doesn't believe he needs a wife and children. Yet. His father disagrees with him, of course.'

'Marriage and children are not to be sneered at,' Ælfgar felt he should counter. He was happy with his wife, robust sons, and daughter, even if they made his life a constant barrage of noise.

'One day, I'll explore the possibility, and of course, the king will soon enjoy his own children.'

'Is the queen with child?' Ælfgar tried to keep his voice neutral but wasn't convinced he managed it.

'Soon she will be,' Beorn shook his head. 'I'm assured the king is assiduous in his duty to his wife, for all some say, he's determined to live as though he were a monk. He might spend much time on his knees, but it's not praying,' Beorn chuckled, forcing Ælfgar to join him, for he'd rather not consider his king and wife in such a way. 'Some say he's an old man and too old to father children, but he's keen to disprove them. If the king has no children, the House of Wessex will falter,' Beorn continued. 'And that can't be allowed to happen.'

'There are others,' Ælfgar offered. 'The children of his brother, Edmund Ironside, survived, although few know where they are.' Ælfgar recalled the king's determination to find the children, and his father's desire to do the same. As of yet, the children remained missing somewhere far from England, not that they were really children anymore. They would have been of an age with Ælfgar.

'And that's a problem. Much easier for the king to produce his own heir, and then there'll be no need to hunt high and low for this missing ætheling. After all, how is anyone to know the man is whom he says he is?' Ælfgar snapped down on his reply to this. He also refused to be baited into suggesting King Harald had a child. It was better if even Beorn didn't know of his mother's involvement in protecting the child. He nodded along, as though he agreed with Beorn. Of course, if the king had no child, as he was adamant, would happen, then there'd be a problem in the future. But was it something to concern themselves with now? All acknowledged Lord Ralph as the king's nephew. Admittedly it was through his mother, but she was still one of King Æthelred II's children. No one would deny the claim.

'Then we should toast the king's success in the bed chamber,' Ælfgar splashed a little watered wine into two goblets and offered one to Beorn. As the two goblets clashed together, Ælfgar couldn't help but hope that the king would produce no heir but that somehow, another would be found, one who wasn't married into the pestilent family of the House of Godwine.

The too-sharp wine hit the back of his throat, and hastily, he reached for his water to drive away the taste.

Beorn once more chuckled darkly. 'Let's hope the king enjoys his duties more than we do the wine.'

Ælfgar grinned, but the action was unnatural. What would the future hold if King Edward had no heir? Perhaps, he considered, he should attempt to determine the location of King Harald's son. Or maybe he shouldn't? Before Edward had been accepted as king, there had been efforts to identify the lost children of Edmund Ironside, the man who'd ruled for less than half a year after his father, Æthelred. It was possible that they'd already been found, but their arrival on English soil would be unwelcome now. He shook his head. It would have been better for everyone involved if King Edward had married someone other than the daughter of the House of Godwine. It would have been ideal if he'd arrived with children already grown to adulthood, as opposed to with his nephew.

'I take it you wished to discuss more than the king's marital exploits and my cousin, Earl Sweyn?' Beorn eventually spoke into the silence.

'I do, yes. It's important to forge an alliance with you. Earl Sweyn has no interest. If anything, he's determined to cause as many problems as possible for the House of Leofwine.'

'I'd welcome the opportunity, but it can be nothing formal. I don't officially have any position in Sweyn's earldom. I'm beholden to the king and don't wish to move against him.'

'Neither does the House of Leofwine, be assured of that,' Ælfgar interjected.

'And yet, the House of Leofwine treads a dangerous path.'

'Perhaps, my father and his father before him were loyal to their kings and Mercia, but maybe not in that order. My grandfather wasn't well served by those who were his king. Equally, few realise that King Cnut was adamant that the House of Leofwine be friendly with his first wife, as well as his second.'

'My uncle was a man who liked to make life difficult for himself,' Beorn commented sourly. 'Two wives, three sons, and all of them wanting to be kings. I knew Harthacnut much better than either of the other two, and he was a clever and deadly man, but he was nothing compared to his father. My mother assures me that Cnut was even more ambitious than their father, King Sweyn.'

'I admired King Cnut, even after he executed my brother.'

'My uncle would have done better to have one wife in England and one in Denmark. He would also have been advised to keep to just one kingdom and not attempt to unite two separated by the bloody sea.'

Ælfgar nodded. It was strange how his perceptions had changed. He'd admired King Cnut as the ideal of what a king should be but couldn't deny that Beorn spoke the truth. King Cnut had held huge ambitions, and his death had come too soon. His empire, for that's what it had been, had fallen to ashes, all three of his sons dead before they could truly accomplish any great things.

Ælfgar shivered at the thought. He prayed his three sons would live longer lives and be able to achieve their full potential, whatever that proved to be.

13

SUMMER, AD1045 , LEOFRIC

Leofric allowed Eowa the command of the crew. It had been some time since he'd been aboard ship, and he'd forgotten it would take him some time to get used to the roll of the ship now that it had left the relative safety of the River Thames.

Olaf accompanied him, a grin on his brother by marriage's face that no doubt matched the one on his.

Behind them streamed the king's new fleet and also the Mercian ships that looked to Leofric for command. However, he was only personally responsible for one of the crafts, and he delegated that responsibility to Eowa.

Mercia might be thought of as land-locked, but the Viking raiders had shown it was anything but, with their stealth attacks via the Rivers Severn and Trent.

The cries of the commanders of the ships echoed through the passage of their journey, sails raised to allow the men to take some ease.

'A fine day,' Eowa called to Leofric. 'A fine day for stretching the confines of winter from our limbs.' Leofric smiled in response. Here, with the ship army, he felt able to forget the worries of Earl Sweyn and the threat of the Welsh. But, he knew it was a fool who entirely forgot them. The king, he understood, would be at Sandwich, and he intended to speak to him again about the menace of Sweyn Godwinesson, especially when the younger man wasn't with the ships. That said, Harold and Tostig were part of the fleet. He would have to be careful what he said. Leofric appreciated that King Edward wouldn't take kindly to being harangued about his decision regarding Sweyn.

Ahead, the sun glinted on the ocean, making it appear tantalisingly golden. If only the water was as warm as it looked. Leofric had heard stories of warm seas far to the south, but he little believe them. The sea was cold and brutal, no matter how it appeared, and that was why the cold-hearted and iron-made Viking raiders had been the ones to make such good use of it in attacking England, and further afield.

'Have you heard,' Olaf spoke to him later, when the first thrill of the sea voyage had passed, and Leofric had gratefully covered his shoulders with his sealskin cloak, 'that Deerhurst is now in the hands of Odda?'

Leofric nodded, the thought making him uneasy. The family home, so long at Deerhurst, had become untenable when the Danish earls had taken command over the border areas with the Welsh. His sister had finally relinquished her hold on the estate, and now Odda, a man rising in prominence and perhaps not as much of a threat to Earl Sweyn, had purchased the estate, and the church.

'I did, yes. I hear he's a good man.'

'Perhaps,' Olaf muttered, 'but it's strange all the same.'

'It is, my old friend. The years have been kind to us, but still, they weigh heavily on us all.'

'They do, yes, and of course, she is much happier with the manor in Much Hadham. There's more room for the hounds.' Leofric nodded. He knew his sister had needed a change. The mention of the hounds, though, reminded him that he had intended to replace his much missed animal.'

'I must speak to her about a new hound,' he murmured, only to be met with a smirk from Olaf.

'She is already preparing a new beast for you. She's a beautiful colour but has a fiery temperament, I can assure you. She can be biddable, on occasion.' Leofric nodded, pleased his sister had seen his need.

'And your son, Leofric, how does he fare?'

'He is still much honoured at Peterborough monastery. His mother thinks he'll make a fine abbot one day.'

Now Leofric laughed aloud. His sister's ambitions for her son were meant to be heard by him. He would have to see if he could assist in any way, although Peterborough was not part of Mercia. Perhaps Bishop Æthelstan might be of assistance, for all his responsibility lay at Hereford.

AT SANDWICH ONCE MORE, Leofric was astonished by the size of the king's fleet, assembled here to protect England from any possible new attack from King Magnus of Norway. There was next to no room along the quayside, and although some of the ships had moved aside to allow Eowa as close to it as possible, Leofric had been forced to climb across two ships to reach dry ground. Once there, he was met by a smiling king.

'The ships are seaworthy?' Edward called to him.

'Indeed, my lord king,' Leofric bowed as best he could while his body felt as though it moved from side to side.

'Tomorrow, I'll join the fleet, and we'll see what they're capable of achieving. Have you seen Lord Harold? His sister bid me speak with him.'

'I saw him in London, my lord king. He and Tostig were joining the fleet.'

'Then no doubt they'll arrive in good time. I hear all is quiet on the borders,' the king continued, although his attention was on the ships and not on Leofric's words.

'Maybe not, my lord king. There are still rumours that Earl Sweyn has forged an alliance with the Welsh king and means to move against Gruffydd ap Rhydderch of Gwent.' If Leofric hoped the king would be angry with the news, he was to be disappointed, for at that moment, Lord Harold appeared and Leofric bowed his way from the king's presence, unease written on his face.

And it only worsened over the coming days. While the king's fleet excelled at the tasks set for it, the king was more often than not in the presence of Harold Godwinesson and Ralph, the king's nephew. Who, Leofric considered, was keeping a firm eye on Sweyn Godwinesson other than his son? And his fears only intensified when Beorn Estridsson arrived at Sandwich as well.

Furious with the king, and with himself for leaving his son alone in Mercia, Leofric watched with disbelief as, the day before the ship army disbanded, King Edward bestowed the earldom of the kingdom of the East Angles on Harold Godwinesson and that of the south-east of Mercia on Beorn Estridsson. He journeyed home, dismayed, aware that if the king announced the queen was with child, the House of Leofwine would be entirely surrounded and, worse, denuded of all power.

The only good thing was that the anticipated attack by King Magnus didn't arrive.

THE ANGLO-SAXON CHRONICLE ENTRY FOR AD1045

And in the same year King Edward went out with his ships to Sandwich; and there was gathered so great a raiding-army that no-one had ever seen such a greater raiding ship-army in the land. (C)

14

AD1046, LADY GODGIFU

ONCE MORE, SHE PACED BEFORE HER HUSBAND. EARL LEOFRIC WATCHED HER, wincing from time to time, and while she'd have liked nothing more than to stop, she simply couldn't.

'The king is a fool,' she seethed. Furiously, she turned and marched back the way she'd just come. 'He was warned,' she continued. 'And he was warned again, and now Earl Sweyn has done all we thought him capable of doing.' She risked a glance towards her husband and took no pleasure from seeing the fury on his face.

'Lords Ralph and Beorn have done nothing to stop Earl Sweyn and his, his intentions towards the Welsh.'

'I,' her husband interjected, but she wouldn't let him continue.

'And now, we're at this situation, where Earl Sweyn has not only allied with Gruffydd ap Llewelyn, he's marched to war against Gruffydd ap Rhydderch, ruler of Gwent. With Gruffydd ap Llewelyn as his ally.' Her words ended in a shriek as she stopped before her husband.

'My dear,' he tried once more.

'And what has the king done to stop his brother by marriage? Sent grown men to watch him, and then they've also failed.'

'Well,' Earl Leofric tried once more.

This time she waited for him to continue speaking. He paused, met her eyes, and realising he was to be allowed to continue; he swallowed before saying more. 'The king was aware of what Earl Sweyn intended this time.'

'And so, what? The king approved of this alliance with the man who killed your brother?' Once more, a flicker of fury on his face assured her he was just as angry as she was.

'The king hasn't told me of his intentions. But, he sent word of what was happening. For that reason, Beorn and Ralph have their household warriors at the border. They, and Bishop Æthelstan, will protect Mercia from whatever befalls Earl Sweyn in the Welsh kingdoms.'

'Does the king believe Earl Sweyn will meet his death there?' The thought brought some small pleasure, she couldn't deny it.

'The king hasn't clarified what he believes Earl Sweyn will do. But he's adamant that whatever it is, Mercia remains safe.'

'And has he sent warriors to Chester, Worcester and Gloucester as well? More than just Hereford needs protection from the bloody Welsh kings.'

'I,' Earl Leofric began.

'No, he hasn't, has he? King Edward, who's never set foot in the Mercian borderlands, does not understand its length or importance.'

'I'm sure that Ralph and Beorn have managed to share that information with him,' her husband countered.

'I don't understand why King Edward thought Earl Sweyn could be trusted with the position and why he didn't take it from him last year.' Her words ended with a plaintive whine, and she winced to hear it. 'If he wished to reward another brother, Harold, then surely he could simply have replaced one brother with another rather than doling out the East Anglian earldom to another of Godwine's sons.'

'King Edward is married to the earl's sister.'

'And that was through his choice,' she finally settled and sat before her husband. The messenger had been sent outside, and even the servants were cowering away from the rage of their mistress. She rested her hands on her crossed legs and realised the one bounced above the other. She couldn't shake the fury that engulfed her. The king should have realised what would happen with Earl Sweyn. If she could perceive the outcome, then the king should have been even more alert to it.

'Indeed, the king married through choice, if you can call it that.' Earl Leofric mollified.

'It was his choice. He could have chosen anyone. A wife from anywhere would have been preferable to one of Godwine's spawn.'

She watched her husband's argument forming and then almost smiled to see him snap his mouth tightly closed.

'We must deal with the situation as we now have it, not how it could have been prevented.'

'Perhaps we should. But I'll not forgive the king for this. He's brought Mercia to the brink of war and all because he couldn't choose a proper bride or harness his bride's brother correctly.'

Her husband's eyes sparkled, and then he leaned forwards.

'My men and I should go and reinforce Beorn and Ralph.'

'You should, yes,' she countered immediately. The thought of Leofric riding to war filled her with unease, but it was the correct thing to do. And if the king wouldn't do it, then her husband certainly would. 'And if Earl Godwine appears, he should be sent back to Wessex.'

'I hardly think,' Leofric started.

'What? That you can send Earl Godwine away? He's already detested in that part of Mercia. Events in Worcester are smeared with his name. It's a wonder Earl Sweyn hasn't been lynched by those with long memories already.'

'I'll send Earl Godwine away. But I imagine it's more likely that Godwine will send Earl Harold. Indeed, Queen Edith will prefer it if her brother, not her father, seeks to bring Earl Sweyn to order.'

'Then you know what to do when you arrive at Hereford. And husband, ensure your son, brother and your nephews are protected at all times. King Gruffydd ap Llewelyn has killed too many members of your family already.'

'My lady,' her husband inclined his head, and she noticed where his hair no longer curled down his neck. Indeed, the top of his head was so threadbare that she could see the entire outline of his head. He looked almost tonsured. She bit down on telling him as much.

'I thank you for such care of your son, nephews and brother by marriage,' Leofric murmured, and she winced.

'And, of course, you, my husband. You must stay safe. Should something befall you, I wouldn't be surprised if the king overlooked Ælfgar and made Harold earl of Mercia.' She spoke with resolve, and the look of defiance that settled on her husband's face assured her that he'd not considered that and, yet, couldn't deny it either.

'Now, if you'll excuse me, I must make arrangements to ride for Hereford again.' As he spoke, Earl Leofric stood, and Lady Godgifu eyed him carefully. He was still very much the man she'd married for love. The intervening years had occasionally worn him down, as had his responsibilities, but she found herself perhaps more in love with him now than she had been for many years. She walked towards him and placed her lips on his bristle-strewn cheeks. 'Take good care of yourself, my love,' she urged him and pretended not to notice how he startled at her touch and then her words.

Turning aside, she smiled a little. It was always good to keep her husband on his toes. But, she had more important matters to consider. If the warband was to ride towards Hereford with all it required, she must see to supplies. Sweeping from the hall, she summoned her steward, thoughts already filled with what was needed and what wasn't. And one thing was for sure. What was certainly required, in her eyes at least, was for Earl Sweyn to lose his position once and for all and be expelled from the kingdom. Nothing less for the earl of Wessex's son. Nothing less.

15

HEREFORD, LEOFRIC

'Bishop Æthelstan,' he greeted the blind bishop warmly once more, despite the sour expression on the other man's face.

'Why is it that you appear so swiftly when there's a problem? No one else, just you?'

'I would take it to mean the king trusts me, but I could be wrong,' Leofric tried to jest, but the words fell flat between them. 'What news do you have for me,' he continued.

'Nothing more than I sent to the king. I'm hoping for more intelligence soon. I've sent some of my household warriors to follow the trail that Earl Sweyn left behind him. It was hardly difficult. Indeed, some of those who've already returned have informed me that even a blind man could have seen it.' Earl Leofric winced at the words, but now Bishop Æthelstan did smirk, his lips parting to show his missing front teeth. 'How many warriors do you have?' the bishop continued, the mirth quickly fading.

'Near enough a hundred. I doubt it will be enough.'

'You doubt correctly. Earl Sweyn has at least double that number if they all still live.'

'And King Gruffydd ap Llewelyn?'

'It's impossible to count the number of warriors he has,' the bishop grimaced. 'My warriors assure me they all look the same.'

'Then we'll settle here tonight, and if news comes before dawn, I'll act on it. If not, I intend to travel south.'

'That's the way my warriors have been going. Do you fear for Hereford?'

'I fear for any part of Mercia which the Welsh king, ap Llewelyn, and his foolish ally think to ride roughshod through. If this war with the other Welsh king goes poorly, every part of the southern border will be in peril, and I'm sure that Gruffydd ap Llewelyn will use it as an opportunity to attack the northern borders as well.'

'I'm only pleased that Bishop Lyfing of Worcester didn't live to see this happen. He would have been devastated.'

'Or involved,' Earl Leofric added sourly.

'Or involved, yes. But at least if he were involved, we'd know what was happening. He was never one to be quiet.'

'No, he wasn't. I take it that Bishop Aldred knows nothing.'

'No. Worcester has been left alone by Earl Sweyn. He knows it's likely to be loyal to your family and not to him, especially after the events with King Harthacnut there.'

'Then he shows some wisdom, at least. But what of Lords Beorn and Ralph?'

'They've informed the king that Earl Sweyn is impossible to keep in line. They tell the king that Earl Sweyn says one thing and does another. I agree with that. I imagine they feel as blind as I am, and at least I have an excuse for being hoodwinked by the slippery eel. Earl Sweyn is just bloody-minded.'

Leofric grunted in agreement.

'I'll have men ride out tomorrow to find where Earl Sweyn is.'

'There's no need. We know where he is. He's in South Wales, at war against Gruffydd ap Rhydderch. The alliance between Gruffydd ap Llewelyn was formed on the proviso that Earl Sweyn would ride at his side. No good will come of it. I suggest you keep your men firmly to this side of the border. What Earl Sweyn intends on his return is impossible to know. But my worry is that it's then that Gruffydd ap Llewelyn will truly show his intentions. I wouldn't be surprised to discover he's trying to claim Hereford for himself.'

'God's teeth,' Leofric exclaimed. The news filled him with rage, and yet, it wasn't unexpected. If anything, it was disappointingly obvious.

'My apologies, my lord.' He murmured.

'No apologies are necessary. I said the same, as have many others. The people of this area feel similarly. Earl Sweyn might believe he's a clever sod, but he's not. He's asking for trouble, and it will come. What do you believe the king will do this time?'

Leofric knew to be careful what he said. What the king's intentions were towards Earl Sweyn were unknown, although he had his suspicions. As such, Leofric's answer was exactly what the bishop needed to hear, even if it wasn't strictly true. 'He'll have no choice but to banish Earl Sweyn. The Welsh kings are England's enemies. It's as though they've made peace with King Magnus of Norway, and the king has built an entirely new ship army to counter that threat.'

'I quite agree,' the bishop nodded, his hands held firmly, one inside the other.

'Then I suggest you split your force. Half to the north and half to the south. You'll need to watch for Earl Sweyn's return.'

'Indeed, my lord. I'll do just that. And I'll travel north, towards lands more likely to be loyal to my family. Earl Sweyn, should he strike there, will likely use them poorly. And I'll not allow it. Not again.'

'Then we have arrangements in place, Lord Leofric. Now all that remains to be seen is who has to draw blood first and whether we should fear King Gruffydd ap Llewelyn or Earl Sweyn more.'

THE FOLLOWING MORNING, Leofric summoned his loyal men to him who led his hundred warriors. He eyed them keenly. He trusted all of them with his life, and with that of his son, Ælfgar, for Ælfgar had now joined him from Oxford. All the same, he determined to protect his son.

'Ælfgar, you'll patrol southwards, staying close to Hereford. I'll take the north of Hereford. We have it on good authority that Earl Sweyn is attacking the southern king, Gruffydd ap Rhydderch, alongside Gruffydd ap Llewelyn, but what happens after that is impossible to determine. If they're successful, then Gruffydd ap Llewelyn should be content. If not, well? I fear nowhere will be safe.'

'Then you should go south, father,' his son urged him, a steely look in his eyes.

'No, I'll go north.' He thought his son might argue with him, but he quickly subsided.

'Send a daily messenger to Hereford. Bishop Æthelstan will ensure we're kept informed of events; likewise, he'll send word to the king.'

'And what will the king do about it?' his son demanded to know. Leofric was surprised his son hadn't thought beyond his initial anger at Sweyn.

'He'll have little choice but to banish Earl Sweyn if he's caught alive. If he's dead, he'll be unable to embarrass his family and his king further.' He caught his son's eyes, trying to convey more with a look than with look.

'I'll believe it when I see it,' a voice chimed, and Leofric made no effort to determine who spoke as such. He wasn't going to berate them.

'Have a care for yourself,' he urged all his men. 'We all know that King Gruffydd ap Llewelyn is a wily warrior. Of Earl Sweyn's battle prowess on land, I've no idea, but I imagine he'll be trying to prove himself or trying not to prove himself. Either could be deadly.'

Without further words, Leofric made ready to mount Oswald.

'Father,' he turned back to face his son. 'Are you sure about this?' Ælfgar asked him softly.

'I am son, yes. I don't foresee a fight for any of us, but if there is one, I imagine it will happen in the north. I've lived a long life, son. If I should fall protecting my kingdom, then I'll have done my duty. Now go. Or your men and my brother will ride off without you.'

Hastily, so his son couldn't see his pride or fear, Leofric mounted up and summoned his nephew, Ælfwine, to his side. Wulfstan would accompany Ælfgar. He also had Olaf at his side. Between the two of them, he hoped they'd make one decent fighting man. Otryggr would escort Ælfgar and fifty of the warriors, alongside his brother, Godwine.

'I'll see you soon,' Leofric called to his men escorting Ælfgar. 'And remember, stay alive, and keep one another alive.'

To the clatter of horses' hooves, he exited the protection of Hereford's walls and turned his horse northwards. Wherever Earl Sweyn was, he wanted to find him first. It would bring him great pleasure to be the one to inform Godwine of his son's death, or capture. This time, he hoped, it would be more successful than last year.

16

ÆLFGAR

Unease settled on him, yet he rode onward, eyes alert, knowing he'd not encounter the enemy. His father had the right to it. If there were to be trouble, it would come from the north, not the south. The two Welsh kings would exchange blows, and the outcome of their fight would either fill Gruffydd ap Llewelyn of Powys with pride or a desire to make amends for his failure. There was nowhere else he could make amends than opposite his own borders in the north. If he managed to claim some of Mercia's lands, he could only hold them if they were close to his existing possessions. Earl Sweyn had failed to steal lands held by the House of Leofwine in Worcestershire, once owned by his uncle, Eadwine. It now appeared that Gruffydd ap Llewelyn would try by force. It was to be hoped that Llewelyn's ambitions wouldn't also focus on the lands held in Shropshire and Cheshire.

Ælfgar called Wulfstan to his side.

'Cousin,' he managed a smile. Wulfstan smirked at him and came closer.

'Well, this is a balls up, isn't it? I thought King Edward knew what he was doing regarding Earl Sweyn?'

'I don't think you're alone in that. Although, well, I think my father was trying to tell me this might be the king's intentions after all. Perhaps, it would be easier all round if Sweyn died in combat.'

'So, now we seem to be at war. Should King Magnus think to attack by sea while Earl Sweyn is dangling his cock in the Welsh kingdoms, the king might be left without the means to defend from either enemy. Do you imagine he considered that?'

'I know,' Ælfgar grunted. 'And no, I doubt he considered it. Now he has his vast ship army, and I think the king feels invincible.' He was trying not to grip his reins too tightly. He didn't want to spook his horse. 'I imagine it won't be long until Earl Godwine arrives and starts causing even more problems. No doubt he'll drag Earl Harold along with him. And you know, I like Harold, but the rest of his family can perish for all I care.' Ælfgar didn't admit that such thoughts closely mirrored Harold's own. Harold and his older brother weren't close. Not for the first time, Ælfgar berated himself for rescuing Sweyn Godwinesson from the sea two years ago. It would have been better if he'd slipped below the waves.

'That whole family are rotten to the core,' Wulfstan growled. While Ælfgar had never known his uncle, Northman, Wulfstan, he realised, must have some memories of his father, murdered at Godwine's hands.

'They are. A pity it wasn't them who drowned in the North Sea instead of Jarl Hakon on the way to marrying his bride.'

'I wish no man an early death, but I agree with you on this. How much easier would it be if Earl Godwine hadn't been allowed to proliferate quite so freely.'

'His wife must once have been very comely,' Wulfstan offered, his lips downcast in disbelief. Ælfgar chuckled. Trust his cousin to think of a way of making him find some humour in their predicament. 'And I hear they weren't small babies either,' Wulfstan winced as he spoke while Ælfgar choked on laughter. He didn't like to be so crude, but sometimes Wulfstan did make a good point.

'So, your father wants all the glory this time?' Wulfstan asked him when they'd stopped laughing.

'He says it's better if he dies than me. So yes, he's after all the glory,' Ælfgar concluded. 'I imagine he hopes to encounter bloody Gruffydd ap Llewelyn and kill him once and for all, the bastard. As well as Earl Sweyn. My father would think it worth the risk.'

'Well, I wish him luck with that. I don't think Gruffydd will come within striking distance of Mercia. Not now. He'll entice Sweyn to help him and not vice versa.'

Ahead, Ælfgar noticed the change in terrain as the hills started to dominate the skyline. That was the problem with this area of the kingdom. The Welsh could hide behind those hills and appear almost without warning. It was little surprise that the English, and before them, the Mercians, had had little luck overpowering the Welsh. Even the lady of Mercia, Lady Æthelflæd, nearly a hundred and fifty years ago, had only enjoyed limited success against the Welsh.

LATER THAT DAY, when they'd ridden as far as was possible before darkness fell, Ælfgar gratefully slid from his saddle and, removing the item, led his horse to a gentle stream to drink. They'd seen few people all day—a lot of sheep, but not many people. The sheep stood out clearly from the green of the hillsides, whereas what people they had seen tended to blend in with the greens and browns of the soil and crops. Many were making the borderlands their homes, and not one of them had eyed the approaching horses with a welcoming smile, not even when Ælfgar had taken the time to explain who they were.

'My arse is numb,' Wulfstan called, bending backwards, his hands on his lower back.

'We did ride a long way today,' Ælfgar confirmed, wincing around his aches and pains. While they rode everywhere, it wasn't often that they spent the entire day in the saddle. Tomorrow it would be difficult to move. Ælfgar didn't look forward to that.

'Can we light a fire?' Edmund, one of his household warriors called.

'Yes, we need hot foot tonight. And, I don't see that the Welsh will want to investigate who's brazen enough to have a fire. Let's use it to our advantage,' Ælfgar decided quickly. He also shivered slightly. The weather had been warm all day, but now, with the sun setting, it was turning cooler. He thought longingly of his wife and warm bed before bending to rip up long grasses to slick the sweat from his horse's body.

The sound of his fellow warriors making camp made the actions comforting, and in no time at all, they were all sitting around a fiercely burning fire, complete with a cooking pot at its centre. The smell of cooking meat filled the air, and Ælfgar's belly rumbled. He was out of practice at sitting in his saddle all day, and only having one warm meal a day. Perhaps it was time they all spent a bit more time out on manoeuvres.

'We set a guard tonight,' he called to his men. 'I don't envision any problems, but I'd rather have three yawning men tomorrow than a seax in my belly.' No one complained, and indeed, later, when he rolled in his cloak, yawning wildly, having taken the first watch, he realised the task should have gone to someone else. Bad enough three yawning men tomorrow, but even worse if one of them was the man in charge of the expedition. He winced around the pain in his legs from riding all day, and closed his eyes, thinking of his comfortable bed, and finally slept.

THE NEXT DAY passed much as the day before. They rode onwards. Ælfgar led the men, his cousin keeping him constant company. He spared a thought for his father, especially how much he might ache from riding all day, but his father was stubborn. He could have stayed in Hereford and commanded his son, nephews, and men to patrol the area. If his father's arse ached as much as Wulfstan's seemed to, if his grunts of pain were anything to go by, then he did only have himself to blame.

A soft rain was falling. Not enough to make travelling uncomfortable, but Ælfgar knew that his cloak would start to weigh even more at some point, and the water would soak into his byrnie. He didn't welcome the thought of scrubbing the rust from it. But that was a problem for another day. Now, he realised, it would be a good time for their enemy to attack, sneaking up on them through the mist of the day. He blinked the rain from his eyes and tried to focus on the view before him, but it was just about impossible. He could only see so far, and it wasn't far enough.

'I hope the bastards don't come for us today,' he grumbled to Wulfstan.

'If they do, we'll be easy pickings,' his cousin offered, which was far from reassuring.

'Why does it always rain in the borderlands?' Ælfgar mumbled. 'Always.'

'Well, not always,' Wulfstan countered. 'And they say the same about the kingdom of the Scots. Once you get beyond Bamburgh, it does nothing but piss it down all the time.' Wulfstan's tone was martyred, and Ælfgar tried to find some amusement in it, but it was impossible. He was bored, wet and miserable. He didn't recall if it had rained when he'd journeyed north.

'My lord,' a cry from behind had him turning, hand on his seax.

'What is it?' he called, squinting into the rain that seemed to be purposefully falling straight into his eyes.

'I heard something,' one of his Æthelred informed him. 'A horse, I'm sure of it.' Ælfgar faced back the way they'd just come. They all strained to hear, but nothing was immediately apparent.

'Are you sure?' he called, only to be hailed by a disembodied voice emerging from the mist.

'Lord Ælfgar. It's Osric. Your father demands you join him.'

'Why? What's happened?' As Osric came into view, Ælfgar smirked to see the other man looking as miserable as them.

'It's Earl Sweyn.'

'What of him?'

'He's taken the nunnery at Leominster. Or rather, he's stolen the abbess and refuses to return her. It's said he's taken her to his bed.'

'For God's sake,' Ælfgar exploded. Bad enough to ally with the enemy and threaten the uneasy peace on the border with the Welsh. But now this. Was there nothing that Earl Sweyn wouldn't do?

17

LEOFRIC

'I'm sorry, my lord, but Earl Sweyn wishes to see no one. He's busy,' the guardsman sniggered. Earl Leofric winced to hear the knowing delight in the man's voice. It was despicable, and yet Leofric could only blame himself for not realising the depths of Earl Sweyn's depravity. A man who could ally with an enemy of England was sure to think nothing of taking an abbess to his bed.

'This isn't a polite request to gain admittance,' he huffed. 'You either allow me entry, or we'll batter down the walls of this place until we've retrieved the abbess.'

'My lord,' there was a shiver of disbelief in the other man's voice, but another appeared behind his shoulders, pushing his head through the thin slit of the gateway.

'Then that's what you'll have to bloody well do,' the belligerent man spoke over his fellow guard. 'Earl Sweyn has made it very clear that there'll be death for any who dare to disturb him, and I won't be the man to lose his life over some whoring.'

'But you would lose it in a battle against my warriors?'

'Earl Leofric, it's well-known that you don't have enough

warriors to hold a sparring competition, let alone make war on Earl Sweyn. Now, be gone before Earl Sweyn hears you and takes your head for your impertinence.' The opening in the gateway slammed in Leofric's face, and he stood back with a grimace. He'd not expected Earl Sweyn to see reason. He had anticipated the guards having some. Would they really face death just so their earl could swive the abbess? It seemed that, yes, they would.

'I take it he said no,' Olaf said as Leofric stamped back to his brother and collection of mounted warriors. The rain was teeming down, and Leofric feared he might slip in the mud.

'Yes, he said no. Or rather, his guards did. I didn't see the earl himself. The men seem to think he's enjoying himself too much.'

Olaf winced at the thought.

'The abbess won't take kindly to this.'

'No, she won't. And it's an outrage. But the guards did have the right to it. We don't have enough to take the settlement. We must wait for reinforcements.'

'And in the meantime?' his brother by marriage queried.

'I've sent word to my wife, and the king. I'm sure that we'll hear back soon. Ideally, we need to have killed the damn fool before my wife arrives and slices his stones from his body. She'll be most displeased.'

Olaf winced at the thought of what Lady Godgifu might do to Earl Sweyn if she ever caught him.

'We need shelter.'

'Yes, we do, somewhere out of the mud and rain. I can't see we'll be leaving anytime soon. It will take at least four days to hear back from the king.'

'And you hope just as many until you hear back from your wife.' For all the seriousness of the situation, Earl Leofric did manage a smile.

'It's to be hoped that she seeks out the king and queen, and they hear all she has to say.'

'I can't believe he's done it,' Olaf commented. They were making their way towards the flimsy protection of a strand of trees. From there, they could watch the gateway and, perhaps, stay somewhat drier.

'He's a bloody fool. Why not just take a wife?' his brother asked.

'There aren't many wives as well-endowed as the abbess of Leominster,' Olaf countered. 'Admittedly, most of them don't come with the added bonus of simultaneously upsetting the king and our Lord God. What's the punishment for taking a nun against her will?' he asked.

'It's not a pat on the back,' Leofric growled. He'd dismounted once more and was trying to hold as much of the wet fabric clear from his body as possible. Oswald looked miserable, and he felt the same.

'Do you think the abbess welcomed his attentions?' Olaf murmured, but Leofric was already shaking his head.

'I think if she'd welcomed it, we wouldn't have been met with the scene of destruction we saw. His men battered down the wooden walls of the nunnery and carried her away against her will. I pity the poor woman. I only wish I could do the same now and return her to the sanctity of the nunnery, but Earl Sweyn has more warriors than we do.'

Earl Leofric shuddered to think of the terror the women had endured. In the heart of England, Leominster should have been safe from attack and certainly safe from being assaulted by the earl for the region.

'He's a grasping man, desperate for more and more land.'

'And does he not realise that getting a whelp on the abbess won't give him control of those lands,' Godwine Leofwinesson quarrelled.

'I don't believe he thinks about anything for longer than it takes to fart,' Earl Leofric complained. He shook his head. They'd been so focused on the alliance between Earl Sweyn and Gruffydd ap Llewelyn and the war against Rhydderch of Gwent, which would have hopefully led to his death, they'd given no thought to Earl Sweyn's other ambitions if he frustrated their ambitions and lived.

'What will the king command?'

'He's a man devoted to his God. He'll also demand Sweyn's stones,' Earl Leofric spoke with confidence. He couldn't imagine the king allowing Sweyn to escape punishment. Not this time. And not when he'd taken an abbess against her will. There were rules about such affronts. The king would have to act. And if not the king, then the queen. After all, she held responsibility for the female religious. She had a say in the running of their land and in ensuring they were safeguarded against the pretensions of men. It had been the same ever since Lady Elfrida had been queen, and her husband had brought about the Benedictine Reformation of the previous century.

'And Earl Godwine?' Olaf queried.

'Earl Godwine's soul is imperilled enough already. I don't see that another mark on it will make much difference to him. He's killed his allies. He'll argue that his son was acting for the good of the kingdom, somehow. Perhaps he'll even decide the abbess was a traitor. But Queen Edith will not accept it easily. As a woman and one devoted to God herself, she'll ensure the king punishes her brother this time, and as I said, she has power over the nunneries should he prove unwilling. But, I don't believe the king will. There are only so many times he can excuse the actions of his earl.'

Olaf nodded, turning to catch sight of Ælfwine. He was dripping with rain as well, his face white and cold.

'They're all inside those walls,' he offered mournfully. 'No others are waiting to relieve them, should they be attacked. Earl Sweyn truly is an arsehole.' Ælfwine shook his head, dislodging more water from where his hair showed beneath his helm.

'At least we can be sure they won't escape us,' Earl Leofric murmured, his eyes not straying from the barred gate ahead of them. Smoke billowed above the settlement, and he'd have welcomed the heat. It was supposed to be summer, but the rain was cold, making him feel miserable, even without knowing what Earl Sweyn had done.

'I hope he gets the pox,' Ælfwine spat. 'Or his dick swells up, so it's too painful to piss.' Earl Leofric grimaced at the thought. 'It's only what he bloody deserves,' he continued. 'He can't ravish a bloody nun.' As with the rest of the men, Ælfwine was furious on behalf of Abbess Eadgifu. She should have been safe in her nunnery, especially with no true enemies on England's soil.

'Even that bastard Gruffydd ap Llewelyn wouldn't have taken an abbess from her nunnery. And he certainly wouldn't have forced himself upon her.' Leofric nodded. It was true.

'Wherever did he get the idea from?' Olaf mused. Behind them, some of the other men were tending to the horses and lighting a fire. Winhus and Cena were also trying to use the tree branches to suspend one of the travel canvases over their heads.

'We can ask him when we finally apprehend him,' Ælfwine menaced. 'I'll take great delight in extracting that information from him when I get my chance.' Still, Leofric stared at the closed gateway. He couldn't stop thinking about what he'd witnessed at the nunnery. The smoke had alerted them of the problem, and they'd ridden with all haste towards the fire, fearful that the Welsh had attacked. Earl Leofric would never have considered that it was Earl Sweyn's work. He still found it impossible to contemplate. And then, when he'd been informed that not only had Earl Sweyn run off with all their portable wealth but had also taken the abbess, it had been hard not to jump into his saddle and ride after Earl Sweyn.

It had taken them two days to track Earl Sweyn to this location. All that time, he'd been prepared to fight him to reclaim the abbess, but with Sweyn and his allies taking control of the walled settlement, he'd have to wait to exact his revenge. He turned the word over in his mind. Revenge. Yes, that was what it would be. He'd never considered himself a vengeful man, but there were some people who had merited all they'd received at his hands. On this occasion, Earl Godwine and his son wouldn't escape without punishment. Hopefully, both men would lose all they currently held. What it meant for Queen Edith, and her brother, Harold, Leofric didn't know, but it could certainly cause them problems.

Equally, what it meant for the House of Leofwine was impossible to know, but certainly, it couldn't hurt them unlike the House of Godwine.

18

LADY GODGIFU

'My lord king,' she inclined her head towards King Edward, trying not to notice the reddened, tearful face of his wife. It seemed that news of Earl Sweyn's latest outrage had reached the king before she could deliver it herself. The look on King Edward's face made her realise she was probably lucky not to be the one to delight in informing him of the abbess's abduction.

'Lady Godgifu,' the king spoke evenly, as she noticed that both Ralph and Beorn were also in attendance upon the king, as were most of his close allies. There was no sign of Earl Godwine or Harold, the queen's favourite brother.

'I fear there'll be outright war in the Mercian lands if due justice isn't served.' She was pleased she managed to keep her words to just that. There was a great deal more she wished to say.

'Indeed, my lady. It's shocking, and I take it there's no possibility of it being incorrect?'

'My lord husband heard it from the nuns themselves. Why would they say as such if it weren't the truth?'

'Indeed, you're quite right. I was just ordering my household warriors, alongside Lords Ralph and Beorn, to travel to Leominster.'

'And what will they do when they get there? The abbess must be returned to her community,' she infused her voice with all the horror the thought of being abducted from her home could give her.

The king's face darkened at the reminder of the transgression. She wasn't surprised. The life of a nun was supposed to be filled with service to God, and, more importantly, free from the interference of men and their sexual requirements on a woman.

'My lady,' a cry echoed through the hall, and she turned, unsurprised to find it came from Earl Godwine. His face was as red with fury as his daughter's was with crying. 'It's outrageous to make such unfounded allegations against my son.'

'They're not unfounded. They're the truth. Unless, of course, my lord, you mean to imply that the nuns are lying about the fate of their Holy Mother.' Earl Godwine thundered forwards, his great bulk making the floorboards vibrate as though he were a horse on the gallop and not merely a man. As much as he disgusted her, and his son's actions offended her, Lady Godgifu was determined to enjoy this, no matter what.

'They're wholly unfounded,' Earl Godwine roared, and now one of the king's household warriors stepped forwards and placed himself between Earl Godwine and Lady Godgifu.

'My lord, stand aside from the good lady. She speaks nothing but the truth.' King Edward's words thundered with fury. She was grateful for the tall back of the warrior protecting her. She'd never felt fearful of any man before, not even the bloody Danes or Norse, but Earl Godwine's entire body was quivering. It was quite possible that he would lash out. However, she had no intention of minding her tongue in his presence.

'We have word from Leominster, my lord. Your son,' and the king's words were sharp and filled with fury. 'Has done this despicable deed. His alliance with the Welsh king was bad enough, but this, this, is beyond redemption. Your son has vastly overplayed his hand. He'll face punishment for his actions once he's caught and dragged here. And this time, I'll not be able to go easy on him, as in the past.'

'My lord king,' Earl Godwine roared once more.

'Mind your tone,' the warrior menaced, joined now by three more of the king's huscarls, gleaming with iron. They surrounded Earl Godwine, and Lady Godgifu took two sideways steps. She didn't want to be unintentionally involved when the stand-off became more physical.

She spared a glance at Queen Edith, but the queen was stony-faced now. Lady Godgifu once more found herself admiring the young woman. It took true bravery to face her own father without a hint of daughterly love.

'My lord king,' Earl Godwine tried once more. 'Allow me to travel north. I'll discover the truth and ensure all is as it should be. My son isn't so much as a fool to have done these things.'

'No,' the king thundered. 'No, you'll have nothing more to do with this other than waiting for your son to arrive here for sentencing. If I catch so much as a hint that you've disobeyed me, then you'll also face my justice.'

Inwardly, Lady Godgifu smirked. This is what she wanted. She'd waited many long years for this.

'My lord king, Lady Godgifu has long hated my son. You know it as well as I do. She speaks with nothing but spite and malice.'

'If that's how you wish to name the truth then yes, Lady Godgifu speaks with spite and malice, my lord. Now, I warn you, calm down, or you can cool yourself down in one of the rooms used to keep the prisoners before their trials.'

Lady Godgifu couldn't see Earl Godwine's face from where she stood, but she could hear his heavy breathing.

'My daughter.'

'Is your queen, and as such, leads the female religious of our kingdom,' the king countered quickly. A sudden silence filled the hall. Lady Godgifu kept her eyes on Queen Edith. She sat, back erect, hands carefully held together, one inside the other. Lady Godgifu approved. But this was what she's always feared. Earl Godwine believed he had the king's ear because his daughter had the king's bed. But it meant nothing. The queen could either be loyal to her husband or her father. She couldn't do both. Not at the moment. No doubt it helped that Queen Edith didn't like her brother, Sweyn. She loved her brother Harold, but Sweyn? Not at all. He embarrassed her.

'My lord king,' Earl Godwine was almost pleading now, but King Edward shook his head.

'Lady Godgifu, please continue speaking. You were using wisdom.'

She inclined her head in thanks and recollected her thoughts.

'The lady will be deeply wounded, I'm sure of it. The bishops must pray for her and absolve her of all sins, for they are not hers, but another's.'

'Indeed, my lady. You're right. The Abbess will be treated kindly. God willing, her wounds won't stop her from continuing her important work, and God willing, the bishops will be able to absolve her, provided she can absolve herself. I take it you wouldn't be disinclined to offer her support.'

'Of course not, my lord king. I would do all I can for the woman. I am but an earl's wife and far from as holy as she, and yet, I'll happily give her all my time and support.'

'You're a good woman, Lady Godgifu,' the king offered her a tight smile, his hands drumming over the arms of his wooden chair.

'Lords Beorn and Ralph, travel to Leominster will all haste. Ensure the nunnery is protected. I'll finance the building of thicker walls, if required. Lord Beorn, you're to assist Earl Leofric in apprehending Sweyn Godwinesson. Lord Ralph, your priority is the members of the community at Leominster. I wish to know everything. There's no need for the abbess to venture to my court unless she wishes to. I would sooner she had time to recover. More than enough witnesses will ensure Earl Sweyn is convicted of this diabolical crime.'

'I would support the abbess as well,' Queen Edith confirmed. 'I will do all I can for her.'

The king nodded at his wife's words, a tight smile on his thinned lips.

'And you, Earl Godwine. You may either stay here or return to your earldom in Wessex until such time as your son is brought before me. I'll send my guards with you. They'll ensure you don't comport with the traitor. Is that understood?'

'My lord king, I would dream of doing nothing to cause further offence,' and yet Earl Godwine's words were far from sincere, and Lady Godgifu wasn't the only one to realise. She watched Queen Edith sweep her father with a twisted look of loathing. Again, she approved.

'I'll remain here until the truth is determined and my son exonerated,' Earl Godwine spoke bluffy.

'Then you'll be waiting an eternity,' Lady Godgifu murmured, and she knew the guards had heard her and hoped Earl Godwine had as well.

'Lords Beorn and Ralph, please leave with all haste and take a hundred of my huscarls.'

'A hundred?' Earl Godwine screeched.

'In fact, make it two hundred,' the king arched an eyebrow as he spoke. 'A hundred to support Earl Leofric and a hundred for the nunnery. Should Earl Sweyn prove truculent, you may reassign them as necessary. I'd hope to see you within two weeks. I'll have the men and women of the witan summoned to listen to the charges laid before the earl. Now, my dear wife, I think we should pray for the safe-keeping of the dear abbess.' The king stood, as did any other in the hall who happened to be sitting. In a procession, the king, his queen, and their attendants streamed from the hall. And still, the guards stood between Lady Godgifu and Earl Godwine.

Only when the king had gone, as well as the lords Beorn and Ralph, did Earl Godwine rise from his bowed position. Lady Godgifu's head had been upright for some time, assessing those still within the hall and Earl Godwine. She'd noticed that some of his younger sons had accompanied him. They stood awkwardly at the rear of the hall, Harold leading them for all it seemed he wished to be with his sister, the queen.

'Now listen to me, you evil bitch,' Earl Godwine reared up before her, the guards still there but a little slow to react.

'I'm not the evil one, my lord,' she spoke coolly. 'It's your son who goes against his king and his God.'

'He's done none of the things you level at him.'

'He has, and I imagine, when the truth is finally revealed, he'll have done much, much worse as well. Your son is the spawn of Satan.'

'How dare you,' Earl Godwine's hand lifted, and she felt, rather than saw, the guards close around her. If he hit her, then the king would hear of this as well. There were many witnesses, and many of them held no loyalty to the House of Godwine.

'Father,' a voice called from the rear of the hall. Earl Godwine's blow faltered, and she cursed. How much easier would it be had the earl just hit her? But no, one of his spawn had stopped him.

'My lady,' Earl Godwine lowered his hand and instead bowed low. 'My apologies for my reaction. It was unmanly.'

'It was yes, but then, it seems few in your family know the true meaning of respecting a woman.' She knew the words were incendiary, but it was time her true feelings were heard.

Once more, Earl Godwine's face filled with loathing, his thick cheeks wobbling with his fury. She waited. There was more to be said yet.

'Did your wife teach those sons of yours nothing? And why did she not teach them? Too busy lying down while you heaved over her?'

'My wife,' Earl Godwine spluttered. 'My wife,' he began once more.

'Has done nothing but beget children for you during the last two decades while you've been too busy trying to win favour and cause problems for others. Well now, my lord, it seems you have six problems to counter, and they're your own sons.'

'Now, my lady, it's unseemly to be jealous.'

'It's unseemly for your sons to show no respect to women, their queen and king. It's unseemly that you're here, begging the king not to listen to the truth. It is you, Earl Godwine, who is unseemly, as it appears, are all of your sons. You should be grateful your daughter has become such a fine woman amongst a nest of vipers.'

'My son,' Earl Godwine began.

'Has made a whore of an abbess. If there are children born to this depravity, how will they feel when they're grown? Your son has broken all the rules, not just of decorum but of morality. He's beyond redemption.'

'He's made some mistakes.'

'If you call having his king wish for his exile and deflowering a nun, then yes, mistakes, my lord, but all will see them for what they are. You had an opportunity to control him, and you failed. And now, you and your family must face the consequences. I assure you, I'll not be alone in pushing for the ultimate justice.'

With that and feeling some smug satisfaction, coupled with her genuine outrage, Lady Godgifu inclined her head to those who'd heard the public argument and walked, head high, to follow where the king and queen had gone to pray. She pretended not to notice the low murmur of appreciation for her words. She pretended not to hear, but it was there all the same. She wasn't the only one to wish Earl Godwine and his coven of sons as far from the English court as possible.

19

ARCHENFIELD, LEOFRIC

'My lord,' he called through the closed gateway. 'My lord Sweyn,' he tried again, turning to face Ralph and Beorn. It had taken them some time to arrive, and indeed, Beorn had appeared without Ralph, who'd first been sent to Leominster, but now both men were together, along with nearly all the two hundred huscarls sent by the king.

'He won't listen,' Leofric said to them both, exasperation in his voice. 'He wants us to assault him.' Beorn nodded while Ralph, much younger than Leofric and indeed even younger than Beorn, looked perplexed.

'But you said he doesn't have enough men?'

'He doesn't, but he believes we won't actually try and attack him. The bloody fool.' Beorn's words rippled with fury. Leofric admired the hot-headedness of Beorn but was pleased he was there to cool wounded pride. He feared, if not, then this place would already be a smoking ruin, and Earl Sweyn perhaps part of the ashes. Not, he admitted, that he could see a different outcome for Sweyn. He would either be exiled or executed. Leofric knew which one of the two options he'd prefer.

'Then we must do exactly that,' Ralph determined.

'We've been waiting for you and your men,' Leofric spoke quickly. He could already detect some unhappiness between the two. It would be bloody typical if he were forced to deal with the king's brother, nephew, and cousin. He could do without that complication.

'Then we should ready ourselves,' Ralph confirmed, already moving to stride away back to the rest of the men. The shelter of the trees remained where they all waited for Earl Sweyn to erupt from inside the settlement, but it was no longer as crude as it had been. Canvases had been erected for the men, and while it could still be boggy underfoot, much of it was almost pleasant, especially with the warm fires to drive the dampness from clothes. The morning had even dawned bright and filled with bird song.

'Which is what I've been saying for days,' Beorn stomped to follow Ralph, and Leofric watched them go, a flicker of amusement on his face, which he saw mirrored on that of Ælfgar.

'Lord Ralph seems to think we've been doing nothing but twiddling our thumbs for the last two weeks. If he'd sent his men to begin with, then Earl Sweyn would already be apprehended,' Ælfgar grouched, but it was remarkably well-natured.

'The impetuousness of youth,' Leofric chuckled darkly. He stood back and glared at the closed gateway. He could hear the door guards behind it. Leofric was far from convinced he couldn't smell them.

'Lord Sweyn, we will strike if you don't release the abbess and give yourself up,' he tried again. He didn't want to attack fellow English warriors, but Sweyn was leaving them with little choice.

For all the times he'd previously encouraged the earl to surrender, he'd had no response to his demands, yet this time, a voice did call back to him.

'Earl Godwine will come and relieve this desultory siege, and then we'll see who must surrender.'

Leofric shook his head, striding away, Ælfgar at his side.

'The damn fool says nothing and then tells us he's waiting for his bloody father to relieve him.'

'Well, he'll be waiting a long time,' Ælfgar confirmed. 'My lady mother assures us that the king has forbidden Earl Godwine from doing anything on pain of forfeiting his own estates.'

Ahead, Leofric could see the king's household warriors preparing to attack the settlement of Archenfield. There had been plentiful discussions about how to gain entry, but through them all, one tactic had made the most sense. A battering ram, or rather, a felled tree trunk, shorn of its branches and leaves. They now had that, and the discarded branches had provided ample fuel for the fires. Now all they needed to do was get inside. Of course, there were other tactics to be employed as well. While they'd decided against trying to burrow beneath the built-up enclosure, they did have skilled archers and spear throwers. All the men were adamant that they could throw a spear over the enclosure or let fly their arrows to do the same. If the tips were aflame, that would also help the matter.

Men ensured they wore byrnies and had their weapons belts ready. Leofric had previously donned his. He wasn't about to get as close as he had done to the gate without a form of protection. He glanced at Ælfgar, his two nephews, and Olaf, and convinced that they, and his men, were as well prepared as they could be, he turned to join Beorn and Ralph. Ralph looked furious. A hot-headed fool wasn't likely to be much use. But then, and he nodded to the leader of the king's household warriors, Æthelwald, there was a man he could rely on.

'What's the plan then?' Leofric asked, aware that as the more senior figure, he was in the position of superiority, not that he meant to stamp all over any plans already devised.

'We aim for the gate,' Æthelwald announced confidently. 'It's not as if there's another way to get inside. It takes sixteen men to carry the battering ram. They'll need their heads protected by their fellow warriors. I'll lead those thirty-two men,' he confirmed. Leofric nodded. He was pleased Æthelwald was there. Between the two of them, he was sure they could bring this unfortunate and unnecessarily elongated matter could be brought to a swift end.

'My archers will fire the settlements,' Beorn added. 'They assure me they can hit the rooves of the buildings without getting themselves within range of any on the interior who might think to counter their actions.'

'And when we gain entry?'

'My men will find the earl and the abbess. They'll ensure she's brought to safety and needn't be fearful.'

'It's almost as though you don't need us at all,' Leofric half-joked. 'My men and I will be here to provide support where needed. I'm sure the king would sooner most of the men left with their lives. It'll be for him to decide on their punishment, not us.' He added as a caution, trying not to glance at Ralph. The younger man was almost thrumming with a desire to kill as many as possible. It seemed this would be his first opportunity to make a warrior's name for himself.

'Then, we should just get on with it,' Æthelwald confirmed with about as much enthusiasm as a wet cloak on a damp day. Leofric nodded.

'We should. Good luck, my loyal warriors.' Leofric couldn't truly see the matter resulting in the deaths of many, if any, of his men, but Earl Sweyn had now had plenty of time to reconsider his actions. Once he realised the protection of his father wasn't to be forthcoming, he might well panic. Then it could get nasty.

'Come on, you ugly bastards,' Æthelwald called to those waiting beside the mammoth tree trunk to be used as a battering ram. Leofric really couldn't foresee the gate putting up that much resistance. As one, the sixteen unfortunate men bent and stood simultaneously, holding the battering ram by a series of hempen ropes tied along its length. Another sixteen men joined them, all of them carrying two shields, and Æthelwald issued instructions from behind them.

'Come on, men,' Leofric called to his warriors. 'Let's get this over and done with, and remember, protect yourselves.'

With Olaf and Ælfgar flanking him, he followed the men and the battering ram. They were also followed by many more of the king's men under the command of Beorn and Ralph. Leofric kept his eyes forward, hoping against hope that Earl Sweyn would determine on a peaceful end to this rather than a blood-drenched one. Not that he was to get his wish.

With a loud crash, Leofric watched the battering ram make its first strike against the wooden gate. He winced, thinking the entire structure shuddered. Yet the gate didn't open. It did bring men to the palisades, and the archers and spear throwers were quick to pick off those who hung too far over the gateway as the battering ram again thundered against the gateway. From his vantage point, he could hear the roar of angry men and the sizzle as the fire arrows struck in thatch that was far from dry but was much drier than when they'd first arrived. He grimaced. This wasn't so much a war as a simple matter of overpowering a weaker force.

No sooner had he thought that than he changed his mind. Again, heads appeared on the ramparts, shooting down at the men with the battering ram and also at those with fire arrows. The smell of smoke drifted to him, and he coughed and blinked the smoke from his eyes. The wind wasn't their ally, but everything else was going well.

For every arrow that those inside rained down on the battering ram, Beorn's men shot two more at them. Indeed, there were so many arrows in the sky Leofric thought Sweyn's men were either brave or foolhardy to take the risk.

He winced as one of Sweyn's men was skewered and, losing his balance, tumbled to land on top of the battering ram with a clatter of wood on wood. The felled warrior made no effort to scramble to his feet, and eventually, two of the shield carriers were forced to pull the man's lifeless body clear from the tree trunk.

'Why doesn't he just surrender?' Ælfgar asked from beside his father. The chin guard slightly muffled his words, but Leofric understood them well enough.

'Because he's an arse,' Olaf quickly interjected. 'Even now, he'll still be thinking that his father will come and relieve him.'

Flames could be seen dancing upwards, the heat unwelcome when the sun was warming them enough.

Another crash from the battering ram, and this time, the gate gave with a shriek of splintering wood. The battering ram swung again, the men screaming as they forced it forward. The gate lay half on and half off, with pieces of wood sticking out all over the place, but Æthelwald had determined enough was enough. Hastily the battering-ram holding warriors exchanged the tree trunk for a shield from their fellow warriors and then began to pour inside.

'Come on,' Leofric urged Cena, Scirwold and the rest of his warriors. 'We need to get in there as well, or it'll be a blood bath.'

'We'll go,' his son and nephews appealed to him, and unwillingly, Leofric nodded.

'Be careful,' he urged all his men, well, all apart from the five, and Olaf, who lingered at his side, watching his nephew.

Leofric watched his son run off and force his way through the gateway. The archers had stopped their labours and hastened to do the same. Leofric glanced around, pleased to see that at least fifty of the king's warriors were holding back. Although there had been no opportunity for Earl Sweyn to escape, it was still not impossible that one of his allies might attempt to provide protection by attacking the attackers.

The sound of bloody slaughter filled the air as Leofric watched Lord Ralph slide in through the broken-down gate. He'd never considered Ralph a warrior, but the young lord seemed keen to prove he had some skill.

'I would wager a hundred pennies that Earl Sweyn will emerge with barely a mark on him,' Olaf offered, eyebrows high.

'And I would take that wager,' Leofric reached out and sealed the deal with his brother by marriage. 'I believe he might fight for his life.'

'I think he'll have others do it for him,' Olaf growled. 'That's what weak men do.'

'You might have the right of it,' Leofric conceded, 'but I hope he shows some stones for once in his life.' He stood beside Olaf in silence. The smell of smoke was pervasive, as was the heat from the fire, but from what Leofric could see, it didn't appear that the settlement would be entirely beyond repair. Every so often, a shriek or cry drifted to them with the smoke, but Leofric was content to wait to gain entry until his son assured him all was well. He was happy to fight, but this wasn't really a fight. It was a simple matter of overwhelming the king's recalcitrant brother.

Yet, for all that, the battling seemed to go on for some time. Leofric was beginning to think he might need to intervene when a crack of wood preceded the broken gate being pulled clear.

'My lord,' Ælfgar called for him. 'It's done. We have Earl Sweyn.' Not too quickly, but with haste enough to show he was impatient, Leofric and Olaf walked towards Ælfgar, the smoke eddying in the wind that had sprung up.

'You're hale?' was Leofric's first demand from his son.

'Aye, father, all is well. Earl Sweyn's men have some cuts and bruises. I don't believe anyone will die because of this. The lords Ralph and Beorn are unhurt. But, there is a problem.' By now, Leofric was level with his son and walked inside the settlement. The smell of too many people being cooped up inside for at least two weeks was ripe in the air, the smoke doing little to alleviate it.

'Problem?' Olaf demanded to know.

'Yes, my lord. The abbess.'

'He's not harmed her? Surely? Other than the obvious?'

'No, father, he's not, and yet, she refuses to be parted from him. She says they're wed in the eyes of her God and that she'll not return to the nunnery.'

'And do you believe she speaks the truth?' Leofric demanded, walking beside his son, nodding to his warriors and those of the king who were apprehending Earl Sweyn's adherents. He winced at the bruises and cuts on display. He hoped they'd not get the wound rot. To die for a man's refusal to give up a woman seemed a waste of a good life.

'I don't,' Ælfgar confirmed quickly. 'I believe she lies. The earl holds something over her, but I don't know what it is.'

'Hum,' Leofric didn't like to hear that, yet he suspected Sweyn was quite capable of such bribery. 'It's clear he means to bind the woman to him to lessen his punishment from the king. Take me to them, but first, did Sweyn fight?'

'No, father, he didn't. He sent his men to protect him, and when they failed, he didn't even raise his seax against Lord Beorn.'

'It seems I owe you a hundred pennies,' Leofric offered sourly while Olaf chuckled darkly.

Ahead, the doorway to the main hall was open, but only smoke gushed forth from it.

'Where is everyone?' he asked of his son.

'Not in there. Come, follow me,' Ælfgar led the way down a long winding path, and Leofric startled when he realised that the way forwards brought them to a church.

'In there?'

'In there,' Ælfgar confirmed. Only now did Leofric see Lords Beorn and Ralph. Both men had some markings on their byrnies, and where Beorn had removed his helm, a bruise was already forming on his chin and lower cheek.

'What happened to you?' Leofric demanded to know.

'A fight between me and one of Sweyn's most foolish allies,' Beorn spat blood from his mouth, and Leofric hoped he wasn't missing a tooth.

'And where's Earl Sweyn?'

'Inside,' both men pointed at the same time. Leofric shrugged and walked inside the church, noticing as he went how many of Sweyn's warriors were moaning on the floor. Some of them had been tied with rope, but others were too bent over in pain to put up any more of a fight.

The interior of the church was free from smoke, although candles danced in the breeze from the open doorway. He could hear the sound of soft prayers but first had to find his way through the mass of bleeding warriors and those who stood as a menacing guard over them. Leofric didn't like seeing the weapons inside the church but kept his complaints in check.

'What's this?' he asked his son, although Beorn and Ralph were also escorting them alongside Olaf.

'They're praying. The abbess was already on her knees when we found Earl Sweyn. He was quick to join her.'

'I imagine he was,' Olaf spoke wryly. From behind, Leofric eyed the abbess and her alleged husband. She was a tall woman, wearing a hood over her hair, even inside the church. The soles of her shoes were remarkably clear from mud, and her words were soft and even, apart from when she ended her prayers with a reverberating 'Amen' that quivered.

Sweyn's hair was lengthy and flowed freely over his shoulders. Leofric noticed his trews were ripped on his left and right leg, even though Ælfgar had said he'd been uninjured.

'My lord,' Leofric spoke over the prayers, noting the shudder of the abbess's shoulders.

Sweyn didn't immediately respond. Leofric waited. Her prayers resumed quickly, but Sweyn's didn't. He paused patiently for Sweyn to compose himself, even though he could hear the huffs of anger from Ralph and Beorn.

'Earl Sweyn,' he spoke when more than enough time had elapsed. Only then did Sweyn turn. His eyes were sullen, and his chin stubborn. Leofric noted that, indeed, the earl carried no wounds on his face.

'Earl Leofric,' Sweyn's tone was even more sullen now. 'I might have known you'd be here. King Gruffydd ap Llewelyn assured me you'd be the one to try and topple my increased power and influence.'

Leofric made no response to that. Mention of Gruffydd ap

Llewelyn was surely intended to incite an argument, but there was no need to have one. Earl Sweyn was entirely overwhelmed, and when he faced the king, he'd be lucky to escape with his life.

'The king ordered us here,' he spoke with conviction.

'So these liars say. But the king would do no such thing. He's my sister's husband. He's my brother.'

'And he's ordered us to capture you, return the abbess to her nunnery, and then have you presented before him.'

'She won't go,' Sweyn stood now. Obstinacy etched into his frame. 'She won't go, I assure you. We're wed, and that's all there is to it.' Leofric noticed that the abbess shuddered as Sweyn spoke with deep conviction.

'Then she'll be presented to the king as well,' Leofric confirmed, a dip of his head towards the abbess's back. He knew Abbess Eadgifu of old. He understood there was much more to this than Sweyn implied.

'The king will merely determine that our union should be made more official, nothing else.'

'The king will do no such thing,' Leofric continued, even as Sweyn stood before him. The man's eyes blazed with conviction, and he placed his hand on Abbess Eadgifu's shoulder proprietorially, and she juddered once more. Leofric noted the movement. He wouldn't get the truth now, but he was sure the abbess would explain everything in time. Still, he tried to speak to her.

'My lady Eadgifu, is my lord correct, and you don't wish to return to your beloved sisters and life of quiet contemplation?' Leofric could hear Sweyn's heavy breathing, although it hitched just once and then resumed its steady pacing. There was something awry here, and he didn't like it. Not one bit.

But the abbess didn't turn to meet him, although she shook her head once. If he'd not been watching, the movement would have been missed.

'Then finish your prayers,' he offered, a tight smile on his lips. 'Horses will be found for you, and we'll ride for the king.'

'What of my men?' Earl Sweyn demanded.

'There are few who live,' Beorn interjected, and Leofric watched as Sweyn's expression faltered, for all Leofric had been assured few had actually died. It seemed Sweyn hadn't been expecting such an answer. 'Perhaps if you'd fought at their side instead of taking to your knees, they might live.'

'Now, cousin dearest,' Sweyn's words dripped with malice. 'I don't believe you'd have done any better now, would you? Not with your family history.' Leofric's hand was immediately on Beorn's arm to stay his hand. This wasn't the place for such arguments.

'Come,' Leofric ordered Beorn and Ralph. 'My son and my warriors will have these two under guard, and then we can journey southwards. The king's determined to pronounce on Earl Sweyn's actions. We don't need to get involved any further.'

For a moment, Leofric thought Beorn might argue, but abruptly, the tension left Beorn's arm, and he turned to Leofric. 'My thanks, my lord,' and the young man strode from the church. Leofric indicated that Ælfgar should step forward alongside Olaf and Ælfwine. Earl Sweyn was roughly trussed up, but Ælfgar was gentle with the abbess, bidding her rise and then allowing her to walk unaided outside. Leofric watched her unsteady steps. He knew the woman had undoubtedly been raped by Sweyn, a heinous crime in itself, but he feared that something else was also deeply wrong.

20

LADY GODGIFU

'SHE'LL ALLOW NO ONE NEAR HERE, NOT THE SERVANTS, SLAVES AND certainly not the queen.' Lady Godgifu spoke in a rush of words to her husband. Leofric, her son, alongside Olaf, Otryggr, Ælfwine and Wulfstan, were resting in the king's hall. They'd arrived late last night, and while Earl Sweyn had immediately been placed under armed guard, Abbess Eadgifu could have gone freely from his side, but she'd clung to him. Lady Godgifu hadn't liked it then and didn't like it now. She'd hoped that the offer of clean clothes and a warm bath would have dragged her from his side, but it seemed not.

'She's not the woman I know her to be,' Lady Godgifu continued, although it was perhaps unnecessary. She knew the abbess very well. She and Leofric had made extensive gifts to the nunnery, alongside many other religious establishments. Leominster was well-endowed and rich. The abbess had listened to her worries and offered gentle instructions in the past. Now, it was as though she'd been replaced with someone who lacked all such wisdom.

'I know, my dear. I don't like it. Although I'd rather not, I suspect this is more than just the outcome of Earl Sweyn's rape.' The use of the word made Lady Godgifu grimace.

'He's a bloody earl. He can have anyone he wants,' she seethed through clenched teeth. She was trying not to pace from one end of the hall to the other. She attempted to recall that here, in the king's hall, many eyes were on her. Bad enough that Earl Sweyn had attacked a nunnery so closely tied to her and her husband. Even worse, if others witnessed her intense hatred of the man and the act. She'd happily geld him herself, given the opportunity. And if the poor abbess was with child, then what then for her?

'Not even the queen?' her husband queried.

'No, she was most adamant that the queen wouldn't see her.'

'Then we can but wait and hope that someone will make her see sense. The bishop or archbishop? It can't just be the shame of it all, can it? The way you speak about her, I would think she had the firmest resolve of all.'

'She does,' Lady Godgifu confirmed, jutting out her chin. She was anxious for the woman, furious at Earl Sweyn and completely perplexed by the abbess's refusal to return to Leominster. She agreed with her husband. It wasn't all as it seemed.

'The king will convene the witan tomorrow,' Ælfgar spoke softly. Lady Godgifu eyed her son. He was as incensed as the rest of them, yet he held himself tightly, his face blank even when he spoke of the coming trial. Lady Godgifu nodded and again went to pace, only to stop herself from doing so. The king's hall was filling with people. It had been some time since a meal had been served. The appetising aroma of freshly caught fish being cooked, and flavoured with exotic spices, made even her stomach growl. And it was bringing others of the king's adherents to the hall with expectation. And that meant it wouldn't be long until Earl Godwine appeared.

Lady Godgifu didn't wish to see him. She certainly didn't wish for him to seek out her husband. There was no excuse for his son's actions, and there would be consequences, for if there weren't, then they had no true king, and that wasn't the truth. King Edward might not be a man of quick action, but his were more reasoned and, normally, more devastating for all that.

She settled beside her son and reached for water to quench her thirst. And all the time, she kept her gaze lowered but was alert. When Earl Godwine arrived, she wished to know about it.

'My lady,' a servant approached her, and she eyed the queen's trusted woman with surprise.

'Yes?'

'The queen seeks an audience with you.'

'Of course,' she inclined her head, a flicker of surprised unease in the pit of her stomach. Meeting her husband's eyes, she followed the shushing skirts of the queen's woman towards wherever the queen was. Lady Godgifu expected to find her sewing with her women or perhaps in discussion with her chamberlain and was instead surprised to be led to the stables.

'You'll ride with me,' the queen commanded, her tone almost making it a question, not an instruction.

'Of course, my lady,' Lady Godgifu looked uncertainly at the queen. She was dressed for riding, but Lady Godgifu wasn't.

'A moment to have my boots and cloak brought to me,' she inclined her head, and the queen startled, a look of contrition on her face.

'Of course, my lady. And your horse prepared?' Queen Edith hastened to add.

'Indeed. I'll be as quick as I can,' Lady Godgifu confirmed, sending a servant to find what was needed while she walked into the king's stables. Her horse was a placid animal but occasionally riled when not prepared as she liked to be. And that would be one of those occasions. As much as it was an honour to ride with the queen, she would dearly have liked some warning. Standing before her horse, she reproachfully eyed the animal, mirroring the horse's own look.

'Will we do this nicely?' she demanded of her horse, only to hear the chuckle of another. Startled, she turned to meet the eyes of her son.

'I had a feeling this might happen,' he informed his mother, already busy with saddle and reins, murmuring to the animal. 'I hastened to get here when you were summoned,' he added by way of explanation. 'I know just what the madame can be like,' he continued.

Lady Godgifu nodded. 'And did you think to bring my riding boots and cloak?' she teased her son.

'I didn't, lady mother, no, but I'm sure that part of the endeavour will be more easily accomplished.'

'Perhaps,' she agreed and then reached out to run her hand along the long neck of her horse, enjoying the feel of the animal's coat beneath her fingers. The horse was no longer young but was Lady Godgifu's favoured mount. Others she found either too docile or too erratic. Her horse was just as changeable as she was, but that wasn't unappealing.

'Here, my lady,' the servant rushed to her, rosy-cheeked and with the boots in one hand and the cloak in the other.

'Here,' Ælfgar summoned her. 'Sit on this, and you can change your shoes.' The stool was really intended to help her mount, but it would suffice, she decided. Better than losing her balance and falling on the horse-shit-strewn floor.

In less time than she thought possible, Lady Godgifu was ready and mounted before joining the queen in the courtyard.

'Inform your father of where I'll be for the afternoon,' Lady Godgifu told her son, the smell of the baked fish making her wish the queen had decided upon this expedition after the meal had been served.

'Ride well,' Ælfgar called cheerily to her. She doubted that this was all about the riding but appreciated the sentiment.

'My lady, I'm ready,' she bowed her head to the queen, and Queen Edith nodded solemnly.

'Are you sure you have everything you need?' she added courteously.

'Indeed, my lady. And I believe my horse is keen for a ride on this pleasant day.' It was pleasant. The terrible heat of the summer seemed to have passed. A gentle breeze blew, bringing with it the smell of the River Thames and other, more pleasant aromas. If it weren't for the issue with Earl Sweyn, the queen's brother, it would have been a perfect occasion to win herself some acclaim for being singled out by the queen. As it was, Lady Godgifu knew this was to be about more than just a ride in the countryside.

Ahead, the gates were cleared, and the queen's guard rode through. Five household warriors were to the front and five to the back. Besides the queen, and herself, there were only three of the queen's companions. This was indeed to be a secretive discussion, far from the ears of those who might think to report back to those with a vested interest, the queen's husband, or her father.

'Lady Godgifu,' they were outside the ancient walls of London, closer to the new church than the River Thames, and yet the queen still spoke quietly. Her voice trembled, and Lady Godgifu bowed her head low.

'My queen,' she intoned. It felt right to show her such respect. Whatever her feelings about the woman's mother and father, it seemed that Queen Edith was an even stronger-willed woman because of that, not thanks to it.

'I'm concerned about the abbess. I fear my brother,' and Queen Edith spat the word, 'has done something to the woman's mind. There's no reason for her to stay at Earl Sweyn's side, even if she is with child. What do you make of it?' The question was genuine.

'I agree with you. Abbess Eadgifu isn't a woman to cower behind a man. He's done something to her. Whatever it is, and if the rape is not bad enough on its own, it is truly terrible.'

'I have an idea,' the queen spoke even more quietly, her eyes on those who might step too close to them than she wished.

'You do?' Lady Godgifu was astounded to think the queen knew the abbess better than she did. She was sure the queen hardly even knew the abbess, if at all.

'I do, yes. My brother is a cruel man. He's always been the same. He's not someone who was kind to me when I was a child. He'll not have changed. And what my brother likes is secrets. He knows something about the abbess she doesn't want anyone to know.'

Lady Godgifu nodded along with the queen. She was sure now that she knew the queen's thoughts. Why they'd not come to her first frustrated her. But the time for such recrimination wasn't available.

'She was no maid when he raped her?' Lady Godgifu did the queen the honour of giving voice to the thought.

The queen opened her mouth to reply, and the word 'yes' was so soft it was barely above an exhalation.

'It's no matter. Many nuns have been wives before they were nuns,' Lady Godgifu defended the abbess. The news was unexpected and yet made every sense.

'But the abbess has staked much on her virginity,' the queen added. 'Even the king is aware of it.'

'And so your despicable brother thinks to make her his bed slave because it's better to be known as the victim of a rape than to have not been a virgin?' Lady Godgifu worked to keep her voice even. It wouldn't do if there were more than just her and the queen to know the truth. Yes, it was something that could be used against Earl Sweyn, but if the abbess was so determined that none should know it, then it wasn't for them to spread the truth of the matter,

'I believe so, yes. The abbess wishes to keep the truth between her and my brother.'

'What a bastard that he's raped so many before he knows that?' Lady Godgifu hissed, aware her words were too loud. She lowered her head, trying to stem the flood of anger that threatened to pour forth.

'What shall be done?' The queen demanded. Her voice was rough with grief.

'We should tell her that we know?'

'And how will that aid her? My brother will still inform everyone, and she'll be humiliated.'

'She'll be further humiliated if she lets him do this to her. She's a woman of God. It doesn't matter if she took up thc veil while a virgin or not. She does good work in Leominster. The nunnery is valuable and tends for the sick.'

'And my brother means to claim that land as his own now he says they're wed.'

'But the land belongs to the nunnery.' Lady Godgifu was frantically considering how much land she and her husband had endowed the nunnery. It was unconscionable to think that might fall into Earl Sweyn's hand when it was for the welfare of the nuns and the souls of her and her husband.

'Some of the land is the abbess's own,' the queen stated. 'Some of it has personally been gifted to her, and so, while the expectation is that it would become the abbey's, there's the possibility that it could be hers should she relinquish her position as the abbess.'

'And Earl Sweyn knows this?' Lady Godgifu questioned. What appeared to be a hot-headed and foolish attack on Leominster was rapidly revealing itself to have been well-thought-out and planned.

'He does, yes.' The queen confirmed, worrying her bottom lip with her teeth. For a moment, Lady Godgifu considered if it was the queen that had informed her brother of this, with her knowledge of the women's religious houses within England. But now was not the time to cast recriminations.

Lady Godgifu felt her horse stir, uneasy with being still for so long after their gentle gallop. She reached down and ran her gloved hand along her mount's long neck.

'Good girl,' she crooned, but her thoughts were far away. Very far away.

'Then we must have the abbess gift the land to the nunnery immediately and before the king gives his decision on Sweyn's future. If the land is no longer there, there's nothing for Sweyn to gain. Perhaps, then, he'll relinquish his claim to her.

'And if he doesn't?'

'Then his motivations will be purely wrathful. There'll be nothing for him to gain but an unwanted wife. The king will not add more landholdings to what he already owns and is more likely to remove what he has from him, dividing it no doubt between Ralph and Beorn in perpetuality as bookland. Surely the abbess would rather weather the embarrassment of Sweyn's truth than live with him in poverty and probably in exile?'

'Will you speak with her?' the queen pleaded. Lady Godgifu nodded, filled with resolve. Now that the solution had presented itself, she was determined to do what she could for Abbess Eadgifu. She couldn't allow the woman to give up her position, wealth and good works just because the sly bastard who'd raped her knew something that should be kept a secret.

21

LEOFRIC

'My lord king,' he bowed low to the king and caught sight of Edward's fingers encouraging him to stand upright. King Edward had summoned Leofric to his private room. This was to be a discussion between them and no one else; whether that was a good development remained to be seen.

'Lord Leofric,' the king began. He was dressed in a simple tunic and trews. They lacked almost all decoration, but the quality of the fabric was hard to deny. And indeed, the nearly purple colour was also a sign of the king's great wealth. 'You've aided me in the past, with King Harthacnut, with my lady mother, and now, it seems, I must call on you once more to resolve this issue with Lord Sweyn. I would welcome your frank and reasoned words. I know your father was known for his honesty even when it won him no favours from his kings.'

'I'll do my best,' Leofric offered, a slight smile on his lips. King Edward would have no memory of his father's altercations with kings. Or at least, he assumed he didn't. Still, Ealdorman Leofwine's reputation was lauded by those looking for the ideal of what it was to be a statesman and a loyal Englishman.

'I'm sure you will. And no doubt, you'll ensure that your arguments lack any bias against Lord Sweyn and his father.'

Here Leofric grinned wider at the king's wry tone.

'I'll do my best, as I said,' Leofric reiterated.

'Then we'll sit and talk. Come, make yourself comfortable.' While the king had a desk in his private room, there was also a setting of two wooden-backed chairs before a small brazier. It wasn't truly cold, but beneath the rafters of the far-distant roof, there was the odd breeze that the heavy tapestries on the walls failed to counter.

Leofric settled himself and eyed the king. He would give his opinion when requested. But, he was very much against Lord Sweyn and his father. He couldn't deny that.

'Now, I believe that my wife is currently speaking to your wife about this unfortunate matter of Abbess Eadgifu. The woman has determined to cleave to Lord Sweyn, and I don't believe I'm alone in having my suspicions as to why. But it's Lord Sweyn who vexes me. The punishment for his crime is explicit.'

'Yes, he must pay her wergild to her,' Leofric spoke quickly. He wanted the king to know he'd taken the time to learn the legalities of the case.

'If it were as simple as she was a maiden, and he taking her against her will, then yes, it would be her wergild. For a maiden, it would depend on her status as to how much the wergild would be,' King Edward mused. Leofric nodded his agreement. The king had also checked the currently operating law codes, or rather one of his clerics had.

'But she's not just a maiden. She's an abbess,' Leofric said, following what the king must be thinking.

'And I don't believe there's a law against the volition of an abbess. It would fall into a combination of her being a maiden and him taking her against her will, and equally, it's a matter of a crime against the church, and by extension, against the king.'

'And that would mean that Lord Sweyn would forfeit his life and all he owns should he be found guilty of criminal actions against the king.' Leofric offered.

'It would, yes, but still, in that judgement, there's no formal recompense for the abbess.'

'But one would be devised for her.' Leofric was unhappy that the abbess would receive nothing for the crime committed against her.

'And how would that change should the abbess wilfully marry Lord Sweyn?' Edward pressed,

'Then she'd marry a man who would have forfeited his life? She'd gain nothing but the status of widowhood. But if there were children, that would make them legal heirs to their father's possessions.'

'Indeed,' and the king pursed his lips, his indecision clear to see. 'If there were children.' The words were not so much a question as a thought.

'It does seem unlikely that there wouldn't be. The Abbess has been his captive for some time.'

'I understand that,' the king confirmed. 'I'm more than aware of how these things transpire,' there was a faint smirk on his lips. Leofric nodded once more.

'And how do you believe the archbishops and bishops will find him?'

'They've made it clear that they intend to charge him with crimes against the church and the king.'

'They want his death, then?'

'I believe that the abbesses have petitioned the archbishops stringently to ensure that Lord Sweyn is held accountable for the most heinous of crimes. And in any case, Archbishop Eadsige and Bishop Aldred of Worcester are incensed, as is Bishop Robert of London. They've cited many old laws which make it clear that the sanctity of the nunnery and abbeys is just that. They don't believe these laws have been rescinded. My clerics confirm what they say. These laws of King Edgar have stood for nearly a century, just as my wife having command over the nunneries, as the queen, has.'

Silence fell between the two men. Leofric knew that the king paid particular attention to Bishop Robert, having been instrumental in having him brought to England from Jumieges. Perhaps, Leofric thought, he should have forged a closer bond with the new cleric, if he was to be outspoken against the king's enemies.

From outside, Leofric could hear people busy with their day's tasks. There was the distant clang of the blacksmith's workings and the familiar clop and whinny from the horses and their hooves. It all felt very normal, and yet they were here, behind these walls, discussing how to punish a man for a reprehensible crime against which there was no written law.

'And of course, if it must be said, then whatever Lord Sweyn's sway is over Abbess Eadgifu, no maiden should ever be forced to marry a man whom she dislikes.'

'But can we argue that,' the king sat forward now, his face alert. 'If she submits to his request that they wed?'

'Lord Sweyn has broken all rules regarding a betrothal. He's taken what he desires, namely her body before he so much as asked for permission to do so. He didn't even abide by the first rule regarding following God's and secular law in pledging that he would maintain her according to God's law as a man should maintain a wife. No priest wed them. Even now, they're not truly wed in the eyes of God. He's made a whore of one of God's holy abbesses.'

'He has, it seems, broken almost all rules with which this kingdom is governed and ruled,' King Edward murmured.

'He's reckless,' Leofric confirmed, finding he could say nothing further without bringing his neutrality into question.

'I don't believe I can have my wife's brother executed?' King Edward fixed Leofric with his gaze. Leofric felt as though the king's request for a meeting now made sense. It seemed he was asking permission to violate his own rules. Not that Leofric was surprised. He'd felt from the beginning that Lord Sweyn was likely to lose his earldom, not his life. Had he died fighting in the Welsh kingdoms, the king would have been content, but to actually order his death? No, the king didn't wish to do that.

'These are the rules, my lord king. I would call your bias into question were they not adhered to.'

'And you would be correct to do so. I am biased, not by love for my wife, and certainly not for her brother, but rather my self-interest means I don't wish to bring my new kingship into such troubled waters.'

'It'll depend on whether your kingship can survive your flagrant disregard for the rules as they're written.'

'Hum,' the king murmured. Now Leofric leant forward, watching the king keenly. Not for the first time, he wished to know what happened in the man's head. King Edward had surprised many by being a warrior and not just a forgotten ætheling. He'd also astonished many by choosing to ally with the House of Godwine, especially when most knew that if not for Earl Godwine, Edward's brother wouldn't have been blinded and murdered. Now it seemed the king would have to astound them again with his actions against Lord Sweyn.

'Earl Godwine has begged me for leniency. He assures me that the abbess gave herself willing to his son and that, other than having to cast aside her veil, Eadfigu will be treated with honour as his oldest son's wife. He's also found some obscure northern law in which it's written that if a man should lie with a nun, both are liable to pay their wergild.'

'And did he also share with you that the abbess has personally been granted lands which were expected to pass onto the abbey at her death but which for now occupy the shadowy realm of only being proposed and not written down as bookland? And that's not even following his line of reason which makes the abbess as liable as Lord Sweyn.'

King Edward shook his head, his shock clear to see in how his hands clenched, one inside the other.

'It seems that even now, Earl Godwine intends to be less than truthful.'

'It's his way,' Leofric consoled. 'He's always thinking ahead to what he can achieve without seemingly intending to accomplish that objective.'

'But on this, he'll not. The abbess must be made to cast aside Lord Sweyn. Should there be one, I'll have her child acknowledged as legitimate and raised at my court,' the king abruptly confirmed. 'And then, it'll be a simple expedient of finding him guilty of acts against the kingship.'

'So he'll be executed?' Leofric pressed, impressed with the king's reasoning.

'No, he won't be. Banishment will be his punishment. Forfeiture of all his lands and resources and banishment.'

'He'll merely seek out the Count of Flanders,' Leofric cautioned. The Count of Flanders was an acknowledged problem for King Edward. What aid he'd provided the king to claim his kingship had long since turned bitter and twisted. King Edward had no love for the count, and not just because he was an ally of his mother.

'Then he can contend with Lord Sweyn and his rapacious ways.'

Leofric fell silent. It wasn't a true resolution. He was sure the king would understand that yet the king offered nothing else.

'He'll seek vengeance,' Leofric eventually felt compelled to advise the king. 'And all the time, his family will still be here, urging you at every witan to reinstate him, to assure you that the abbess was willing. It might even be that your bedchamber won't be free of such imprecations.'

'The queen has no love for her brother.'

'And yet she will still be his sister,' Leofric retorted. 'And her father and mother will still be Lord Sweyn's parents as well as her own.'

For a long moment, silence once more reigned between them. Leofric thought the king must be thinking frantically about what could and couldn't be done. Only then, King Edward spoke once more.

'I've erred, I don't deny that, but the crime must be punished, and no matter how much I might want to, I can't have my wife's husband executed. More's the pity. It would, my lord, have been better had he been killed in the fight to bring him to my side.'

'It would, yes, my lord, but the instructions were clear. No harm was to come to Lord Sweyn or Abbess Eadgifu, and all know that the king's orders can't be disobeyed without facing justice.'

Leofric didn't miss the slight grimace on his king's face at those words.

'You're indeed correct, Lord Leofric, but perhaps, on this occasion, your punishment would have been particularly mild.' The king's words ended on a wistful note.

22

LADY GODGIFU

She found Abbess Eadgifu where she expected to, praying in the church. Lady Godgifu looked at her rigid back, listening to the shush of her prayers, and felt renewed pity and not a little anger towards the woman. How much easier would it be if she denounced Lord Sweyn? It wasn't as if others weren't already doing the same. And yet? Well, she would have the truth from her, no matter what.

But for now, and with a nod towards those guarding the abbess, Lady Godgifu settled to wait for the abbess to finish her prayers. Unsure if Eadgifu knew of her presence, Lady Godgifu hoped the woman wouldn't be too long at her task. It was cold within the church, but then churches always seemed to be. She couldn't help thinking that her God, and certainly Jesus Christ, born in the warmer climes to the far south, would have welcomed some warmth against the vagaries of the English weather. Her thoughts brought a smirk to her face, pulling her cloak tighter around her shoulders. It was only September, and yet the wind was fierce.

Lady Godgifu eyed the richness of the church before her. St Peter's was particularly dear to the king, and he'd endowed it with wealth, for all there was the annoyance of building work close by.

The altar cloths flashed with shimmering threads, and while the windows lacked coloured glass, the fact they were sheeted in glass was worthy of note. She tried not to judge her own dear establishments against the king's wealth, but it was hard not to. She surmised that some of her churches were far better endowed, but then the king had put much of his wealth into only this one church, so it was bound to benefit from his largesse.

Eventually, she realised the shushing words of Abbess Eadgifu had come to a stop, and indeed, the woman was standing before her, uncertainty on her face.

'My lady,' she dipped her head. Lady Godgifu hastily stood and offered her the same. After all, as the abbess of Leominster, Eadgifu was her superior in spiritual matters.

'My dear Eadgifu,' Lady Godgifu broke with protocol and spoke her name warmly. 'I have sought you out to offer you the assistance of me, my husband, the king and queen, and the archbishop, bishops and your fellow abbesses.' Lady Godgifu didn't miss Eadgifu's sharp inhalation or the look of panic that touched her pale cheeks.

'Come, sit with me.' She offered.

'I'd sooner not, my lady. The church is no longer my home. It's only where I come to seek salvation for my soul.'

'It's no such thing,' Lady Godgifu rejected those words and then regretted it. She was here to be tactful, not dismissive.

'Then outside, in the grounds.' Without waiting for Eadgifu to formulate a reason to reject the idea, she looped her arm through the other woman's and drew her close. Over her shoulder, she cast a look at the men guarding Eadgifu, and they acknowledged her and made ready to follow them. She was grateful for that.

Outside, the sun shone brightly, but there was a bite to the air, and she looked to the abbess. She wore a cloak, but it wasn't a warm one. Over her shoulder, she beckoned a servant closer and asked for a warmer cloak for her companion. Before they could truly make much headway, a new cloak was brought for Eadgifu and slipped over her shoulders without complaint. Lady Godgifu muttered her thanks and hoped someone wasn't shivering with the inconvenience of losing their cloak nearby.

'Now, my dear friend,' Lady Godgifu spoke softly, head bent towards the other woman. 'I've come to you, as I said, as a friend. I'm here to help you, and others are as well. We're devastated by what's befallen you. Even now, I understand my husband is closeted with the king, discussing how that bastard can be punished.' The vehemence in her words wasn't forced, although she felt Eadgifu flinch away from her.

'It's good of you to offer these words,' the abbess spoke with some verve to her voice. 'But there's little that can be done now. The earl and I will be wed before God.'

'Lord Sweyn won't be an earl for much longer,' Lady Godgifu was stung into replying.

'Perhaps you may be right, but I don't believe an earl has yet lost their position for proposing marriage to a woman.'

Lady Godgifu hoped her face was bereft of all expression. To hear Abbess Eadgifu speak as she did was heartbreaking and infuriated her all the more.

'But you were no mere woman. You are an abbess, a nun, a wife of Christ not of some earthly man.'

'And yet we'll be wed.'

'It is usual for a man to betroth himself to a woman rather than just take what he desires,' Lady Godgifu tried once more.

'We will be wed before God, if not in the eyes of all.' Eadgifu retorted. Lady Godgifu frantically tried to think of another way to have Eadgifu admit that the marriage was illegal. Not that there had truly been a marriage yet. If there had been, that might change everything.

'It is, yes, but the earl was too keen, I admit that.' The woman turned to smile at Lady Godgifu, her lips trembling, tears forming in her eyes. 'He was not gentle with me, no. But it was God's will, what happened between us. And I'm grateful to him for that.' Lady Godgifu's eyes were sharp, and she noticed the abbess's movement to rub her hand over her belly. Inwardly, she cursed. It seemed that their worst fears had come to fruition. The Abbess was indeed with child thanks to the bastard's unwanted advances.

'You're with child?' Lady Godgifu questioned her.

'I suspect I am, yes,' and the abbess's pale cheeks flushed a deep pink at the admission. 'And that's also a gift from God. I never thought of having children born of my body. I was merely to mother my nuns.'

'There are means of disposing of an unwanted child,' Lady Godgifu pressed her. She was unsure whether a woman of Eadgifu's standing would know of them. 'I have a woman I trust. She will bring them today if I send word to her.'

'My lady,' the abbess abruptly stopped, yanking herself free from Lady Godgifu's arm. 'To speak as such is to defy God.'

'It is not,' Lady Godgifu jutted out her chin in defiance. 'Men are bastards and think nothing of spilling their seed. Not all women can carry a child without risking their own life.'

'I'll do no such thing, and Earl Sweyn will be a kind father.'

'Will he know? A traitor and a rapist will be a kind father to a child who's entirely in his command? I don't believe so.'

Swift fury touched Eadgifu's shadowed eyes, yet she held her tongue. It seemed she couldn't deny those words.

Lady Godgifu tried again. The woman was entirely conflicted.

'Whatever Lord Sweyn thinks he knows about you is irrelevant. The king, the queen, the archbishops and the bishops, my husband and I, we are not unaware that an abbess is not always an abbess. Some youthful indiscretions. Some fumbled experienced before taking the veil are to be expected.'

'My lady,' this time Eadgifu's rage was bright and hot, her hand straying to her belly, even while she glowered. 'I'll not have such aspersions said about me. I came to God whole, as a woman should.'

'Then what is it that Lord Sweyn holds over you? It must be something. He abducted you, and yet now you cleave to him. That's unholy. He should be whipped for what he did to you. He should be cast out of the communion of God. You should not reward him with such loyalty.'

'He'll be the father of my child,' Eadgifu cried. 'He'll care for me and the child.'

'He'll see you as the instrument of his downfall from the king's high favour. He'll not be good to you or your child, and as we've seen, he puts no store by the laws of God or of the king. He can't be trusted.'

'He has assured me that when we're legally bound, all will be forgiven and forgotten before the king.'

Lady Godgifu couldn't help herself, she chuckled, the sound dark and filled with derision.

'You think you know him, but you're innocent in the ways of vainglorious men. You are also, luckily for you, unused to having any contact with the poisonous family of the Godwines. Whatever he's promised you will not come to fruition.'

'My lady,' Eadgifu spoke quickly, her chest heaving. 'Earl Sweyn is a man of honour, great wealth, and influence with the king. I'll not denounce him. One day, my children will be kin to England's future king. We will be wed, and the king will forgive all.'

'The king won't forgive all, and your child will never be kin to the king's heir, I assure you of that,' Lady Godgifu was riled into replying.

'You seem to know a great deal about the future,' Eadgifu countered just as angrily.

'I know more of men and women than you do; that's a certainty. I came to you as a friend, but you want no friend. And you'll have none. The king won't welcome Lord Sweyn to his court, and your current family, the women of the abbey, won't seek out your company as you're no longer one of them. I wouldn't wish such ostracisation on my enemy, let alone my friend.'

'Then it seems, my lady, that we're not friends and never will be. If you'll excuse me, I must return to the king's palace. My future husband will be there, waiting for me.

'Lady Eadgifu,' Lady Godgifu called to the woman's back. 'When you change your mind and realise the truth I speak, I will not forsake you; remember that. I'll be your friend then, as will the king and queen. Remember that. Don't think yourself alone in this, even though you're set on this current path.'

Abbess Eadgifu stopped to listen to those words, and Lady Godgifu watched her shoulders shudder, and yet she walked on regardless. Lady Godgifu cursed under her breath. The damn woman was determined to make this as difficult on herself as possible. And in doing so, she was making it challenging for the king to banish Lord Sweyn. That was frustrating and somehow entirely consistent with how the entire pestilent tribe of the House of Godwine managed to maintain their hold on all that they had and worse, profit when they should be doing entirely the opposite.

23
LONDON, LEOFRIC

Leofric eyed the king almost in disbelief as he gave his pronouncement before the witan on the abduction of the abbess by Earl Sweyn. After all they'd spoken about, it seemed Sweyn wouldn't be punished after all. No matter her efforts, his wife had been unable to prevail over the abbess. She held that they were married, and nothing Lady Godgifu, the queen, the archbishops or bishops said could sway her from such a statement.

As such, the two were to be married. The only consolation, if it could be called as such, was that Swein wasn't to benefit from Abbess Eadgifu's, or rather, Lady Eadgifu's now, landed interests.

'As such, Earl Sweyn will be released and return to his earldom. However,' and the king paused, meeting the eyes of Earl Godwine before he went on. 'There will be some adjustments to Earl Sweyn's earldom. Already, Lords Ralph and Beorn have an interest in the earldom. Now, Earl Harold will do the same.' Leofric could barely contain his ire. Not content with allowing Sweyn to go virtually unpunished for striking an alliance with the Welsh king, and stealing an abbess against her will, the king now intended to allow even more of the troublesome family to have a say in the governance of Mercia. Admittedly, Leofric knew Earl Harold was a far more sensible character, beloved of his sister, the queen, and the king must hope, the man to finally hold Earl Sweyn to account.

'Earl Sweyn has escaped without punishment once more. But if there are any more problems, he'll be banished.'

Not expecting today to resolve in such a way, Leofric temporarily found himself unable to think of a single argument to make. He knew, without doubt, that the king had erred in his resolution. There wasn't even mention of the wergild due to the abbess for what Sweyn had done to her. He could blame the abbess for refusing to speak out against Sweyn, but Leofric knew that at the heart of the matter, the king was too weak. He'd assured Leofric, on the day of his fateful marriage to Lady Edith, that he had no intention of allowing the might of the House of Godwine to grow, and yet that not only couldn't be denied, the king seemed to be making excuses for his wife's older brother – almost desperate not to have to exile him.

Leofric considered where the king's resolve towards his wife's brother had gone. When they'd spoken together of the legal options available to the king, Edward had seemed eager to follow through with them. Now, it appeared that he'd forgotten all of that.

Leofric felt his wife's rage beside him. It was a miracle that she hadn't spoken out. Leofric knew that the words of the law codes were meant to ensure that justice was served. He also understood that the good of the country could occasionally override the intention behind the law codes. But he could see no way that this was for the good of the country.

Earl Swein had caused problems with the Welsh that still reverberated up and down the border with Powys and Gwent, and his brother and nephews were even now reassuring those who looked to the House of Leofwine . Putting aside his hatred of Gruffydd ap Llewelyn and his involvement in the death of his brother, Leofric still understood that the king was giving his tacit acceptance of what was happening there. Was King Edward determined to have enemies everywhere? King Magnus of Norway remained a threat. And now the Welsh as well. It was beyond imagining.

THE ANGLO SAXON CHRONICLE ENTRY FOR 1046

Here Earl Swein went into Wales, and Gruffydd, the northern king, together with him and he was granted hostages. Then, when he was on his way home, he commanded the abbess in Leominster to be fetched to him, and he kept her as long as it suited him. (C)

And Magnus won Denmark (D)

24

AD1047, LEOFRIC

He shivered despite the cloak, two tunics, fur covering his knee and the hot fire blazing before him. Damn, it was bloody cold, and it only seemed to be getting colder. Not even his fury at the king and Earl Sweyn could warm him, that was how cold it was.

Leofric looked to his family, servants and household warriors. Everywhere he looked, there was a red nose, blue skin and dripping noses. No one was warm.

No one, it seemed, but his wife.

'If you sit around like this all day, you'll never get warm.' Her tone was acerbic. He noticed more and more people shrug aside their furs and rise from where they were sitting, some almost within the blazing hearth fire.

'We need more logs, the animals need tending, the grain store needs checking, the animal traps as well, and that's before I've even considered what more needs to be done.' The groans of his servants and warriors assured Leofric that they were about to venture outside. The wind had been bitter all night, blowing through the hall as though the wattle and daub on the exterior walls, and the thick, heavy tapestries, on the interior, didn't exist at all.

'And make sure the cows give up their milk,' Lady Godgifu called to the women tasked with such an endeavour. At least, Leofric thought, they'd have warm fingers from the cows housed in the barns.

'I include you in that, my lord husband. There's no point in sitting here all day, shivering. Put on your warmest fur, and thickest linen cap, and get busy. It will warm you better than hovering over the hearth and demanding more and more hot drinks.' He wanted to argue with her, but she was right. The bitter winter, after a reasonably good harvest, was unexpected, but he knew to be grateful, for they had all they needed to survive. There were others who wouldn't.

He forced himself outside, his new hound close to him, sniffing the sharp air and perhaps thinking better of it. His sister had relinquished the new animal to him, satisfied she was trained as a hound of the House of Leofwine should be. He welcomed the animal's constant attention. And her warm body over his feet at night, that couldn't be denied. But Olaf had been correct to warn him. The new hound was not biddable on occasion. He'd named her Hunter in honour of his father's beast when he'd been a boy. He hoped the name would make her as obedient as that hound had been.

The cries of men, women, children and animals rang through the frozen forecourt. The crack of someone trying to force their way through the ice-crested water barrels also split the air. It had been so cold two nights ago, that the water barrels had been frozen all the way through. Only moving them inside, next to the hearth, had allowed the ice to thaw.

He shivered once more, a doleful look back towards the smoke rising into the sky from the hearth fire, but he knew better than to try his luck. He wasn't expecting to hear the sounds of another rushing towards him.

He turned, startled, and caught the plume of hot air from a horse and rider, asking for admittance at the gate.

'Good day,' he hailed, fearing bad news.

'My lord, the king has sent me.'

'Allow him entry,' Leofric called to the gate warden that morning, Godwulf. The man, grumbling as the gate was unwieldy in the weather, bent to his task all the same. Leofric watched the rider. The horse seemed badly used. Leofric was far from sure the animal should have been out in such weather.

'Here, I'll have the animal taken to the stables,' he offered, moving to help the man dismount. It seemed his legs and hands were cold, and the man struggled to move.

'It's a bitter day,' the man juddered.

'Indeed, and the king thought this too important not to inform me.'

'You'll realise why soon enough, my lord,' the man offered, wincing as he jumped to the hard ground, jarring his legs. Leofric flinched at the evident pain the other man was in.

'Here, take the animal into the warmth and ensure it's fed well and allowed to warm up.' Leofric didn't berate the messenger or the king, but all the same, he thought it.

Eager to be inside, the messenger scampered towards the tightly sealed doorway. Leofric followed him, more mindful of where he needed to step to avoid slipping. He was too old to absorb such an impact.

Inside, he caught his wife's furious stare, that only disappeared on catching sight of the messenger.

'What's this?' she demanded. Leofric noticed that she and the female servants had decided to take part in what amounted to a good clean of the hall after a long winter. It was far too early for such a task, but it was certainly warming them all up. Even the small children were helping, running from one end of the hall to another with tasks assigned them by either his wife or another of the women.

Hunter slunk to the floor beside him with a soft sigh, and Leofric would have happily done the same. At least, he reasoned, going outside had ensured he appreciated how warm it was in the hall.

'A messenger from the king,' Leofric provided. 'Bring warm food and wine, if we have it.'

The messenger had seated himself before the fire without being invited, but Leofric wasn't about to stand on ceremony. The man must be all but frozen rigid.

'What news,' his wife stood before the bleached man, observing him closely.

'Bring warm water for his feet and hands as well,' she called.

'Earl Sweyn,' the man began, rubbing at the ice that had formed on his brown beard and moustache.

'Has been causing trouble for three years. What was so urgent now?'

'The archbishop and bishop have finally prevailed upon him to give up the abbess, on the threat of excommunication. She is even now, round with child, back at Leominster. Mind, the king has given the land into the care of his wife, to prevent her brother from appropriating it.'

'Then that is good news,' his wife exhaled quickly, and Leofric agreed. Why then had the king sent this man running to them, and indeed, why had the archbishop and bishop done the same to whoever had brought the news to them?

'There is more, alas.'

'When isn't there more?' his wife countered quickly. A warm beaker had been slipped between the man's frozen fingers, and Leofric could see him visibly thawing.

'My lady,' the messenger inclined his head. Not in agreement, but not denying it either.

'Earl Sweyn has retaliated by taking command of the churches in Shropshire, at Maesbrook, Hopton and North Cleobury. Bishop Aldred of Worcester, is, as you can imagine, furious. The king has determined that Earl Sweyn must be out-lawed.'

'And he expects us to go and hunt him down?'

'Quite, my lord, alongside Earls Harold, Beorn and Ralph. The king requests it's done before Easter.'

Leofric shook his head, at the thought of venturing outside. It was March. Admittedly, he understood that the Easter festivities would be late this year, but he didn't believe they stood much chance of meeting the king's commands with the snow and ice on the ground.

'It is what you've wanted for many years,' his wife commented, although without admonishment. Leofric eyed the messenger with unease.

'And you're to inform Harold, Beorn and Ralph of this.'

'I have, my lord. Their response, I confess, was similar to yours. They have advised that you will meet in three weeks, at Worcester and from there, track down the earl.'

'Then let us hope the weather improves in the next three weeks.'

'Indeed, my lord,' the messenger's words were fervent.

'And will you be staying here until the weather improves?'

'If you would allow it, my lord, I would greatly appreciate it.'

'Then, yes, you may,' his wife agreed before he could. 'But be warned; there's no sitting around all day before the hearth. As you can see, we're all busy trying to keep warm, and you will be put to work as well. Tomorrow. I will give you some time to recover.'

'My thanks, my lady,' the messenger bowed low, and Leofric felt his wife's eyes on him. It seemed, no matter the news from the king, he was still expected to warm himself by assisting others outside. He bowed towards his wife and with Hunter trailing him, made his way once more outside.

This time, the blast of cold air that enveloped him brought with it the warmth of knowing that the king was finally going to outlaw Earl Sweyn. It was just a pity that he'd waited so long that all involved would have to endure the terrible weather to bring it about.

'My lord,' Earl Leofric found himself outside Hereford once more, and this time, those on duty at the gate had been unwilling to allow them entry. Fifty cold and frozen men at his back and the presence of his brother, cousin and the king's nephew, as well as the Earl of

Mercia, had ensured that they were allowed inside, no matter orders from Sweyn. Now, they were standing before a belligerent looking Sweyn.

'The bitch is back where she should be,' Sweyn began without preamble.

'It's too late, my lord. The king's orders are clear.'

Sweyn, the bite of cold on his cheeks, despite the heat in the hall, didn't meet Leofric's eyes but rather gazed at his brother.

'What did our father say to this?'

'It doesn't matter. These are the orders of the king.' Earl Harold's voice lacked all inflexion.

'And my sister?'

'Is merely the queen. She isn't the king.'

'But the woman is back where she should be?'

'Round with your child.' Leofric interjected, earning himself a swift glower from Earl Sweyn, or rather, not Earl Sweyn. His title had been taken from him. That pleased Leofric, although it infuriated him that the king had left them to fulfil the most difficult part of the bargain, actually removing Sweyn from Hereford. Not even the bishop had been able to bring that about.

'And you took from the bishopric of Worcester, and the bishop is a powerful man. The archbishop has his ear, and now you will leave England. Brother, you are outlawed.' Leofric admired Harold's poise. Ælfgar had assured him that Harold was unlike the rest of his family. Only now did he begin to realise that might be true.

'I will give the land back,' Sweyn dismissed with a wave, as though despoiling churches was of no concern, just as despoiling a professed abbess wasn't.

'It's too late. Now, collect what possessions you have that don't belong to the earldom, and come with us. It would be better if there weren't a fight. But there are men here who will fight you and your warriors, if the need arises.' Leofric spoke quickly. This time Sweyn wouldn't be able to wriggle free from the king's commands. This time, the abbess wouldn't be able to protect him by saying they were wed in the eyes of God, and neither would his father be able to stop what was happening. And not only because he was too old to ride north to protect his son while the weather was so bitter.

'You may have until the morning. A guard will be set over you. Our men are now in command of the gatehouses, and you'll be unable to escape us.' Leofric intoned this, and noticed how Sweyn flinched as each avenue was lost to him. 'Should you consider seeking sanctuary with any of the king's enemies, in Wales or Bruges, then the king will take your child, once it's born, as surety against your behaviour. Should you prove unwilling, the child will lose its life.' This part of the king's orders sat ill with Leofric, but the children of treasonous bastards were so often tainted with the sins of their fathers. Leofric knew this only too well. Perhaps then, the king should have given this instruction to one of the other men. Not Beorn, who was the son of a man executed on the orders of King Cnut. And not Leofric, either. He was grateful his nephews weren't here to witness the words being spoken.

'I care little for the child,' Sweyn jutted out his chin as he spoke. 'It's not even born yet if it survives. And you can inform the king that I will go where I please and make alliances where I want.'

'But they'll not be within England,' Beorn spoke for the first time. A swift look of fury descended over Sweyn's face at the words. Beorn was his cousin. But Beorn was furious with Sweyn. Furious and Leofric suspected, embarrassed as well.

'The discussion is at an end,' Leofric quickly interjected. 'Now, prepare yourself. Men,' and he turned to two of the king's huscarls. They were fearsome-looking warriors, carrying the scars of battles won and lost. They had no loyalty for Sweyn. They had sworn their lives to the king. Leofric trusted them to carry out the king's orders.

'Now, food and drink,' he called to the fearful servants, trying to hide in the room's shadows. 'And fear not, you'll not lose your positions. There will be a new lord within this hall.' Those words were greeted with the thump of a door being loudly smashed, and

Leofric's eyes jumped to where one of the huscarls was prying the door open, while the other growled low in his throat.

'Less of your games, my lord,' Leofric called as though scolding a small child. 'Or you'll find yourself in chains this night, and it won't be a pleasant experience.'

As the huscarls gained entry to Sweyn's chamber and a low mumble of outrage reached his ears, Leofric turned to eye the younger men to determine how they were feeling about their place here, and Sweyn's belligerence.

Harold's eyes were cold and yet blazed with fury. Beorn looked disgruntled, and Ralph was doing his best to show no emotion. None of the men was perhaps as skilled as they thought at hiding their emotions.

Leofric took himself to the hearth and beckoned one of the servants close.

'Please send word to Bishop Æthelstan that we'll call upon him shortly and will require the use of some of his scribes.' The man bobbed and hastened away. From outside, a heavy thud could be heard, and while all glanced upwards, no one moved. The sound of snow tumbling from the rafters wasn't new in the last few months. It had become an almost daily occurrence, and indeed, the problems were more likely to appear if the snow didn't slide free. Then men and women would need to scamper up high and attempt to clear the stuff before it either melted into the thatch or, worse, caused damage to the roof because of its great weight.

Along with the thud, Leofric felt the tension rise from his shoulders. At last, Sweyn Godwinesson would be banished from England, and with him gone, Leofric hoped they could do more than worry about Sweyn's next actions. Of course, much of that would depend on who was made an earl in place of him. Leofric imagined he already knew the answer.

25

EASTER, AD1047, LONDON, LEOFRIC

'He's gone?' King Edward had taken him aside to determine the success of his endeavours to remove Sweyn from England.

'Yes, in a ship that left two weeks ago.'

Edward, enclosed in a thick fur cloak, looked all of his years, and Leofric realised with a start that while he had a son grown and four grandchildren, Edward, at ten years his junior, had none of those things, and it appeared, was unlikely to. The king had been married for over two years. The queen showed no signs of carrying his child. Perhaps, after all, there was some things that the king had been truthful about to Leofric.

'He made no fuss?'

'Oh, he made as much trouble as possible, denouncing his brother, his cousin, and your nephew. He's a spiteful man.' Leofric thought those words were rather too general to truly explain how difficult Sweyn had been about being ejected from his earldom. 'The bishops are ensuring everything is restored to how it was before.'

'And the abbess?'

'Twins,' Leofric offered, eyebrows high.

The king's eyes boggled at such a statement. 'Both healthy, two boys, Hakon and Tostig. The nuns have ensured they have all they need, and the abbess has returned to her duties. She's much changed by her ... ordeal.' Again, Leofric knew that was a word that masked what had truly happened to her.

'My, my,' Edward offered, a faint smile on his lips. 'The queen will be pleased,' he provided, and Leofric realised that was an admission that the king's secret perhaps weighed heavily on him. It seemed the king was fond of his wife. Certainly, she brought a vibrancy to the court that had been missing since King Cnut's death.

'But to more practical matters. Earl Harold will retain his earldom in East Anglia but will also have responsibility in some of the counties on the Welsh border, and on the coast, to the south. Beorn will take the southern Mercian holdings, alongside those he will also hold in the east of Mercia, close to Harold's. It is best this way. The two at least get along, unlike Sweyn and everyone else.' The statement was dry, and yet Leofric didn't miss the irony.

'Indeed, my lord king,' Leofric spoke without showing his unease that his son was still yet to be provided for. Would an earldom, after all, simply come to Ælfgar after his own death? Was the king so determined to have allies who were his family members that he could look no further? Certainly, the king had slowly begun to build a following of men from his time in Normandy. But, in England, while he relied on Siward and himself, the rest of the governance was in the hands of the relatives of the king, and more often than not, those relatives were members of the House of Godwine, and not the House of Leofwine. Only amongst the churchmen was Edward truly starting to build a wider circle for himself. Robert of Jumieges, now bishop of London, had been just the first to be invited to England.

Leofric knew his wife would be unhappy once more. He was beginning to believe she was right to be so outraged.

'For the future, I assure you, I will provide for your son once I'm able. I haven't forgotten the loyalty of your house, Leofric. In time, good man, in time. And now to more pleasant matters. I will be calling on the ship army once more this summer. We'll amass at

Sandwich. Reports from Denmark assure me that King Magnus is still determined to war against Svein Estridsson, who threatens to undermine his hold on Denmark. I believe Magnus will happily attack anywhere else to fund that war. And of course, I'm not blind to the potential for Sweyn Godwinesson to get involved somehow. And perhaps Osgot Clapa as well. Both men were unhappy with what happened to them. Maybe even Lady Gunnhild. It's one thing to rid England of the menace of them, but quite another to ensure they don't enter into alliances with England's enemies.'

'Will you require the earls to attend upon you, or shall I send the youths?'

'Ælfgar and his cousins will be welcome additions. I would ask you to remain in Mercia for the summer. Just to ensure that Sweyn doesn't return, and of course, to ensure that the abbess and her twins are well-protected. I'll carry out my threat to those children should Sweyn become problematic.'

'And what of Earl Godwine?'

'He's pig-headed and angry, his wife demands the children are brought to her. My wife is firm with them both. They're to have nothing to do with the children. And, of course, Queen Edith now holds much of the Leominster possessions. She'll provide for the nuns, the abbess, and her nephews, I assure you of that.'

'Very good, my lord king.' He thought to bow and leave the king, but Edward didn't dismiss him.

'Leofric, tell me, are you pleased with how events have transpired?' This perplexed Leofric.

'With Sweyn?'

'Yes, and also in general? Earl Godwine is embarrassed?'

'But while he's lost one son, another has simply absorbed more power?'

'Harold is to be trusted, perhaps of all of them. I understood you thought highly of the man?'

'My son does, yes, but he's still a plaything for his father. Perhaps

Harold will show his true abilities when his father is no longer troublesome.'

For a moment, the king's eyes narrowed, and then his lips twitched in a cross between a smile and a grimace.

'I think you may be right. We'll endure until then. I assure you.' And with that, Leofric was dismissed, and strode from the king's presence. Leofric realised the king was correct, and yet, did he truly wait for the death of the man to release him from the oppressive power of Earl Godwine? What if he met his death first? There was little in age to differentiate the two. He didn't wish to think he'd wasted so much of his life.

No, he resolved, stepping into a bright, but clear day. If the other man died before him, Leofric realised, he'd probably miss the pestilent bastard. He and Earl Godwine had been uneasy allies and almost enemies for many years.

26

SANDWICH, AD1047, ÆLFGAR

'Row in time, or we'll look like arses,' the coarse call of Eowa brought a smirk to Ælfgar's face, even while he sweated and laboured to keep in time with the rest of the rowers. Perhaps, he realised, he ought to relinquish his hold on the oar. But he wasn't prepared to, not with his cousin on the ship as well, and knowing full well that Earl Harold was in attendance, and he was a much better shipman than his brother had ever been.

'The king's watching,' Eowa reminded them as Ælfgar gritted his teeth. Edward was indeed watching. He was aboard one of his ships, nominally in command of the entire fleet. While they might not have faced an enemy since King Magnus, that didn't mean they weren't alert to the fact one might appear. There were rumours that Sweyn Godwinesson was in Bruges and that he'd gone to Denmark to help his cousin, Svein Estridsson, against King Magnus of Norway. Not that it was going well. The latest reports were that Magnus had overwhelmed the Danes. Ælfgar imagined his father's ally, Lady Estrid, was displeased about that.

And so, the threat never diminished. Those who could pull

together a group of ships and command them to go where they demanded were powerful. They didn't need the wealth of a country at their backs, not if they could win tribute by attacking others. And to that end, Ælfgar was mindful of Earl Godwine. While providing the king with a fine ship to win his favour, the earl had also been building his own fleet. His father had only one personally owned ship for Mercia. Earl Godwine had many more than that number. Some of them, admittedly, were captained by his sons, Earl Harold amongst them. But many others had professional shipmen, just as good as the king's. Ælfgar knew he needed to mention this to his father. It was a new development. It seemed clear to Ælfgar that the shipbuilders used by the king during the winter, two years ago had found suitable employment with Godwine since then.

'Put your backs into it,' Eowa hollered again. Ælfgar bent to the task once more. This wasn't something new that the king was trying, but they'd never performed such manouevres in peace time. But the king was determined that they'd be ready and prepared for all eventualities. Having to encircle an enemy craft, so similar to when he'd had to rescue Sweyn Godwinesson from the waiting depths of the ocean, was not easy. And certainly not when the sea was so choppy. They couldn't hoist their sails, and neither were the oars having the desired effect.

Later, resting with his oar balanced on his knees, Ælfgar watched more of the king's fleet trying the same. He found a smile on his lips. None of them was exactly succeeding, but some of the ships had more skilled commanders than others, and others, he was sure, were just being bloody lucky to hit a sudden moment of peace between the waves.

The wind ruffled his hair, drying the sweat from his back, as he admired his father's shipmen. Eowa, as always, was firm but fair. He knew how to make his crew work together. Now he watched the exercise with interest, never taking his eyes from what the others were doing.

'Earl Harold's a good shipman,' he muttered, just so Ælfgar could hear. 'His young brother Tostig is as much of a fool as his brother.' Ælfgar had already been thinking the same. Tostig was far too like Sweyn.

'At least Lord Godwine's not here.'

'Aye, and that man prides himself on being the son of a skilled shipman and commander. If it's true, then he didn't learn anything from his father.' Eowa spoke without malice. The fate of Godwine's father wasn't dissimilar to what had happened to Northman. Both men knew how easy it was to fall from grace with a ruling king.

'But the earl certainly has the funds to build good ships,' Eowa continued. 'They're as good, if not better, than the king's. Is your father worried?'

'He will be, when he knows,' Ælfgar murmured. He could detect that Ælfwine was listening to their conversation. He wasn't surprised. Ælfwine liked to know everything.

'Aye, well, I would be as well. The king should be too. If the earl doesn't stop his building programme, he'll have more ships than the king, and we all know he's still unhappy about what happened to his oldest son.'

Ælfgar nodded and then smirked.

'You're very well informed for a man who spends so much of his life at sea?'

'Well, it's imperative to keep track of politics, as well as who has the most blades to command. It's always bloody politics that leads to war,' the commander complained. Ælfgar nodded along. Eowa was a wise man.

'Right, you lazy sods, get your backs into it. It seems we're done for the day.' And with that, Ælfgar once more bent to the oar, ignoring the callouses forming on his hands. The other men were more seasoned to the wooden oars than he was. They wouldn't have the same marks on their hands, but despite it all, he found himself enjoying the exercise and the honest sweat that beaded his back.

After the terrible winter, it was good to be alive, and to be out on the sea.

Perhaps, he considered, he might broach the subject of having more ships built in his father's name. Then he might be able to have one of his own to command. Although, what his wife might think of that he was unsure. But, his sons would undoubtedly approve.

27

AD1047, LEOFRIC

'My lord king, I must complain. Earl Leofric has made it clear that he doesn't support my family. Isn't it enough that my beloved Sweyn has been banished?' Leofric didn't react to Earl Godwine's whining. The man was making a fool of himself. While the king might be keen to agree with Leofric on this, it was only because he thought the same.

'My lord Godwine. England's fleet is to secure England's safety. It's not to win a kingdom for your wife's son, which he's been foolish enough to lose.'

Leofric nodded along with the king, pleased to hear he had no intention of casting the blame at Leofric's feet. The missive from Lord Svein Estridsson had caught them all by surprise. Lord Svein demanded support against King Magnus, who'd claimed Denmark as his to rule and had roundly beaten Svein earlier in the year. Svein had been forced to flee to stay alive, but Leofric knew that Lady Estrid, his mother, had remained in Roskilde, not quite pledging her support to King Magnus but doing enough to be able to remain in the kingdom of her birth.

He didn't glance at Svein's brother, Beorn. He knew that the brothers had shared a difficult past. Beorn had determined to come to England with Harthacnut rather than stand as a second to Svein and his ambitions within Denmark. Yet, Beorn had spoken in favour of his brother's endeavour in Denmark, as had Earl Godwine, although Harold was markedly quiet about the whole thing.

Neither had Ralph or Svein and Beorn's stepbrother, Asbjorn spoken in favour of supporting Svein. It was no surprise that Asbjorn had been corralled into attending the king's witan now that Sweyn had been banished. Earl Godwine was eager to keep his cohort of supporters high, and of course, family could usually be relied upon to remain loyal.

'But, my lord king, it would aid England if Magnus were removed from Denmark and our ally, Svein, ruled in his place.' Lord Godwine was far from resolved to the king's decision.

'And yet, at this time, the conflict between Magnus and Svein also keeps Magnus from England's shores, as it does, Svein.' The king spoke well. Leofric nodded along once more, aware that, at his side, Earl Siward was perhaps more conflicted.

Siward owed much of his elevation to the House of Gorm in the figures of both Cnut and Estrid, the uncle and mother of Svein and Beorn.

'The ships, Earl Godwine, are to protect England and not Denmark. Can you imagine what would happen if we sent ships to support Svein and our enemy, Baldwin of Bruges or even some of the new Viking raider pirates, decided to try their luck? I'll not allow my kingdom to be made weak to make another stronger.'

The tension in the room was palpable. What should have been a mild-mannered witan to discuss the coinage, taxes and witness a land confirmation the king was bestowing upon the church in Holme had become anything but that.

'I'll take my ships, then,' Earl Godwine was militant. Leofric understood why. His son, Sweyn, was believed to have gone to Denmark to join his cousin in fighting King Magnus. Whether there was truth in that, or not remained to be seen.

'Ah yes, your ships?' Leofric had the distinct impression that Edward might have been waiting for such a statement. 'I understand you've built yourself quite the fleet, my lord,' the king's words were cold, and Leofric noted that Queen Edith had stiffened beside the king.

'My ships, yes, my lord king, paid for with my coin and crewed by men of Wessex.'

'Indeed. And my lord, does that not strike you as somewhat counterproductive? Should the earldom of East Anglia or Mercia be attacked, will your men be keen to defend them?'

'My lord king?' Earl Godwine sounded outraged, but Leofric knew the king's question was genuine and highlighted a real problem.

'I'll order you to reassign your men. Half of your ship men will become crew to the royal fleet, and half of the royal fleet will become crew to your ships. You'll still meet all funds for the shipmen's wages, but my scribes will take on the responsibility of distributing the payments.'

'My lord king,' it seemed, to Leofric, that Earl Godwine had no answer to the king's commands. He could hardly refuse to do as the king ordered, and beside him, Leofric was aware that Earl Siward's body was gently shaking. He risked glancing at him, seeing the mirth on the other's face. Earl Siward was enjoying this rather too much.

'And we'll hear no more of this request from Lord Svein Estridsson. If you must, inform him that the English king has refused. The ship army is to keep England secure. Send my sympathies for his plight but nothing else. You can, if need be, send him coin, Lord Beorn. After all, he is your brother, and I'm sure you wish him to prevail.'

Beorn looked relieved at the king's words, whereas Earl Godwine was still floundering. Leofric felt he'd had to say little but a refusal. He'd not even truly had to argue for his words to sway the king. King Edward had been keen to retain his hold on the ships and shipmen he commanded.

'And now, and somehow, we can never get away from ships, we must discuss Baldwin of Bruges. I understand that while he supported the disgraced Sweyn Godwinesson during the year, he's now moved on. However, Baldwin threatens my sister, Lord Ralph's mother.'

Leofric hadn't known about this. He listened carefully as the king detailed the matters taking place over the Narrow Sea. Baldwin of Bruges had involved himself in English affairs for several years, most notably when he sheltered Lady Emma from the wrath of King Harald. However, it appeared the man was determined to do more than just infuriate English kings.

'He's putting pressure on Countess Godgifu's second husband. I fear that the weak-willed man will do as Baldwin demands and repudiate my sister. Therefore, I request permission from the witan to allow her safe passage to England.'

Leofric didn't miss that while Edward was determined not to allow Earl Godwine to assist his nephew, the king wished to protect his sister. Not, of course, that the two actions were similar. Lord Svein Estridsson wanted ships to wage war against King Magnus. Countess Godgifu, and Leofric remembered meeting her when he'd been asked to approach Edward about returning to England, wanted a safe haven, if she were to lose her husband. And it wasn't as if Countess Godgifu would need to be provided with land. She already had manors in her name, gifted to her by her father, and managed by Ralph on her behalf.

'But, my lord king,' of course, it was Earl Godwine who spoke, no doubt quick to jump on the irony of the king's request. 'Will this not bring the eye of Lord Baldwin to rest once more on England?'

'I believe he has more than enough problems with the Emperor. But, if it does, then yes, we'll face any seaborne attack he thinks to carry out. But, my lord Godwine, we'll be protecting England, not denuding her of her precious ship army.'

Leofric nodded along with the king. In many ways, he and King Edward had failed to forge the alliance he might have hoped, but in this, they were of one mind. Countess Godgifu was welcome to come to England and return to the home from which she'd been absent for even longer than her older brother. Lord Svein Estridsson, despite Leofric's close association with his mother, would need to fight his own battles. For now, at least.

THE ANGLO-SAXON CHRONICLE ENTRY FOR 1047

‘And in the same year Earl Swein travelled out to Baldwin’s lands, to Bruges, and lived there all winter, and then towards summer went out.’ (E)

28

COVENTRY, MAY, AD1048, LADY GODGIFU

'What was that?' She spoke urgently, shaking her husband from his loud snores beside her.

'What?' he asked groggily.

'Didn't you feel that?' she demanded.

'Feel what?' now he sat upright, and stared at her. From close by, other cries could be heard, and she shook her head, convinced that it was that which had woken her husband more roundly than her yelp.

'The ground shook.'

'No it didn't,' he countered quickly. 'I'd have felt that.'

'Would you, my dear,' she asked wryly, reaching for her over-dress. She could hear the loud voices of others and knew she'd not made it up. 'Get up,' she called to her husband over her shoulder, aware that Hunter slunk out of the door at her feet. She ran a calming hand over her thick coat.

No eyes met her arrival in the hall, and that wasn't surprising, for the door was wide open, and she could see almost everyone was awake, apart from her husband.

'Did you feel that too?' she called imperiously, forging a path through the men, women, children, and animals that stood too close to the door.

'Yes,' the gate warden was the first to agree. 'And the horses felt it too. One of them has kicked their way right out of their stable, look.' She followed where the man pointed, unsurprised to find the new, high-stepping stallion cavorting in the closest field, unheeding of the crops he was trampling while bucking and dancing in the gentle breeze. It was daylight, but still early enough that dew coated every surface.

'We must check for injuries and if any of the outbuildings and the main hall have been damaged.' Now outside, she could also hear men and women calling to themselves from their homes, dotted throughout the manor where she and her husband spent much of their time. In the distance, she could see Coventry. 'And we must ensure the people of Coventry are well.' She was beloved by the inhabitants of Coventry. Through the terrible winters of late, the awful harvests, the wet summers, and the demands of King Harthacnut, she'd kept her people safe. And she'd do so now.

'What happened?' Leofric was in the doorway now, looking around, suddenly alert, as he saw all the people on his manor arranged before him.

'The earth shook,' Lady Godgifu found herself explaining once more. 'Your damn horse has bolted, look. We must ensure any repairs are carried out quickly.'

Leofric licked his lips and nodded along with his wife. She was pleased to see he wasn't about to question her again. Not that he could. Not when the majority of people had also experienced it.

'What does it mean?' a frightened voice called. Lady Godgifu knew how to counter any panic that might infect her people.

'It means we'll have a busy day,' she spoke briskly. 'And this evening, we'll attend the church and offer our prayers that no one has been unduly injured. It's similar to a bad storm, that is all, nothing to fear. And husband, have your horse restrained before we have no beetroots to eat during the summer months.' Her tone was acerbic but she noticed the mirth in her husband's eyes. She felt a moment of pride that her husband was content to allow her to control the situation. They'd been married for many years. They were settled in their ways. And they both had strengths that contributed to the other. In the matter of her home and her beloved Coventry, she knew what was needed.

'We must check all the animals and fences remain in place,' Leofric called to his men as he strode towards the stables. She could hear him complaining about the damage the stallion had done. She looked at the women and children crowded around her.

'Has the morning meal been prepared?' She arched an eyebrow at the woman who ran the kitchen.

'My lady,' she ducked a quick curtsey and hastened on her way, beckoning her assistants to her side.

'Have the chickens been fed,' she called to the woman responsible for the hens.

'My lady,' another curtsey and the woman scurried on her way. Lady Godgifu watched as the others with tasks to accomplish realised they'd be called upon next and instead hastened on their way.

In no time at all, she was stood there, alone apart from her personal servant, surveying her manor and all the people and buildings within it.

'We'll check the grain stores,' she informed the woman. Again, a curtsey. 'And bring me my cloak while you hunt out the tallies,' she continued. Only now did she allow herself to shiver. An earth tremor. They weren't unknown. In fact, she knew, far to the north, they happened often in the country called Iceland, usually accompanied by puffs of smoke and grey clouds pouring forth into the sky. Not for the first time, she considered why such didn't occur within her kingdom. Not that she wasn't grateful it didn't. That would have been something else to worry about.

As she turned to stride towards the grain stores, the sound of hooves over the hardpacked earth running close to the property infiltrated her thoughts. She turned, meeting the eyes of someone she didn't know well. No doubt, she realised, it was a messenger for her husband, from Lady Estrid. It had been some time since he'd had such a messenger, and the man was certainly not from the king or her son. They didn't wear the correct livery on their clothes.

'Good day,' she called, eyeing the rider. The gate warden had returned to his position, and as he heard the question, he opened the gate.

'Good day, my lady. I've come to seek Lord Leofric.'

'He's busy, trying to restrain his stallion.'

'The tremor was felt here, as well then?' the man asked, quickly dismounting and offering her a bow of his head. Lady Godgifu was aware that the king employed many men as messengers, but this man spoke with a strong Danish accent. She was convinced he was from Denmark.

'It was, yes. Did you see any damage as you came through Coventry?'

'A few scrapes and bruises. The monks were busy tending to the people.'

She smiled, relieved to hear as much.

'And why are you here, if you don't mind me asking?'

'News from Denmark, my lady. King Magnus is dead. I'm sure all will know soon enough.'

'Then who's king now?'

'King Svein Estridsson is king in place of Magnus.'

She nodded. The day had started poorly, but this was good news.

'And he doesn't mean to pursue a claim to the English kingdom?'

'No, my lady. He was always only able to claim his cousin's kingship of Denmark.'

'I imagine Lady Estrid is pleased?'

'Indeed, she is, as is his brother.'

'Go,' she smiled. 'Go and inform my husband. I know he'll be satisfied, despite everything.'

The messenger bowed again; no mention of Leofric's reticence to support Lord Svein against King Magnus the previous year.

'Ah, but, my lady,'

'Yes?'

'I can confirm that Sweyn Godwinesson has indeed made his way to Denmark.'

She nodded but felt the smile sliding from her lips. It seemed they could never have everything they wanted at the same time. It was good that Svein was king of Denmark. What was less appealing was any support he might give to his outlawed and excommunicated cousin, Sweyn Godwinesson.

While she and Abbess Eadgifu had made peace with one another, and Godgifu couldn't deny that the children were delightful babes, they could, if need be, be used against their father. It was a poor man who didn't put his children before all else, but Sweyn Godwinesson had never been concerned with the outcome of his illegal marriage, only with the wealth of the nunnery, which had now been redistributed and was safely in the hands of Queen Edith.

'My lady?' recalled to the aftermath of the earth tremor, Godgifu attempted to dismiss all thought of Sweyn Godwinesson, and yet she feared, or rather knew, that they'd not heard the last from him, and now that he had the ear of another king, things could go poorly for England.

29

AD1048, ÆLFGAR

THE WITAN WAS IN A FURORE. ÆLFGAR WASN'T USED TO SEEING MEN WITH fearful faces when they addressed the king.

'Where are they from?' Edward demanded loudly over the unwelcome rumble of unease running through the witan.

'We don't know, my lord king. They've already been successful, though.'

'Do they fly a sail with distinctive colours? Showing the Danish emblem, or the one that Baldwin of Bruges uses?'

Ælfgar was able to see the perplexed expression on the breathless messenger who'd been allowed immediate access to the king, despite the witan taking place.

'Neither, my lord king. Neither, I'm sure of it.'

King Edward's face wore a similar expression to that of the messenger's, and Ælfgar could almost hear him thinking.

'Then it's not a concerted raid?'

'Perhaps not, my lord king. They attacked Sandwich, and stole much wealth from the church and the people of the settlement, even some supplies from the king's fleet.'

'And where was the fleet at that time?'

'Patrolling the Narrow Sea, as requested.'

'Very well, and have the enemy gone now?'

'It's believed that they've gone elsewhere, further north.'

'Then, even now my people could be threatened. What of the ship army?'

'They've been informed and think to track them.'

For a moment, silence reigned, the king's fingers drumming on the armrest of his chair.

'Then we're doing what can be done. Earl Godwine?'

'My lord king?' Ælfgar's lips curled at the obsequious tone the other man had adopted.

'Have your fleet mobilised. Ensure Wessex is protected. The king's fleet will remain divided between Sandwich and the mouth of the River Thames.'

'My lord king,' Ælfgar didn't watch the earl, but he could imagine him bowing low, perhaps almost mocking the king.

'Earl Harold?'

'My lord king?' Harold spoke with more respect and Ælfgar was pleased to hear it.

'I fear your earldom might be threatened as well. Hasten home, to Ipswich or Maldon, and ensure your people are protected from attack. I'll not allow pirates to take what they want when England is equipped with the largest ship army it's known since the early days of King Cnut's reign.'

Ælfgar did glance to see Earl Harold hastening from the meeting. He doubted there'd be much more discussed today other than the fleet that had attacked Sandwich. His father would be pleased not to have missed more when he was unwell and unable to attend upon the king. All the same, Ælfgar didn't feel it had been a wasted journey. He was sure he would also be called upon to support the king.

'Now, I have two of my ships in London, and Lord Ælfgar, I believe you also have two ships?'

'Yes, my lord king, the new one, and the old. And the rest of the Mercian fleet as well, ready and at your command, all ten ships.'

King Edward nodded. It might seem small numbers to someone such as Earl Godwine, but Mercia had never felt the need to be overly reliant on ships to protect it. It had been many long years since the Viking raiders had encamped deep in the heart of Mercia at Repton and Torksey. Instead, defences were much closer to the source of the River Trent.

'Then you'll escort me. We'll sail with the tide today and ensure these pirates are dissuaded from ever attacking again.'

'Very well, my lord king,' Ælfgar was pleased with the task. While Earl Godwine and Harold had both been instructed to see to their coastlines, neither of them had been asked to sail with the king. It was certainly an honour that would please his mother and which wouldn't be overlooked by Earl Godwine. The man was still far from favoured by the king, despite his daughter's marriage, and Harold's elevation. The spectre of Sweyn's missteps chimed against any good the House of Godwine could bring about.

'Ah, my lord,' Eowa was as jovial as ever. He already knew of the king's command, for Ælfgar had sent word to him while he prepared for the journey, and rumours were running rife through London anyway following the attack on Sandwich. Ælfgar was always amazed how bad news spread so quickly and good, so much slower.

'You're ready?' Ælfgar called. He didn't have either of his cousins at his side this time or Olaf or his nephew. After all, it had been a witan called to London, not an army called to defend the country.

'Always, my lord. And the new ship isn't bad either. Here, I'll introduce you to the man I've set as commander over that ship, with your father's permission, of course. Beorhtric, come here,' Eowa lifted his voice and called over a harassed-looking man. Ælfgar recognised him. Beorhtric was well-known to him. They'd sailed many times together.

'My lord,' Beorhtric nearly tripped over his feet, and Ælfgar remembered the man had better sea-legs than land legs.

'Beorhtric, well met. It seems we're to test her sooner than we might have thought.'

'Yes, my lord. But she's ready, as are the crew.' Beorhtric stood taller now, a glimmer of pride on his wind-roughened face.

'Well, they're nearly ready,' Eowa interjected, his tone somewhat sour. 'They still need to show they can survive the curse of the Viking raiders,' he added quickly, to counter the dismay on Beorhtric's face. 'Come on, man, cheer up. This is what we live for.' Ælfgar chuckled, and Beorhtric tried to do the same, but Ælfgar could tell he was nervous, and that didn't surprise him. He knew he'd be nervous in the same situation, suddenly responsible for the lives of so many others than just himself.

'We leave with the tide,' Ælfgar offered, hoping to distract the new ship's commander from his duties.

'It's been high the last few days,' Eowa quickly confirmed. 'Almost as though the sea knows we need a smooth passage to the open sea.' With that, he turned aside, and Ælfgar took the time to admire the new ship he'd managed to convince his father to have built the previous winter. The cost had been astronomical but Ælfgar believed it well worth it. While Earl Godwine had a host of ships to defend Wessex, it was about time that the Mercian earl could offer similar.

Later, Ælfgar settled in the ship that Eowa commanded. He felt it unfair to position himself in Beorhtric's when the men were only just learning to work together. He'd also realised that while he knew Beorhtric, many of the men on the ship were new to him. Better, he decided, to be with men used to him as he was to them.

With sails raised to take advantage of the steady wind, the many ships left London. People had come to see the king leave, including his wife. She stood stoically on the quayside, as the ships sailed away. Harold had already left for his earldom, but it was impossible to ignore the imposing façade of Earl Godwine in the crowd. Earl

Siward hadn't been at the witan, attending to affairs in the north, and neither had he sent a representative, as Leofric had done. But, it was much further for Siward to travel, as opposed to him.

It was imperative that they discovered the extent of the damage to Sandwich. Not that they managed to make it further than the opening of the River Thames on that first night. It had been late in the day when they'd set out, and already, the sun had stained the horizon, and darkness wouldn't be long in arriving. The ships didn't make for land, though. Instead, they waited, guards on watch duty all through the night so that they could resume their journey as soon as it was light the following day.

Ælfgar watched the coastline as he rowed with his fellow shipmen. He'd been this way many times before. The coastline felt familiar, and in no time, they rounded the Isle of Sheppey, Thanet the next place they would encounter.

The sea was almost calm, encouraging them onwards. Ælfgar had seen the king standing with his ship's commander, discussing the journey, or so he assumed. But, within sight of Thanet, a ship suddenly surged towards them.

From the king's ships, swift commands were given, eight of the ships coming together, including the one that Ælfgar was on, while the one under Beorhtric's command was kept further back, just in case it needed to dash towards where it was hoped the East Anglian fleet would soon be appearing from. A further two hung back, in case they were needed to rescue any from the sea's grasp.

'My lord,' a coarse voice hailed them, before suddenly seeing the king, and bowing low, despite the rough seas suddenly buffeting the ships in such close proximity.

'My lord king,' the man spoke again, his voice filled with awe.

'Speak,' the king demanded urgently. It was evident that the man was a seasoned shipman, as were the men who'd powered the ship towards the king. It wasn't a craft made for defending the kingdom, but instead a fishing vessel, Ælfgar was sure of that.

'The Viking raiders have tried their luck on Thanet, but we

rebuffed them and sent Lothen and Yrling fleeing for their lives, alas, with most of their ships intact.' The man smirked as he spoke. It looked as though he'd been in a fight recently, the shimmer of a slowly recovering black eye visible on his face. His nose also seemed bent, pointing towards the land.

'Well done, I'll send reparations to the people of Thanet,' the king offered, his voice filled with respect.

'No need, my lord king. We lost no lives and indeed, managed to acquire some of their stolen treasure. Not all of it, but some of it.'

'What's your name?' the king queries.

'I'm Hering, my lord king. I'm a fisherman and the portreeve combined.'

'And tell me, have you heard what happened at Sandwich?'

'I have, my lord king, yes. I hear many good men died there, including their portreeve. People think it's all taxes and nothing else, but it's a dangerous position, I assure you.'

'We're away to Sandwich then, if all is well here. But, do you know where the enemy went?'

'North, my lord, as we saw it. It's too be hoped they've slunk back from where they came by now. Fierce resistance, we meted out to them, all of them. They thought to overpower us, but we're a people who know the secrets of our coastline, and we used it.'

Ælfgar grinned to hear the man's pride. Comparing his ship to those of the king's ship army was far from favourable. It wasn't built for great speed, but still, it had overpowered men bent on destruction.

'I'll send word to the people of Thanet,' the king called. 'But remain on your guard. Earl Godwine and his son, Earl Harold, will be patrolling the coastline, as will the remainder of my ship-army, and the ships of Earl Leofric as well. Stay alert until we're sure they've left our shores.'

'Very good, my lord king,' and while the ship began to turn to head back towards Thanet, the king's fleet remained on course for Sandwich. While it was good that Thanet had survived, Ælfgar decided, it was unfortunate that they'd lost sight of the enemy fleet. He spared a thought for Earl Harold, hoping that he'd made it to Ipswich or Maldon quickly and even now wasn't engaged in a fight with the enemy.

Ælfgar could tell that the rest of the shipmen were eager to engage with the enemy. While they'd fought King Magnus four summers ago, it hadn't been more than a skirmish. This might give them all the opportunity that they wanted to fight an enemy and overwhelm them.

SANDWICH WAS REACHED as the day once more came to an end. They'd been forced to row through the middle part of the day, but now, as the horizon coloured in vibrant reds and yellows, the sail again powered the craft onwards, and Ælfgar was pleased to give his hands a rest. He rubbed the fingers of one hand over the callouses on the other. He was sure they weren't as bad as in the past, but still, they did hurt. Practising with sword, war axe and seax and shield wasn't enough to make the skin on his hand firm enough to withstand the wood of the oar.

They came into the quayside slowly. Ælfgar could see it was busy, despite the time of day, and all turned to face the ships approaching them, some with hands on weapons belts.

'We're the king's force,' Eowa bellowed towards men he'd known for many years. They relaxed at that, and Ælfgar's eyes swept the desolation before him. While the king's fleet had been far from Sandwich at the time of the attack, the fishing craft had been wrecked. He could see where some of them wallowed in the water, while others had been pulled onto the quayside to undergo repairs.

There were also blackened timbers and some of the people carried injuries.

Ælfgar watched as the king hastened to disembark. He quickly moved amongst the people, while his ships took up defensive positions, come to protect the quay, although it all seemed too little and too late.

'I better disembark, as well,' Ælfgar murmured to Eowa, and effortlessly, Eowa directed the ship to the wooden quay so that Ælfgar could join the king. Ælfgar could already see that a monkish-cleric had made his way to the king, bowing low, still carrying his parchments onto which he must surely be making a reckoning of what had happened here.

'Ah, Lord Ælfgar,' the king noticed him and beckoned him closer. 'We'll remain here tonight, and get a better view of everything in the morning. Order your ships and those of Mercia, to join mine. They'll take turns to patrol in order to prevent further attacks on Sandwich.'

'My lord king,' he bowed low and turned to convey the king's wishes, deciding a cloak was also in order. He was astounded by what he could see. He'd visited Sandwich almost yearly for the last four or five years. It had been a prosperous place, well endowed with ships, fishing craft and a vibrant market place, but now it seemed broken and more than half-burnt. It would take a great deal of money to set everything to rights once more, but Ælfgar didn't imagine the king would be slow to offer those funds. His face, while welcoming to the survivors, showed his determination.

ONCE MORE OUT at sea and racing back the way they'd come only two days before, Ælfgar felt reassured that much of the king's fleet had joined the few ships they'd taken to Sandwich. They'd received reports that the fleet had been close to Essex, and now they raced back towards the mouth of the River Thames. Somehow, they'd missed them while they journeyed to Sandwich.

The king was in a belligerent mood. He was determined to encounter the men directing the fleet, Yrling and Lothen. Some of the shipmen had met them before and knew of their reputation.

Ælfgar couldn't help feeling how ineffectual the king's response seemed. Or rather, not ineffectual, but too late. They'd had no warning of the attack. Indeed, how could they have expected a band of Viking raider pirates to strike out towards England. They were, he realised, taking advantage of the discord between Baldwin of Bruges and the Emperor and all the other areas drawn into the fight. He wouldn't be surprised to discover the raiding spree had begun in Boulogne.

Earl Godwine's fleet had also joined that of the king's ships, but only as they'd been moving towards East Anglia. There had been no time to do more than instruct them to follow the rest of the king's fleet, all aside from those ships that had been tasked with ensuring Sandwich, Thanet, and the other coastal regions remained free of all menace.

'Will there be a fight?' Eowa asked him. It was impossible to tell whether the other man hungered for a fight or not.

'It'll depend on whether we find them,' Ælfgar replied. He wasn't convinced. While the ships of Yrling and Lothen had done much damage at Sandwich, as of yet, there had been no sign of other successes. The fisher people and traders had ensured news of the attacks had reached other settlements even before the king had been aware. Everyone had been on their guard ever since.

'I don't see it,' Eowa mused. 'I think the arseholes will know they've had their chance. Now they just need to escape England before the king's fleet entirely overpowers them. These Viking raider pirates don't make coin and earn the allegiance of other ships by killing off their ship men and being sunk.'

Ælfgar bit his lower lip as Eowa spoke. He couldn't help thinking the other man was correct. While they all wished for a fight, it didn't seem possible. After all, how were they to find them when the enemy could be anywhere along the east coast?

30

AD1048, LEOFRIC

Coughing and generally feeling sorry for himself, Leofric was roused from his stupor by the sound of horses outside. He tried to sit a little straighter in his bed, but found it impossible to do so. His entire body ached, and he'd be pleased when whatever ailed him passed, if indeed, it did pass.

His wife had berated him for such morbid thoughts, but he was an old man in the eyes of many. Not many lived to such a great age, and his current illness, kept reminding him of that. This year he'd celebrate his fiftieth winter.

'Uncle,' he met the eyes of Ælfwine, who'd opened the door to his private chambers and poked his head inside, although he didn't seem to want to draw near. 'Aunt Godgifu won't allow me to come any closer, but there's news.'

'What news?'

'A Viking raider fleet attacked Sandwich. The king, and your son, left the witan to counter it, but although it's all but destroyed the fishing fleet at Sandwich, the scum have turned tail and run to Bruges.'

'Bloody Bruges,' Leofric coughed. 'Nothing but trouble either comes from Bruges or leaves there. And my son, he's safe?'

'He is, my lord, yes, and the king as well,' Ælfwine added with a cheeky twinkle in his eye.

Leofric glowered at him before subsiding into another coughing fit. When he could speak again, Ælfwine had closed the door, and his wife had appeared.

'Drink this,' she commanded acerbically. 'It seems you need to be better sooner rather than later. While you're lying abed, England is threatened.' There was no give in her voice that was filled with iron resolve, and Leofric smiled to hear it. Lady Godgifu was not kind to those who showed weakness, and being ill was, to her, a weakness.

'Our son is well,' he informed her.

'I know that. Ælfwine told me everything. Now, hurry, and get better. No good can come from Viking raider pirates, and, as you say, Bruges.'

LEOFRIC FORCED himself out of bed the following day, and would admit to no one that it made him feel better.

Ælfwine had remained in Coventry.

'Tell me everything,' he demanded from his nephew.

'I told you all I knew yesterday. The Viking raider pirates have run away, but not without destroying much of Sandwich. I believe the king thinks Osgot or Sweyn Godwinesson may have been involved.'

'But not Lady Gunnhild?'

'No, not her, or her sons. No one knows anything about them.' Leofric nodded and then coughed, cursing his weakness.

'And what did Earl Godwine say of the king's fears?'

'He was belligerent, as you might expect. Since Countess Godgifu arrived in England last year, the king is much firmer in his dealings towards the House of Godwine, don't you think?'

'Certainly, having his own family has made him reassess some of his earlier decisions,' Leofric agreed. His wife joined them now, her face pensive.

'There are others with your cough,' she complained.

'Well, I've been in my room for near-enough two weeks. Surely, I can't be to blame?' Her refusal to answer, somewhat pleased him. It meant that she might well agree with him.

'And what news from Denmark?

'King Svein is king. He says his mother is Queen Estrid.'

'And they don't plan on turning to England for assistance or to invade?'

'Not as far as is known, but of course, if Sweyn Godwinesson has the ear of his cousin, it's possible.' Leofric nodded. He felt sure that Svein Estridsson would be content with the kingship, or so he hoped. He was aware he'd been firm that Edward not support Svein in the past. He hoped that Lady Estrid and her son wouldn't take that too badly now they had what they'd long coveted.

'Then all is well, for now,' Leofric coughed, reaching for his soothing drink to stop the coughing.

'Perhaps, husband,' his wife offered, her tone hardly comforting. 'But these things never tend to last for long. Sweyn Godwinesson will return, mark my words. It's to be hoped he doesn't do so with half of Denmark's ship army at his command.'

Leofric wished to glower at his wife's doom-laden words but merely coughed again instead.

Damn his illness. Perhaps, once he was well, his wife would be less miserable.

HALE ONCE MORE, Leofric took himself to the witan. He knew, thanks to reports from his son, that the Viking raider pirates had done untold damage not just to Sandwich but also within Essex. The thought of men stolen away, if those rumours were correct, to be sold at the slave markets, infuriated him. He was determined to speak to the king about Lady Gytha. All knew that she made much of her money in the Dublin slave markets. Not for the first time, he thought the woman quite wealthy enough. And to profit from the misery of others was obscene. It spoke too much of her Danish origins.

All seemed quiet in London when he arrived, accompanied by Olaf, and, rarely, by his sister as well. It had been some time since he'd last seen her, and he was surprised to see grey threading her hair.

Ealdgyth eyed him sharply as they settled in one of the family properties far from the River Thames at Isleworth.

'I'm sure your wife must have silver hair as well, stop looking at it.' Her tone, Leofric realised, was perhaps too sharp. She had three hounds at her feet, two of them softly growling at one another as they fought over a bone. Hunter was eager to stay clear of the brewing argument. As he realised, Olaf was as well, the other man busying himself with some small task that involved his cloak and hanging it just right on the hook.

'I've not seen it on you before,' he countered.

'Then that's because you're a terrible brother and don't visit often enough.' She harumphed as she spoke, and Leofric found a smile playing on his lips. She was right. He had been remiss of late.

'Then, I apologise and will stop looking. How are you and your son and daughter?'

'My son is well, thank you. He's rising in the abbey. My daughter shows no interest in marriage.' Leofric detected the censure in that summation and determined not to ask for more details. He was bound not to like whatever argument there might be between his niece and his sister.

'And Ælfwine, I hear, is to wed?'

'Is he?' Leofric was shocked, and he realised so too was Olaf, who'd finally finished his messing around to join them before the hearth.

'Yes, a good woman from a good family in Derbyshire.'

'And Wulfstan?'

'There's no chance of that boy ever taking a wife, I assure you,' Ealdgyth spoke firmly. 'Despite his mother's pleading, he can see no reason for it.'

'And Lady Mildryth?'

'Is well, despite some worries about her health. She's rallied and has no intention, so she tells me, of dying before both of her sons are wed.'

'Then Wulfstan would do well to find a wife if he wants some peace,' Olaf chuckled darkly. Leofric grinned along with him, whereas Ealdgyth looked shocked at the pair of them.

ANGLO-SAXON CHRONICLE ENTRY FOR 1048

'Here in this year was a great earth-tremor widely in England. And in the same year Sandwich and Wight were raided, and the best men that were there were killed; and King Edward and the earls went out after them in their ships. And in the same year Bishop Siward resigned the bishopric because of his infirmity and went to Abingdon, and Archbishop Eadsige again succeeded to the bishopric; and within 8 weeks of this he [Siward] passed away on 23rd October.' (C)

'Here Swein [Svein Estridsson] came back to Denmark; and Harald, the paternal uncle of Magnus, went to Norway after Magnus was dead, and the Norwegians accepted him; and he sent here to this land about peace. And also Swein sent from Denmark, and asked King Edward for support with ships that would be at least 50 ships, but all the people opposed it. And here also, on 1 May, was an earth-tremor in many places; in Worcester, and in Droitwich, and in Derby and elsewhere. And there was also a very great pestilence among men and pestilence among cattle; and also the wild-fire in Derbyshire and elsewhere did great damage.' (D)

'And in the same year Lothen and Yrling came to Sandwich with 25 ships, and there took untold war-booty, in men and in gold and in silver, such that no-one knew what it all was. And then [they] turned around Thanet, and wanted to do the same there, but the local people resolutely withstood and kept them both from landing and from water, and completely put them to flight from there. And they turned from there to Essex, and raided there and took men and whatever they could find, and then turned east to Baldwin's lands, and sold there what they had looted, and afterwards travelled east from where they came earlier.' (E)

31

AD1049, COVENTRY, LEOFRIC

'My lord.' Leofric eyed the man before him, his heart already sinking.

'Yes,' he offered softly. He recognised the man, Ælfwold, as a messenger of King Edward. He felt as though he'd only just returned from the Easter witan. What could have happened in such a short space of time.

'The king regrets this, but he summons you to attend him at Sandwich. Have your shipmen meet you there as well.'

'Sandwich? Again?' he felt his heart still. The shock waves from last year's attack by those bastard Viking raider pirates were still being felt in many of the communities. He hoped they'd not returned or some other bastard hadn't decided to try their luck as well.

'Problems with Baldwin of Bruges, alas,' the messenger offered grimly. 'The fleet is called upon, and the king is determined to support the Emperor against him.'

'Very well,' Leofric inclined his head. 'Are you heading north to Earl Siward?'

'I am, my lord, yes. The king prefers all of his allies together, but he's aware that Siward must also protect his coastline, as must Earl Harold.'

'I will hasten to Sandwich,' Leofric nodded, only to startle as he heard the sound of a hurrying horse on the roadway outside his home. He held his hand above his eyes and caught sight of his nephew, Wulfstan.

'Wulfstan. What ails you?' he called, the grey horse foaming at the mouth. Wulfstan, atop his fine steed, scowled at his uncle, and then noticed the other messenger.

'Damn it,' he huffed. 'Has the king heard already? I only sent word yesterday.'

'Heard what?' Leofric demanded quickly, his eyes sweeping from the messenger to his nephew.

'Gruffydd ap Rhydderch of Gwent has forged an alliance with a fleet of Viking raiders. They mean to attack Gruffydd ap Llewelyn of Powys and the border's in uproar.'

Leofric nodded, absorbing the information, torn between his duty to the king and what might befall Mercia if he didn't support his nephew. While Sweyn Godwinesson's lands had been distributed between his brother, Beorn and Ralph, Harold was already called upon to support the king on the east coast, and Beorn and Ralph didn't have the resources that Leofric did.

'Come inside, both of you,' Leofric decided quickly. 'The king has summoned me to Sandwich with the ships,' he explained to his nephew. The messenger, his brown eyes perplexed, followed Leofric to the hall, men from the stables coming to tend to the two horses.

'You shouldn't have ridden him so hard,' Leofric murmured to his nephew.

'I know, but the animal wanted to run. I tried to rein him in more than once.'

'Ensure the animal is well rested,' he called to his stableman. The man nodded, offering reassurances to the horse, who still blew.

'What now?' Lady Godgifu called to her husband, from where she sat, embroidery to hand before the heat of the hearth.

'The king orders me to Sandwich, but Gruffydd ap Rhydderch has allied with another band of Viking raider pirates.'

She looked up at that, eyeing her nephew with concern.

'It must be bad if you're here in person,' she murmured, sitting upright and beckoning for drinks and food for the riders.

'Ælfwold heads north, to Earl Siward.'

'Is it two fleets of Viking raiders?' Lady Godgifu queried.

'No, the king is determined to hold against Baldwin of Bruges. The Emperor has decided to take action against him.

'Does Baldwin act alone? Are Osgot and Sweyn Godwinesson involved?'

The messenger shrugged his shoulders, pausing in the act of eating.

'The king has been contacted by Emperor Henry, the third of his name, that's all I know. Baldwin has been meddling in affairs that don't concern him. Emperor Henry wishes to ensure he received no aid from others, and of course, the king is aggrieved that Baldwin forced Countess Godgifu's new husband to cast her aside.'

'I imagine Baldwin must think the king might favour him for supporting his mother.' Lady Godgifu's words were ripe with amusement. All knew that wasn't likely to happen.

'Then the threat isn't immediate?'

'No, my lord, it isn't.'

Leofric nodded. He didn't wish to deny his king. But obviously, at this moment in time, the king was unaware of events close to the Welsh kingdoms.'

'You sent word to the king?'

'I did, father, yes. I was unsure where Earls Harold and Beorn might be. I knew of the witan called by the king for Easter.'

Leofric grunted at this. Wulfstan had done the right thing, but still, it was a conundrum.

'Has the fleet been sighted yet close to the Welsh kingdoms?'

'Only on the coast. Traders informed me at Shrewsbury. It's been at least a week since they were seen.'

'It's early for the Viking raiders to leave their winter camps,' Ælfwold murmured alongside them.

'Then, I'll ride to join the king and send Ælfgar to aid you. By rights, it should be Harold and Beorn who counter the threat from the South. I imagine it's possible that any attacks might use the River Severn, but I hope your people and manors will remain safe.'

'Then I'll return as soon as possible. Ælfwine has remained in my place. He would have come himself, but he's unwell, with this pestilent cough all seem to have. I couldn't allow him to risk himself.'

'Keep me informed of what's happening.'

'I'll travel to Oxford,' Lady Godgifu announced. 'I'll be closer then, both to the borders and Sandwich. Coventry shouldn't be threatened,' she continued, and Leofric grunted his agreement. 'Two potential enemies, and it seems Sweyn Godwinesson is attached to neither.' She arched an eyebrow as she spoke.

'For now,' Leofric murmured. Like his wife, he found it impossible to believe that Sweyn wasn't involved in some way. And Baldwin of Bruges was a troublesome man. In the past, Leofric had thought him a magnanimous lord. But, he was ambitious beyond all imaginings. After all, he'd risked inciting the might of Emperor Henry III against him as well as King Edward. And the Emperor had resources that far exceeded those of Edward.

Leofric considered Denmark. He'd heard little from Lady Estrid since her son had become king, and she'd had the courtesy to send word to him. The last information received from her had reassured that the son of King Harald and his unacknowledged wife was safe and growing well.

Leofric prayed that continued.

He also hoped that no one ever knew the truth of who the boy was, for there were, Lady Estrid had warned him, rumours that King Harald had married and fathered a son. That could only cause problems if King Edward ever found out.

~

LEOFRIC FOUND the king at Sandwich. He was welcomed into his presence without fanfare and could tell that news of worries with the Viking raider fleet to the west of England had already reached the king.

'Earl Leofric, I would speak to you,' the king announced, making it clear the intention was to continue his walk along the largely rebuilt quayside. The smell of freshly cut wood sweetened the salt-laden air, and Leofric was surprised to see so much repaired and worried by just how much had needed replacement. His son had told him, but there was a huge difference between being told something and seeing it for the first time.

'My lord king,' Leofric offered half a bow, wincing slightly. He'd ridden a long way in the last week, and his backside was aching. He was getting too old for such exertions. Edward watched him with a knowing smile.

'It creeps up on you,' he commented wryly.

'It does, my lord king, just like the pestilent Viking raiders.'

'Yes, what news from the west?'

'My nephew brought his fears to me. I've sent Ælfgar to assist him, and my two ships should be making their way here to Sandwich alongside the rest of the Mercian fleet.'

'Yes, they arrived with the tide,' the king confirmed, but his face was twisted in thought. 'This leaves us with a conundrum. While I welcome the eagerness of your nephew, the land is Earl Harold's, but he must also protect the East Anglian earldom from anything Baldwin attempts.'

Leofric nodded. He didn't think he needed to agree with the king. It was self-evident.

'For now, I fear the threat from Baldwin of Bruges more than these Viking raiders. As soon as Gruffydd ap Llewelyn hears of this, he'll think to counter Gruffydd ap Rhydderch. I don't like to leave things to chance, but I believe Gruffydd ap Llewelyn will do most of defeating the force for us. If not, I'll send the Mercian fleet.'

Leofric nodded. He tended to agree with the king, as much as it worried him to think of what his son and nephews might encounter.

'Explain why Baldwin of Bruges might attack?'

'Henry III, the emperor, has had enough of Baldwin. He's raised a huge army against him, and in the spirit of our family connection, for he was wed to my stepsister before her death and is the father of my niece, I've said we'll watch the seaways to ensure Baldwin doesn't escape. The man has caused me so many problems, it's a worthwhile endeavour.'

'Indeed, my lord king. It would be prudent to have the threat of Baldwin countered, once and for all.'

'Yes, he's always too keen to provide safe haven for those dismissed from England. Lady Gunnhild. Osgot. And, of course, my brother by marriage, Sweyn.'

'Then I'll ensure we're kept up to date with news from my nephews and son. The Mercians will be pleased to defend England, and counter Baldwin of Bruges, you can rely on them.' Leofric spoke with pride. Whereas the Wessex fleet of Earl Godwine was lauded as the largest, it was far from as loyal, despite the king's attempts to curtail the might of Earl Godwine by splitting his force with that of Godwine's.

While it had been a clever idea, if it came to a fight between Godwine's force and that of the king's, Leofric was unsure that those who'd once been Godwine's shipmen and now crewed the king's fleet, would remain loyal to him.

32

SHREWSBURY, AD1049, ÆLFGAR

He eyed the swell of the river with some trepidation. The River Severn was a contrary beast. Those who used it to ply their trade were always wary. Those who lived close enough to be subject to its floods held it in healthy regard. And for those who didn't know it well, it could often lead to their death.

Here, at Shrewsbury, the river curved around the main settlement, and he considered just how likely it was that a Viking raider fleet might make it so far inland without first being waylaid by anyone else. But then, the problem with that was that Gruffydd ap Rhydderch could allow ready access inland, and the Viking raiders weren't above carrying their ships overland to get to the next river or sea. Anything to discomfort the English and of course, his hated enemy, Gruffydd ap Llewelyn.

Ælfgar eyed his cousin. Ælfwine was furious, and Wulfstan had only just returned from sharing the news with his father.

'The king thinks we can keep a big, bloody fleet of Viking raider ships and those scum on board from causing untold damage within Mercia. All he cares about is the threat from the east, which, as far as I can tell, is non-existent.

Ælfgar nodded along with his cousin. He didn't like to publicly disagree with the king and his actions. His father had always advised against doing so, but right now, he concurred with his cousin. Even though he'd been part of the fleet last year, countering the attacks of Lothen and Yrling, and was more than aware of the damage they'd caused, he could sense that the arrival of such an enemy fleet on the west would be the very thing that undid the uneasy accord that was currently keeping the borderlands safe for the English king.

'I'm confident my father will do all he can to ensure the king takes the threat seriously.'

'I'm know he will,' Ælfwine nodded. 'But there are the voices of Earl Godwine and Harold to counter as well. I doubt they care about matters here.' That was true, for Leofric and his family held much of Shropshire, of which Shrewsbury was the largest settlement. Further north, Wulfstan and Ælfwine had the landbook for many manors and settlements at Ditton Priors, Wellington Ford, Ellesmere, Emstry, High Ercall, Crudington and Doddington amongst others. Sweyn Godwinesson had failed in his attempt to take them from Ælfgar's cousins.

'I'm sure Harold must do, surely? He's the earl of Hereford since his brother was outlawed.'

'And he's here in the west, is he? Or at his other possession in Somerset. No, he's in East Anglia, or Sandwich, with the king. The king has given one man too much to order, and so he has too little with which to defend half of it.'

Ælfgar remained silent. It was useless trying to argue with Ælfwine when he agreed with him. With more men in control of such important places, no doubt the Viking raider fleet and their ally wouldn't even consider causing as many problems as they were. And now, if the attack happened, it was left to them to defend possessions that owed them no allegiance. And they'd get little thanks for it.

Ælfgar met the enraged gaze of his cousin. It was impossible not to see the same thoughts swirling through his cousin's mind. How much easier would it be had King Edward simply given him the earldom after Sweyn's outlawing? With this family's reputation and base in the northwest, he felt sure they'd have been able to prevent the incursion of the Viking raider fleet along the Rivers Severn or the Wye. Now, he'd need to see what could be done, while the king's eyes were on the east.

'Come on, we need to ensure the river can't be used to get north from here. We might not be able to do everything we'd like, but we can certainly protect what we can.'

So spoken, Ælfgar met the heated gaze of Ælfwine and saw grudging respect there. Perhaps Ælfwine's marriage into a good, local family meant he could think more of what they did have, as opposed to what they could have had.

33

SANDWICH, AD1049, LEOFRIC

He'd remained in Sandwich with the king despite his fears about what might happen in the west on the borderlands with the Welsh kingdoms. Until now, all had been calm. But that calm had been disturbed, and not by Baldwin of Bruges, but by the arrival of Sweyn Godwinesson.

Leofric tried to keep his expression neutral as he eyed the man before him. Sweyn was little altered since he'd been last seen. Despite his outlawing, he had command of five ships, and he'd led them into Sandwich, unheeding the king's force there, which numbered more than eighty ships. It was evident that the commanders of the ships Sweyn had encountered hadn't known what to do. As such, they'd asked for advice from the king, and Edward had given permission for Sweyn to come ashore, but only for the afternoon. By the time the tide turned, he'd be gone from Sandwich.

News from the Emperor was that Baldwin of Bruges had been cowed, and he didn't require Edward's help anymore. But that no longer concerned those at Sandwich. The return of Sweyn Godwinesson overrode all else. If he had five ships to command now, then did he have more elsewhere, and were the rumours correct that he'd forged an alliance with the outlawed and equally furious, Osgot?

The king had gathered his earls and thegns to him, none of the holy men being in attendance at Sandwich at that time. They fought their battles on their knees, not on board a ship. Inside the hall where Leofric had witnessed so much in the past, the return of Harthacnut and Edward prominent in his mind, he looked from his king to the exiled Sweyn and considered what would happen next.

He didn't miss that Sweyn's brother, Harold, was doing less well keeping his emotions from his face. Initially, Beorn, Sweyn's cousin, had been eager to see him, no doubt keen to hear how his brother fared as the king of Denmark, but that had quickly faded as Sweyn had spoken.

'My lord king,' Sweyn's homage was excessive and had made the king's lips twitch with either amusement or suppressed fury; Leofric wasn't quite sure.

'I come now, begging to be returned to my position within England. I'm a loyal man to you. I'm a father who's been banished from his children, from his sons. I would return to England and reclaim my children and my lands, and on my oath, I'll swear my small ship army to you alongside my lifelong allegiance. And so will my children.'

Leofric wanted to bark with laughter at that. Abbess Eadgifu wasn't interested in the man who'd married her against her will. Once more, she was assured in her position, and the landed wealth of Leominster was safe in the hands of Queen Edith. Edith, as well as his wife, were absent. His wife, Lady Godgifu, had remained in Oxford. Queen Edith was at Winchester, alongside Countess Godgifu, the king determining to have his wife and sister there as London was too exposed with the River Thames at its side. He risked a glance at Earl Godwine. His expression was impossible to decipher. Was he pleased to see his son or not? There was an uneasy alliance between Earls Harold and Beorn. Would that be disturbed? Would the king truly listen to Sweyn's words?

'Lord Sweyn, your words have no effect on me. You were outlawed and will remain so.' The king spoke firmly. He showed no sign of unease at having Sweyn appear before him

'My lord king.' Now Earl Godwine revealed his true allegiance. 'I would hope that further consideration might be possible. Perhaps, you should seek the advice of your earls and king's thegns before making such a decision?' Leofric didn't miss the glower Harold directed at his father nor the fury suddenly blazing in the king's eyes.

'My Lord Sweyn,' the king began, his words sharp and decisive. 'We'll take this under advisement. For now, you have no safe passage in England. Return to your ships, and stay away from Sandwich or elsewhere. I'll summon you once a decision has been reached.'

With a gleam on his lips, and a sharp nod of his head, Sweyn turned aside, but not before flashing a welcoming smile towards his father. Leofric was sure this hadn't been prearranged, and yet, well, perhaps it had been. If so, Harold was furious about it.

Commander Eowa was tasked with ensuring Sweyn and his ships followed the king's instructions, and the sound of the ships taking their leave echoed through the hall. Only then did the king turn to those attending upon him. Leofric appreciated that the king hadn't wished to ask such questions before Sweyn. The answers, he quickly understood, would only have fuelled further problems.

Indeed, he was hardly called upon to give his opinion.

'My lord king, brother,' Harold demurred, for all his voice was as determined as the king's. 'I'll not give up my holdings for Sweyn. I'm sorry. He's my brother, yes, but even now, and as we all know, unease ripples through his previous holdings. Men and women are aghast at his outrages against the church, and should he return, Gruffydd ap Rhydderch will do much more than allow the Viking raider pirates to raid his enemy's lands.'

Harold didn't glance at his father as he spoke, but Earl Godwine's furious response was audible to all.

'Now, Lord Godwine,' the king intervened. 'You'll have time to speak your mind when the men who've dealt with Sweyn's depravities have been consulted. Now, Lord Beorn?'

Beorn, Leofric admitted, looked torn. Leofric was far from convinced he'd agree with Harold's stark assessment of a future where Sweyn was allowed to return to England.

'My lord king, cousin,' Beorn began, inclining his head as he did so. The weight of Earl Godwine's stare seemed to disturb the younger man, and Leofric felt some pity for him as he turned to meet the gaze of the older man.

'I agree with my cousin, cousin,' Beorn nodded as he spoke, as though convincing himself. Beorn hadn't made it clear which cousin he agreed with. Leofric waited.

'Cousin Sweyn shouldn't be allowed to return to England. And I'm sure that Lord Ralph would agree with me.'

Leofric felt his eyes boggle at that. Of the six earls, himself, Godwine, Siward, Harold, Beorn and Ralph, two had so far spoken against Sweyn, and all knew that he wouldn't welcome the return of the problematic man. If Ralph agreed with Harold and Beorn, then it wouldn't matter how much Lord Godwine demanded from the king, he wouldn't get it. Sweyn would remain outlawed. There was also the added problem that the church had excommunicated Sweyn. The king wouldn't wish to allow a man such as that back to England, and if his earls were against it, then he couldn't even prevail upon the archbishops to overturn their actions.

'My lord king, uncle,' Ralph, the youngest of all, and nervously licking his lips, spoke with a slight wobble. 'I agree with Earls Harold and Beorn. Lord Sweyn is too problematic. He's anathematised and a troublemaker.'

'My lord king,' Earl Godwine roared over the whispered conversations springing up, but King Edward turned to face him.

'My lord, my earls have spoken. I'm not eager to see Sweyn return. I'm sure that Leofric would agree with me, wouldn't you?' this was finally directed at him.

'I do, my lord king. My wife wouldn't welcome it, and nor would Sweyn's wife, come to that.'

'But,' Earl Godwine tried once more.

'My lord, don't speak unless addressed. The witan has decided. Lord Sweyn may return tomorrow to hear of this. And he'll be expected to remove himself from England's shores. You would do well to advise him of that necessity and that a firm response will be made to any attempt to circumvent my word.'

ONCE MORE, Lord Sweyn was before them all, swaggering with all remorse wiped from his face His brother was there, watching him, while Earl Godwine bolstered himself with the support of young Tostig at his side. Earls Beorn and Ralph had absented themselves on the king's orders. Perhaps, Leofric appreciated, the king sensed that they were the weakest in their determination. It would be good not to have them here, to allow Sweyn to harangue them. Earl Harold was made of stern stuff, to stand against his brother in person.

'I may return,' Lord Sweyn bowed low, his voice slightly muffled, his confidence impossible to ignore.

'No, you may not. You remain outlawed from England and excommunicated by the church. Now, take your leave. Be assured no port will welcome you.' Leofric didn't miss the satisfaction in the king's voice, or the glower that Earl Godwine directed towards the king and then his second-oldest son.

'My lord king?' fury in Sweyn's words had the king's huscarls reaching for their blades. 'You can't go against the command of your witan.' His tone was indolent.

'I have not,' King Edward countered. He wore, not the clothes of a king but rather the garb of a shipman. His boots and trews as proofed against the water as possible. The scent of salt water was difficult to ignore.

'But, my lord king, we all know that Earl Leofric would never counter my return. He's but one voice.'

'He is yes, and not at all the casting vote.'

The smug expression on Sweyn's face slipped for a moment, and his eyebrows furrowed. Leofric could see him trying to calculate who could have voted against his return.

'Earl Siward is absent?' he demanded. 'He should be sent for his opinion.'

'He remains absent yes, but again, his vote wouldn't alter the voting.'

Only now did Sweyn truly understand what the king was telling him. Furious, he turned to face his father.

'Who did this?' he demanded.

'Lord Sweyn, your time here is finite. I suggest you leave before my huscarls forcibly remove you.' A flick of the king's fingers and the armed men moved closer.

'I've a right to know who voted against my return,' Sweyn demanded, his eyes daring the four huscarls to lay their hands on him.

'Lord Sweyn, and I use the term only to be polite, for you are no lord. You have no rights within England. Now, I've listened to you, and my earls, and you remain outlawed and excommunicated. Now, leave, before I change my mind and retract your safe passage for this morning.'

'Father,' Sweyn demanded from Lord Godwine. Godwine could only shake his head, his fat lips tight with fury.

'Alas, my son, your crimes were too heinous for even me to sway the king.'

'What of my children, my wife?'

'It really is a little late for you to be considering them,' the king announced, as though bored with the conversation. 'They're safe and protected under the order of myself and the queen. The woman is no longer your wife. And your children were never yours in the first place. Now, huscarls, remove this man from my presence.'

But Sweyn hadn't finished yet, with a lunge, he reared up before Earl Harold, his hands reaching for his brother's throat.

'You damn bastard,' he roared, spittle flying into Harold's face. Leofric moved to intervene, but Harold had control of the situation, stepping back from his brother's attack and going so far as to kick his left leg at his brother's right so that Sweyn lost his footing and sprawled to the floor with a resounding thud, as though a ship coming into the quayside.

'Pick him up, and get him out of here,' Harold commanded, and the huscarls were swift to obey.

'Remember,' the king spoke once more. 'As an outlaw and anathematised, your life is forfeit should you return to England without my express command.' The words thrummed with intensity, and Leofric was forced to clamp his lips together to prevent his jaw from falling to the floor. These were not words he was used to hearing from his king, and certainly not in such an implacable tone.

Sweyn, roughly handled to his feet, paused to glower at his brother, and then his father, and only then turned to the king, somehow recollecting himself, to bow before him before allowing the huscarls to escort him from the hall.

'Earl Godwine,' the king spoke into the growing silence. 'I caution you against rash behaviour concerning Sweyn, and I'd extend that to your wife as well. You're the father by marriage of the king. You, of all people, must be above reproach. Now, go and say farewell to your son, and ensure he knows my resolve on this. I'll order his death should he return.'

With a puff of effort, Earl Godwine followed his son, while Leofric watched young Tostig, unsure what to do, until Harold encouraged him to follow their father.

Silence grew between them all, and then King Edward recovered himself and looked to Leofric.

'I've decided that the Mercian fleet may return to London, well, half of them. The other half will journey to the west. Aside from Lord Sweyn's unexpected arrival, I believe the threat from Baldwin of

Bruges has passed. But, I'll keep the fleets that usually guard these waters. Earl Godwine, Earl Harold and Beorn will command.'

'And me, my lord king?'

'I would ask you to remain with me, until the raiding season has come to an end. I welcome your advice, and trust that your wife and son will manage your lands in your absence, your nephews as well.' Leofric nodded. He'd sooner have returned to Mercia, but he could understand the king's reticence. He was convinced that the threat from Sweyn Godwinesson was far from finished with. It seemed that the king knew the same.

'As you will, my lord king. I'll speak with my men.'

'As you see fit, my lord,' the king encouraged him. 'I would have those with the most experience to the west, but I'll leave it for you to decide.'

'I agree, my lord king. The River Severn and the estuary is a tricky beast, as we all know. Here, the men of East Anglia and Wessex know the waters well, and can assist if the Mercian fleet is needed again.'

'Then, I'll be about today's business,' the king announced, striding towards the door, which opened for him. Leofric watched him go thoughtfully, unable to dismiss the idea that the king was keen to watch Sweyn leave Sandwich. He remained, as did Earl Harold. Only when the king had been gone for some moments did Harold speak.

'You must think me a bastard, my lord, but I assure you, the bastard is Sweyn. I don't trust him, even now, and I trust my father even less. You're lucky to come from such an honourable family. I wish I could lay claim to the same.' And with that, Harold swept from the hall as well, and now Leofric did allow his mouth to fall open in shock. He knew his son had spoken to him of Harold's unhappiness with his older brother. Now, it appeared, that family ruction had grown. It would be interesting to see what would happen. Like the king, he didn't trust Sweyn, or his father, Earl Godwine, and he didn't believe it would be long until his fears were borne out.

34

AD1049, ÆLFGAR

He sighted the Viking raider ship army with unease. While Shrewsbury had remained safe, as had many of the places along the River Severn, there had been reports of attacks at Gloucester and down into the estuary, as well as on the kingdom of Gruffydd ap Llewelyn. That news didn't surprise him.

He turned to Commander Eowa.

'The king sent you?'

'Yes, well, the king divided the Mercian fleet. Your father sent his more experienced men this way. The rest have returned to London, should the king need them once more.'

'And will we counter the threat?' Ælfwine queried. Eowa had come ashore at Gloucester, amongst the smoking remains of the quayside which had been attacked seven nights ago. They'd managed to fight them off, but there was much damage to repair. By rights, Earl Harold should be here assessing the damage, but the king had determined he should remain on the east coast.

'We'll certainly make the effort,' Eowa confirmed. Ælfgar had received a message from his father along with Eowa. If needed, he was to join the fleet and assist Eowa. For now, it remained to be seen what the fleet would do. They'd sailed further west three days ago, but had now returned. While they remained within sight, Ælfgar was unsure what to expect.

Eowa pursed his lips.

'They're just taunting us, now they know the English king has taken the challenge seriously. What remains to be seen is what the outcome might be. I don't believe they'll attack again. It's one thing to make raids and steal wealth and people for the slave markets in Dublin, it's quite another to encounter a fleet sent to fight them. These pirates are mostly weak men.' Eowa spoke firmly. Olaf, to the side of Ælfgar nodded along, despite the fact he shared ancestry with most of the Viking raider pirates. He was, on occasion, more English than even Ælfgar and his father.

'We'll watch and see. Obviously, we can't protect everywhere at once, but a few ships here, and perhaps one or two further along the Severn, just in case, and we should have eyes on them. However, I imagine they'll turn their eyes south when they realise they're scuppered here. The king might need to reassess his plans.'

Ælfgar grunted his agreement. He'd seen the aftermath of the raids. He was keen to steep his seax in the blood of the enemy. He hoped that much of Eowa's assessment would be correct but that he'd get some chance to counter the arrogant bastards.

'If they attack the lands south of here, then Earl Harold will have to bring his fleet as well,' Olaf confirmed. 'Mayhap that's what the king plans on doing anyway. It's taken you some time to get here, perhaps he's already on his way.'

'Possibly, but I suspect the king is keen to have all of the Godwines close to hand, in case Sweyn reappears, or there are further problems. Rumours persist that Osgot has a large fleet to command, as well.'

'The king would have done better to kill the bloody fools,' Olaf murmured. His tone was rich with disgust. After all, Edward's father had been quick to kill those who committed treason, and Cnut and Harthacnut had been the same. While some might argue Edward was a more reasoned king, it couldn't be denied that killing enemies was a sure way of concluding such disagreements.

'He would,' Eowa confirmed, and Ælfgar felt his gaze switching between the two men. They had more experience than him. Some might say they were soured by their years supporting England's kings, but maybe they had the right to it.

'Right, enough of that. Are you joining us today?' Eowa directed this at any one of the four men before him. Ælfgar nodded.

'Today, Olaf, because he's more experienced than us. When you next come ashore, one of us will replace him. Olaf speaks with the voice of my father. His decisions are to be obeyed, unless they're damn foolish ones, and then, feel free to tip him overboard.' Ælfgar smiled to take the sharpness from his tone. Eowa, never one to smirk, offered him a rare flash of what few teeth he had remaining.

'You heard him, Olaf, if you make damn foolish decisions, I can pitch you overboard.' Olaf didn't smile, but fixed Ælfgar with a grimace.

'And you can explain to my wife, should that happen.'

Ælfgar's smile slipped from his face, and to Eowa's retreating back he called, 'keep him safe. Lady Eadgyth will make my life most unpleasant if not.'

'Sorry, my lord,' Eowa turned to face him. 'I didn't quite catch that,' but before Ælfgar could repeat himself, Eowa ambled to a run and was quickly out of earshot.

'Damn it,' Ælfgar complained while his cousins grinned at his discomfort.

'Lady Eadgyth will feed you to her hounds,' Wulfstan offered without sympathy, hastening to follow the others into Gloucester. Only Ælfwine remained.

'One day,' he offered his cousin. 'You'll be earl of Mercia, and then, you won't be able to say such as that,' and laughing, he also left Ælfgar to his thoughts.

He sighed heavily, considering Eowa and Olaf. Surely both men would be wise enough not to cause more problems. Or at least, he hoped they were.

35

AD1049, LEOFRIC

Leofric yawned wildly. The night have been rough, and a fierce wind had blown throughout much of it. He'd been pleased the ship army had been ashore, but knew that there would be damage to be inspected. However, at least such terrible weather would have kept ships in their harbours all along the Narrow Sea. The threat from Bruges had diminished, but now, there was a new one. Only last night, before the storm had closed around them, had come news of the outlawed Osgot and his fleet of ships, currently held at Wulpe but with a clear intention to attack England, if the traders who'd brought the news were to be believed.

'I'll recall the Mercian fleet from London,' the king had confirmed, even as the wind had howled outside. 'And what I can of the Wessex fleet. I've sent it westwards, to counter the threat from Gruffydd ap Rhydderch, but it seems there's more trouble for us here.' Leofric had agreed with those decisions, but now much would have to wait until the storm entirely ceased and the sea settled once more.

His head ached from the shrieking wind, and he shivered, despite it being mid-summer. He could hear the sound of others waking and roused himself more fully. He felt as though he'd spent the entire year at Sandwich, escorting the king, but it had only been since just after Easter. Still, there were some months to go until the summer raiding season would be considered finished, and he was missing his bed, and his wife.

He stroked a hand along the back of Hunter's back, and the animal responded by yawning just as widely and exuding a meaty breath into his face. He grimaced at the stink and realised he'd probably done the same to the dog.

Stretching, he left his private room, a luxury in a settlement so filled with the king's household and shipmen, and struggled to inhale against the sharp tug of the wind. Hastily turning aside, his back to the gale, he strode to the hall, fully expecting to find the king inside. But first, he heard angry voices raised against one another. He groaned. What was this now? He recognised the voice of the king but was unsure who else he spoke to.

The door was opened for him, and he stepped inside, already prepared to deal with the consequences of whatever was happening. The hall was filled with men just waking from their slumbers, and servants bustled around, everyone trying not to watch the argument being played out before them. Leofric was far from surprised to find Earl Godwine there, his son, Tostig at his shoulder, and Earl Harold to the other side of him.

'My lord king,' Lord Godwine spoke loudly and arrogantly, assuming that if he could drown out all other voices, his would be listened to.

'Lord Godwine, you've woken the men, please speak more quietly,' the king commanded, a quick glance meeting Leofric's eyes, and encouraging him to join them.

'What's this?' Leofric asked quickly.

'An argument about the Godwine family,' Harold offered quickly. 'And one, which somehow, my father thinks should include the king.' His voice was tight with fury.

'And what's the argument?'

'Sweyn has been sighted with his ships close by last night. Earl Godwine wishes permission to approach him. I said it goes against the king's wishes, so now my father thinks to get his way by shouting about it to the king.' Leofric nodded. He could see the king was unhappy at having his orders questioned again.

'I understood Earl Godwine and Earl Harold, alongside Tostig, were to join the fleet to the west.' Leofric questioned, although it was more statement.

'They are, yes. Earl Beorn's taken command of Harold's fleet that remains close to Sandwich.'

'Then why are they now returned to Sandwich? The threat from the Viking raider pirates and Gruffydd ap Rhydderch isn't one to be ignored. My son, and nephews, and the portion of the Mercian fleet ordered there could easily be overawed by such a fleet.' Leofric spoke angrily. The king had delayed in giving the order, and now that it had been given, Godwine had countered it, placing Leofric's family at risk.

'I don't believe I could have said it better myself,' the king glowered at Earl Godwine.

'The weather delayed us,' Godwine rumbled.

'It hasn't stopped you from returning here, though, has it, against my wishes. Earl Harold, I expected more from you,' the king met the younger man's eyes, and Leofric saw Harold flinch.

'I'll depart immediately,' Harold confirmed, turning but not before fixing his father with a furious expression.

'And Earl Godwine, you'll join Lord Beorn in ensuring Sandwich remains safe from all enemies, while Harold commands most of your ships. And that includes keeping it safe from your oldest son,' the king's words were colder than midwinter, and Leofric nodded. It was good to see the king so determined. And yet Godwine wouldn't let it alone.

'But my lord king, he's my son.'

'Then you should have ensured he knew what treason was and that the right of the church is just that. My kingdom is a holy one. It won't allow someone cast out of the church into it. Inform your son of this when you see him, as I know you will. Now, there's to be no more talk of Sweyn. He bedevilled the earldom I gave him. I've had enough of listening to the problems he causes.'

Leofric watched Godwine fight with himself, his mouth opening and closing as he tried to decide what to say while the king turned his back on the earl. Tostig, beside his father, looked beseechingly towards Leofric.

'I suggest you return to your ship,' Leofric commented, taking pity on the young man. Tostig almost leapt to obey, and all the time, his father stayed immobile.

Only then did Leofric approach the other earl.

'The king is firm on this, Godwine. Understand that. Nothing you say will undo the damage that your oldest son caused. Be grateful the king allowed your grandsons to live and your other sons to flourish.'

'But he's my son,' the cry was anguished.

'And he's a poor son,' Leofric countered, his head tilted to one side. 'And more, he only claims you as his father when it's politically expedient to do so. He's not worthy of your damn name.' Leofric turned to follow the king, not wishing to witness Godwine's tears that fell from his fat cheeks. All these years, Godwine had been a pain in Leofric's backside. Now, he found it strange to watch the man realise his limits had been reached. King Edward was not one to play the games of which Godwine was so fond. No. King Edward was determined to rule, and now, he was evidently confident that he could do so without the aid of Earl Godwine. Leofric thought it a pity he'd not realised as much sooner.

LATER THAT DAY, the wind had still not abated, as Leofric watched the quayside in some concern. Earl Harold had been true to his word and had departed westwards, but Earl Godwine had been unable to leave, no matter the king's orders, the wind and sea too wrathful to allow it. In this, it seemed, the might of God would prevail as the wind howled into what should have been a sheltered harbour. Leofric took solace in knowing that while the wind blew as it did, there would be no way that Osgot would be able to threaten England's shores. Yet, out there, somewhere, was Sweyn Godwinesson, and Leofric wasn't fool enough to think he wouldn't use the storm as an excuse to stay close to England.

'What will he do next?' Leofric hadn't heard the king approach over the roar of the wind, and startled at the words, spoken loudly to counter the shriek of the gale and the sharp slap of the sea against the wood of the quayside. The ships docked there heaved with the wind and the turbulent tide. Leofric considered it might have been better to bring the ships onto the quayside rather than have them battered.

'I doubt he'll simply retreat,' Leofric replied, hopeful they spoke of Sweyn.

'He's a persistent bastard, that's for a certainty,' the king replied, his words filled with dismay. 'I must apologise, Lord Leofric, for my poor decision in making Sweyn an earl. I know you were displeased, and you were right to be so. He's done nothing but cause problems. Even outlawed and ostracised, he's still a pestilent boil on my arse.'

'And he'll remain so,' Leofric concurred. 'Better he'd met his death fighting the Welsh.' He expected the king to be surprised at such venom but Edward merely chuckled darkly.

'I agree. I thought I'd given him enough incentive to do just that, but instead, he surprised me and caused me fresh problems.'

'Earl Godwine will not stop his petitioning of you,' Leofric cautioned.

'I know, and my wife will not stop urging me to stay true to the rule of law and ensure Sweyn never steps foot on English soil again. She has no love for her brother. As devout as she is, that plagues here, but not all men are born worthy of our respect.'

'They aren't, no,' Leofric agreed.

'Whatever happens next, Leofric, for something surely will, you have my permission to remind me that this is all my fault. I need a man such as you to do so. As your father did for my father, so you will for me. I fear it will get nasty quickly. Sweyn is a man who has no problem in taking what he wants, no matter the consequences.'

'Perhaps, my lord king, it would be better to instruct an assassin?' Leofric felt the words roll from his tongue, only to gasp in surprise. It wasn't the way of an honourable man to suggest as much.

'I would wish it were so easy, but that would only make me like Earl Godwine, and I despise that man and all he's done in his long life. I won't be tainted by Sweyn. I will find a way out of this. I assure you.'

'Indeed, my lord king, and you know I'll support anything you do, but like you, I believe Sweyn Godwinesson is capable of the most heinous crimes. I only hope there's a law we can apply to his actions in order to seek retribution for those affected.' Leofric spoke forcefully. He was reminded of just how difficult it had been to seek recompense for the abbess Sweyn had captured, raped and then said he'd marry, only to have the archbishop and bishop excommunicate him. Leofric couldn't help being surprised that it had been so effective. He'd not have imagined Sweyn being a man concerned for his soul.

'If there is not, Earl Leofric, I will enact one. I give you my word.' The words were heartfelt, but all the same, Leofric felt a shiver of unease course through his body.

36

GLOUCESTER, ÆLFGAR

'TELL ME,' HE URGED COMMANDER EOWA. IT WAS EVIDENT THAT SOMETHING had disturbed the usually unperturbed man.

'Ships, my lord, many, many ships. They've been sighted close to the kingdom of Gruffydd ap Rhydderch but I suspect they mean to use the rivers to get even closer to Powys.'

'How many?' Ælfgar had been sure that with half the Mercian fleet, as well as his father's two ships, that they could at least match the size of the enemy force.

'At least thirty,' the words were doom-laden. With such a number, the leaders of the expedition, and Ælfgar was still unsure of the name of the man who could command so many men to follow him, but imagined it would be a Halfdan or an Olaf, would quickly overwhelm the fleet they had.

'Why will they not sail north around the coast, and simply attack Gruffydd ap Llewelyn from that direction?'

'Because Gruffydd ap Rhydderch means to punish Mercia for involving itself in their fight, no doubt,' Olaf spoke dolefully. The wind buffeted them. It was strong, meaning that Eowa and his shipmen had been able to make good time returning from their scouting mission. But, it also meant the enemy fleet would quickly reach their shores.

'What should we do?' Ælfgar asked. He felt hopeless, and yet, he was the senior of the royal men there. His father was in Sandwich. Earl Harold was there as well. While this area of Mercia wasn't his to command, he was the man everyone looked to in the absence of a more senior figure.

'We prepare for their attack,' Eowa confirmed. 'We station the ships in the Severn estuary.'

'But it can be deadly.'

'It can, my lord, yes, but not as deadly as Viking raider bastards,' Eowa spoke with conviction, and Ælfgar was surprised to find Olaf and his nephew nodding along with him. Olaf and Otryggr had Norse blood in their veins. They thought as Viking raiders did. He swallowed against the unease that made his breath come too fast and his chest tight with fear.

He'd fought few enough battles on land, and even less on the unsteady surface of the sea, but he knew his place was with the shipmen.

'I'll join you,' he announced, expecting to be refused, but the refusal didn't come. Ælfgar swallowed again. It was bad if no would deny him.

He looked to Olaf and Otryggr and also to Ælfwine and Wulfstan. All of them were determined. All of them had faces whitened by fear of what would come.

'Today?' he questioned Eowa just to be sure.

'Yes, my lord. They'll come today, and we'll prepare to counter their aggression. We won't allow them to breach the River Severn or the River Wye provided we hold the estuary.'

'Then we'll have the warriors ready to counter any attempt to land, and we'll take to the ships.' He spoke with far more confidence than he felt. The pressure of a hand on his upper arm had him look to Olaf.

'We'll prevail,' his uncle assured him. 'We always do,' but Ælfgar heard some desolation in those words. Yes, they always prevailed, but at what cost?

THE WIND BUFFETED THE SHIP, and Ælfgar swallowed against his nausea. The roll of the sea had looked vicious from on land, on Eowa's ship, it was even worse than he'd feared.

Eowa stood, facing away from the wind, what vestiges of hair he still held onto, blowing into his face. It had been like this for some time. Overhead the sky was heavy and threatening rain, or worse. For now, the wind was enough to contend with.

The shipmen were sullen as they held the ship as steady as possible, oars digging deep into the grey-tipped water. The remaining ships were spread out. They couldn't risk being too close together, for fear one of the ships would crash into the other if caught by a particularly violent gust of wind. As such, he couldn't see his uncle, or his cousins, and indeed, he could barely make out land. Here there was a rolling seascape of sky and water, and little else.

The shipmen had donned all they could to keep themselves dry from the slap of freezing water surging over the sides of the gleaming ship. She'd been a part of Ælfgar's life since childhood. Now he hoped the old ship, with its creaks, was fit for the task that lay ahead. Admittedly, she'd been entirely rebuilt on more than one occasion, but she still remained his grandfather's craft at heart. He thought back to the tales he'd been told of his grandfather's journey to Shetland, of his journey home having been attacked by King Swein of Denmark and not for the first time, he cursed the bloody Viking raiders, even if he'd never have known Olaf or Otryggr without his grandfather's participation in that perilous journey.

His sealskin cloak was held tight against his body, as the ship faced towards the west. When the Viking raiders came, they would see them first, of that he was sure.

More than once he glowered southwards. He was expecting the

king to have sent reinforcements to assist them. The threat from Gruffydd ap Rhydderch and the Viking raiders was greater than anything Baldwin of Bruges could throw at the king, and with Magnus of Norway dead, the real threat was here, not at Sandwich.

Yet, no matter how much he wished, or prayed, no new crafts emerged from the deepening gloom. He feared the storm was gaining in intensity, and yet Eowa held firm. He didn't urge them to make a run for land, beating against the violence of the Severn Estuary. No, he waited, and he watched, and Ælfgar couldn't take his eyes from the view either. He felt sure that should he look away, the enemy fleet would appear from out of the gloom.

The day dragged, and Ælfgar's body grew cold and aching from the tension running through it. He tried to take calming breaths, but it was to no avail. Neither was he alone. There was little noise on the ship, and not just because it was impossible to talk without shouting. No one wanted to make a joke, or sing a rousing song. No, fear ran through the shipmen and it was more insidious than the howling wind.

The sky darkened, and Ælfgar was convinced that the day must be drawing to an end. Soon, he was sure, Eowa would order them to return to the safety of the nearest harbour, having decided that the enemy ships wouldn't come. No sooner had Ælfgar allowed the thought to settle inside him, a tendril of warmth working its way through his body, than he saw them.

They came close together, their sails down, oars stretching into the greyness of the sea, and he wasn't the first to give voice to it.

'Ready yourselves,' Eowa's voice, so silent for much of the day, shot through Ælfgar with more force than a blade. Ælfgar reached to his side, his hand finding the comforting presence of his seax as the waves beneath the ship intensified, forcing him to grip the side of the ship to stay upright. He heard a thud and looked, horrified to find that Eowa, the steady ship's commander, had lost his balance with the violence of the squall.

'No,' he huffed, hurrying to hit feet, despite the uneven tipping of the ship. 'No,' he shouted again, reaching Eowa and running his hands over the older man's body, seeking out wounds.

Eowa met his concerned gaze, eyes glazed, shock showing in the whiteness of his face.

'You hit your head,' Ælfgar informed him, hastily grabbing a piece of cloth and holding it the bloody gash that ran across Eowa's forehead. How he's taken such a wound was difficult to tell. Ælfgar thought he'd fallen backwards not forwards.

'Help me,' Eowa growled ferociously. 'They'll not see me on my knees,' he cried. The bilge water had drenched his clothes where his sealskin cloak hadn't protected him, and now Ælfgar realised that he too wore sopping wet trews. Not that it mattered. As they stood, the rain that had been threatening all day, began to fall and in only moments, all were just as wet as he and Eowa.

'You're wounded, sit and let me tend to you,' he urged Eowa.

'No,' the other man growled, his face running with red, the wound bleeding copiously, the rain making it seem even worse. 'I'm fine. Get back to your seat. The bastards are coming.'

And they were. In the brief moments it had taken Ælfgar to tend to Eowa, their foemen had come even closer. He could see them now and pick out the expressions of the shipmen as they surged against the pull of the choppy sea and the sheeting rain.

'Prepare yourselves,' Eowa roared at his shipmen. Ælfgar risked a glance to them. All looked shocked at what had befallen Eowa, but quickly, they returned to the task at hand, and Ælfgar followed them.

He licked his salty lips and once more prepared for the coming fight. It was impossible that all would survive what was coming. He whispered a prayer for his wife and children, for his father and his mother, and an even more fervent one for himself, his uncle, and his cousins. They would survive this. They must do.

37
SANDWICH, LEOFRIC

The commotion had him running from the hall where he'd been sat with the king, towards the quayside. He didn't know what had happened, but fear stalked him.

Earl Godwine had managed to sneak from the harbour late two nights ago, taking advantage of a brief lull in the storm to do so. Was he back? Was it the enemy? Had Osgot also noticed the lull in the wind to head for England, or was it Sweyn Godwinesson? The previous day had passed as peacefully as one could while the sea heaved and surged towards land, the wind making it impossible for any other to leave the safety of the harbour.

Leofric's eyes were everywhere as he hurried onwards.

'My lord,' the cry of one of the king's ships commanders had him coming to an abrupt halt. He met the gaze of the man, trying to recall his name, but realising it wasn't the most important thing at that moment. The man's accent marked him as at least half-Danish, if not more. Leofric recognised him as one of the men who'd been loyal to Earl Beorn.

'Tell me,' he demanded. The man nodded. He looked weak and

drained. 'Are you wounded?' Leofric questioned when the man didn't immediately speak.

'No my lord, no, only in spirit.'

'What's happened?'

'I must tell the king,' the man prevaricated, although the thought of it made him falter in his swaying steps as he struggled to stay upright on dry land.

'Tell me, and I'll inform the king,' Leofric assured him.

The man's shoulders lowered, relief covering his wind-roughened face.

'Treachery and treason,' he began. 'Sweyn Godwinesson,' and the man spat as he said Sweyn's name, 'has murdered Earl Beorn Estridsson.'

'What?' In Leofric's worst imaginings, this possibility hadn't crossed his mind.

'Truly? How do you know this?'

'I was with the fleet, at Pevensey. I witnessed Sweyn try and speak with his father, and when he was rebuffed, he sought out Earl Beorn. The fool, the damn fool,' and now tears fell from the hardened man's eyes, 'he went with Sweyn, in good spirits. I watched it all. I followed on. I should have intervened, and then, and then Sweyn had Beorn murdered, and his body buried in a shallow grave at Dartmouth. I must return for it, see him correctly buried. The bastard.' The final word was edged with blades.

'I'll notify the king,' Leofric confirmed, although now he wished he'd been less eager to assure the man. That was it, his name was Edwin Haroldsson, attesting to his mixed heritage.

'Will you, my lord?' Edwin gasped.

'Yes, here, come with me. We must get you and your men warm and dry. Order them to leave the ship, and follow me.'

Leofric didn't stop to see if Edwin followed his orders. He was intent on intercepting the king before he had to inform him of this terrible news in front of all. His steps were hurried, his hound rushing beside him, as he erupted into the king's hall.

Edward met his gaze in surprise, as he prepared to leave the hall. He was brought up short.

'Leave us,' the king called imperiously, the waver in his voice almost unnoticed.

Leofric waited, as the rumble of men and women leaving the king echoed away to nothing.

'My lord king,' Leofric found himself faltering as much as Edwin Haroldsson had on the quayside. He swallowed heavily. Already outrage was making itself known outside, the news spreading quickly. Leofric needed to force the words through his dry lips.

'My lord king,' he began again. 'I regret to inform you that Earl Beorn Estridsson has been murdered by Sweyn Godwinesson and his body left in a shallow grave at Dartmouth.'

The words hung like seax blades in the air, and King Edward shuddered, as though pierced by those very same blades, and then cold rage thrummed replaced it.

'I'll kill the bastard, the *nithing*,' he all but whispered, and Leofric nodded, tears shimmering from his eyes, as well as the king's.

Lady Estrid, Beorn's mother wouldn't take the news well, he was sure of it.

If there had been family strife caused by Sweyn Godwinesson before, it was only going to multiply now. The king's brother was a murderer. And he'd not even been wise enough to ensure his actions went unwitnessed.

38

THE SEVERN ESTUARY, ÆLFGAR

THE CRASH OF THE ENEMY SHIP AGAINST HIS OWN THUDDED THROUGH HIS body. He gripped his seat for balance, and then sprang forward.

Eowa, already looking as though he'd fought with the devil himself, shouted his orders, and Ælfgar obeyed.

All thought fled him. Nothing else mattered but surviving the attack.

His blade shimmered with the grey of the sea, and the iron of the sky, the rain adding to the slickness of the ship's wooden struts.

The enemy flashed with red and grey, their intention to overpower them impossible to deny. The enemy ship was of a size with their own. They faced fifty men, but fifty men keen to kill them all.

With shield in hand, Ælfgar joined his fellow shipmen in their shield wall, while others laboured to force the enemy ship away from their side. They'd met side-on, somehow, the sea playing its games and turning the enemy craft aside at the last moment so that it hadn't attempted to breach their side. Death then would have been swift and watery; now it threatened to be longer, and not quite as inevitable.

'Defend,' Eowa cried from his place close to the rudder. The enemy ship didn't quite reach him, and Ælfgar spared a thought for him. He had a shield yes, but Ælfgar was aware he wavered, the wound to his head having done far more damage than Eowa was prepared to admit.

In defiance of that command, Ælfgar heard the enemy captain give his own orders to attack, his accent thick and thundering. Already the shrieks of men caught in a bloody fight to the death filled the air, defying the roar of the waves and the thunder of the rain.

Ælfgar gripped his seax and shield firmly, awaiting his turn to engage the enemy. He didn't spare a thought for his cousins or uncle, not now. Now he needed to stay alive, or his wife, and his mother, would kill him. He knew that for a certainty.

The ship shuddered and bucked, the two ships, so close together, forcing water to surge upwards from where they just about met and then surged apart again, only to meet once more. A rain of salty water covered him, and he spat aside the sour taste from his lips, as he made his way forward, the reaching hand of a wounded man grabbing his leg, as he did so. He gazed into the eyes of one of Eowa's shipmen, and lent him his arm to aid him upright. The man, staggering as much as Eowa, streamed with blood from a wound to his neck. Ælfgar winced at the sight.

'Help Eowa,' he urged the man, roughly shoving him away from the fighting. He would be lucky to survive this with such a wound.

A scream rang through the air, and despite himself, Ælfgar turned to hunt out the sound, only to glimpse a man, caught between the two ships, being slowly crushed between them. Ælfgar swallowed against his nausea, although he didn't know if the man was English or Viking raider, his back to him. One moment he shrieked in pain, and the next, the waves battered the ships apart, and the trapped man disappeared beneath the waves.

A thud on his shield restored him to the fight ahead. The enemy threatened to overwhelm them, as a leering face met his eyes, long hair and an even longer beard, plastered to the enemy's chest.

'I'll kill you,' Ælfgar shouted, but he knew he couldn't do it alone.

'Together,' he urged his fellow ship-men. With Eowa wounded, there was no one to truly give the orders.

'Together, attack,' he roared, his shield battering against his enemy's head with a satisfying crunch. But the man didn't fall, and Ælfgar felt the cold blade on his seax hand before he could withdraw it. A thin line of blood appeared on his right arm, but he couldn't feel it, not when he was so wet and cold.

'Together,' he roared again, and now all of his fellow ship-men followed his orders. The concerted sound of every single shield hitting the enemy full in the face overwhelmed even the roar of the storm.

'Attack,' he bellowed, and his seax slashed outwards, aiming for his enemy, but content to draw blood from any one of his enemy.

'Together,' he called again, his seax back at his side. And so it went on. He and the shipmen worked together, using their strength and shields to block the enemy, and then wound them. It took precious moments for the enemy to understand their intent and change their tactics accordingly. By then, Ælfgar knew they'd killed some of their opponents, bodies falling away between the two ships.

Ælfgar didn't hear the call, but abruptly, the enemy ship surged away from them. He lowered his shield and saw enemy oars being used to lever some distance between the two ships. He sucked in much needed air, and looked at the carnage. Some of his fellow shipmen bled copiously, others had fallen still in the murky bilge water.

'Oars,' the cry came from Eowa, and Ælfgar hastened to obey, unsure why the order had been given. Only then, as Eowa ordered the right side of the ship to row, but not the left, did he understand. The enemy had decided to try their initial tactic against them. Provided they could mirror the movements of their ship, there'd be no possibility of the enemy trying to smash through their hull.

The pull on his shoulders was immense. He watched with fascination as blood welled from the thin cut on his arm with each heave on the oar. His shoulders burnt with exhaustion in no time at all, and still the enemy played their games.

'Row you bastards,' Eowa called, but Ælfgar appreciated they couldn't continue against the rage of the sea, and the spite of the rain. They would have to try something different.

He turned to call to Eowa, but despite his bloodied face, Eowa seemed only too aware of their predicament. The cry of the other ships around them was clearly audible, but little could be seen. The clouds had descended so low, that he didn't know which way would lead them back to land, even if they had the opportunity to flee the attack. And they couldn't, anyway. They needed to defend England from the murderous bastards.

They couldn't let the ship slip by them, and neither could they maintain the frenzied rowing. Something needed to happen. Ælfgar was unsure what. His experience of sea battles was limited. Yes, he'd taken part in the manoeuvres of the king's ship army, but they'd never practised anything such as this. Only then there was a hand on his shoulder. He met Eowa's lopsided smirk, and nodded at the whispered command. As Eowa walked unsteadily down the ship, bending to deliver his message to those still hail enough to row, Ælfgar tore his gaze away from the enemy, and looked all around him. The sea was still rough. As his ship crested a rise, his oar failing to dig into the water as it was lifted so high, he spotted two of the other Mercian ships, both engaged in a bloody battle. He swallowed his fear, as men fought on the precarious struts of the ships, and then prepared himself for Eowa's command.

With his commander returned to the steering board, he waited, continuing to row as commanded. Sweat beaded his face, despite the icy blast of the sea and the wind, and his throat felt dryer and dryer. His shoulders strained, his back as well, and he thought the order would never come.

'We can't circle them forever,' an aggrieved voice called. Ælfgar agreed but had no air to voice it.

And then, when he thought it was hopeless, and they'd flounder, Eowa lifted his voice and roared his orders.

'Ahead.' For one horrifying moment, the ship was perched once more on the tip of a wave, and despite his best efforts, his oar didn't bite into the water. Only then the craft stabilised and the oar caught, pulling his shoulders once more, his hands bleeding from the cold and the callouses, but he didn't let up, and neither did his fellow ship men.

With a mighty effort, they ploughed through the wave, the enemy ship ahead, finally showing its broadside to theirs. With a satisfying crash and crunch of wood on wood, his fellow shipmen struggling to lift their oars clear from the other ship, they smashed directly through it, as though butter and a hot seax, and then they were clear. Two halves of the enemy ship wallowed low in the water, the horrified cries of their enemy filling the air, as Eowa calmly ordered them to steady their pace and turn the ship once more.

With every other oar hauled on board the ship, Ælfgar and his fellow warriors went to the grisly task of killing their floundering foemen before any other could rescue them. Ælfgar killed enemy shipman after enemy shipman by thrusting his seax into their scalps or hacking their hands clear from where they grabbed the side of the ship.

He took little pleasure in it, other than knowing he had no choice.

Finally, chest heaving, blood staining his already bleeding hands, he turned to meet the smirk on Eowa's face. The sea had miraculously calmed now that the enemy had been killed or routed. Some of the ships had slunk away, the occasional lucky Viking raider first hauled on board, but Ælfgar had eyes only for the ships where his cousins and uncle had battled. Did they live? How he hoped they lived.

39
LEOFRIC

'My lord king,' Leofric spoke softly, not wishing to unduly alarm his king, but it was time Edward made some decisions. Since news of Earl Beorn's fate had been known, the king had brooded and done little else other than order that his cousin's body be removed from its shallow grave. It was to be brought to Winchester. Beorn was to be interred beside his uncle, King Cnut. Leofric thought it only right.

'My lord king,' he repeated. The storm had blown itself out. Now, the only tempest to be heard came from the king's ship men—those loyal to Earl Beorn above all others. Leofric knew the king was in an even more difficult situation now than ever before.

'I hear you, Lord Leofric,' the king murmured. 'I hear you, and I know something must be done. Do we know more? Has Earl Godwine returned, as demanded.'

'We know more, yes, but there's no sight of Earl Godwine yet.'

'Then, I'd hear what happened to my cousin. Bring those to me who witnessed it all.'

Leofric nodded, thinking nothing of the fact the king ordered him as though he was a servant. After all, he was the king's servant, and had been for almost all of his life.

He didn't have far to go, Edwin Haroldsson was waiting within the king's hall. He'd been joined by one of Earl Beorn's most loyal warriors. The man had been poorly used, and a bandage covered his chest and a livid pair of blackening eyes starred at Leofric. There was no denying that Osbeorn had fought for his friend's life.

'The king will hear you now,' Leofric told the pair. Edwin stood, resolved. Osbeorn was slower to respond, and when he stood, he swayed. With a quick look to Edwin, they both took one of Osbeorn's arms, and held him steady.

Close to the hearth, the king watched their steps, while servants hastily brought chairs and arranged them close to the king. While all might have now learned of Earl Beorn's fate, this was to be a private conversation. With Osbeorn and then Edwin settled, Leofric made to move aside.

'No, Lord Leofric, you must listen as well. I'd not repeat the truth of this matter again.'

'My lord king,' he inclined his head, and sought a chair.

Silence grew in the small group, and then he cleared his throat. It appeared he must begin the conversation.

'Osbeorn, good man, please, tell me and the king what befell Earl Beorn.'

Osbeorn nodded, but didn't look up. He was twisting something between his fingers, and Leofric wondered what it was, but didn't ask.

'My lord king,' Osbeorn's words were accented with the Danish tongue, but he spoke English well, as did so many. 'That bastard Sweyn,' and he made no apology for his language, and the king didn't so much as flutter an eyelid, 'came to Pevensey and prevailed upon Earl Beorn to speak to you, on his behalf. He'd been to Bosham, one of the Godwine estates. He'd not left England, as you commanded.' The words were tight with fury. 'Earl Beorn, he didn't wish to help Sweyn, but Sweyn told him stories of how Beorn's brother, King Svein of Denmark, had pledged his assurance to Sweyn that Beorn would aid him. Sweyn Godwinesson said that Svein Estridsson had said if he did not do so he would never again be welcome in Denmark, and would never again be able to see his mother. I'm sure the bastard lied, but Beorn has, or rather had hoped for reconciliation with his brother. He reluctantly agreed to do as Sweyn asked and to come with him, to speak to you, my lord king.'

This deceit on the part of Sweyn Godwinesson pulled at Leofric. He knew Lady Estrid would never have refused to see her youngest son.

'They returned to Bosham, and Earl Beorn believed they'd ride to Sandwich, the weather being so terrible, but then Sweyn Godwinesson changed his mind, and said they'd come by ship, after all, but not in Beorn's ship, only in his.' Osbeorn's words trembled as he spoke.

'Earl Beorn was uneasy, I could tell from where I watched all. Sweyn Godwinesson was filled with good humour, and kept embracing him, and talking of the estates he would soon reclaim as his own. Beorn wished to argue, but then, he was overpowered by Sweyn's shipmen, and there was nothing we could do against the greater force that Sweyn commanded, and had turned to his terrible deed.'

'I rushed to Sweyn's ship, to follow where it went, but we couldn't catch it. The storm pushed us away from it, and when we finally caught the ship, close to Dartmouth, it was too late. They'd murdered Beorn. We witnessed them burying the body, and hastened to attack them, but after only a brief sea battle, the wind aided them and they escaped.' The man let loose a low moan, as though keening for his lost lord, and Leofric laid a soothing hand on Hunter's back, where she'd rushed to her paws, as though needing to defend him.

'And what of Earl Godwine?' King Edward's tone was sharp with anger.

'He wasn't there.'

'He must be informed of what's happened,' Edward announced, already summoning a servant to him and muttering that he needed fast riders to carry a message for him. 'I'll also issue a writ that should Sweyn Godwinesson be seen on English land, he's to be detained, or executed, if he can't be detained. Lord Leofric, please, will you arrange to send word to Lady Estrid, and King Svein of Denmark. I want them to know as soon as possible.' His words were decisive, but filled with sorrow. Beorn and Edward's friendship had been unlikely, but firm.

'I'll find a ship immediately that's going to Denmark,' Leofric confirmed, standing and walking away from the king. At the door to the hall, he paused and turned back to gaze at the king, Edwin and Osbeorn. All three men had heads bowed with grief.

Leofric swallowed his sorrow.

Earl Beorn had been a good man. He hadn't deserved to die at the hands of Sweyn Godwinesson. All the same, he allowed a sad smile to play on his lips. Just how, he considered, did Earl Godwine expect to escape from this fresh catastrophe unscathed?

40

GLOUCESTER, ÆLFGAR

THEY MORE STAGGERED THAN JUMPED FROM THE SHIPS. EYES WIDE, ON unsteady feet, he helped Eowa, and then turned to assist others of his fellow warriors.

Some wore bandages, sea-stained and rusty brown while others lay, forever staring in the bilge water. But he had eyes only for those other ships that had survived the storm and the attack.

His uncle. His cousins. He hoped they yet lived.

The Viking raiders were gone. None had followed them into the estuary and then further inland to Gloucester. If any survived, then they were running back to wherever they'd come from. Ælfgar hoped this would put an end to Gruffydd ap Rhydderch's involvement with the Viking raiders, but he wasn't sure. Truly, it was Gruffydd ap Llewelyn who should have borne the brunt of the attack, but that wasn't what had happened.

'Ælfgar,' his name thrummed through the air, as he turned and met the haunted expression of Wulfstan. They embraced, even with Eowa between them. The older man had fought through his wound, but now his eyes lacked all focus, and Ælfgar knew he needed warm clothes and rest.

The men and women who'd flocked to the charred quayside, rushed to aid those who came back. The soft sobbing of those who had only a body to return to them, meant Ælfgar's grin of relief at seeing Wulfstan slowly slipped from his lips.

'Ælfwine? Olaf? Otryggr?' he asked, but Wulfstan shook his head.

'I don't know,' he cried. 'I've only just seen you. I thought you lost as well.' Wulfstan had a strip of cloth tied tightly around the top of his right arm, and his face was pale. Ælfgar sniffed, and then regretted it for Wulfstan smelt of vomit and piss.

Together, they manoeuvred Eowa to the ground, clear from the water and the hurrying feet of others. They stood, side by side, heaving in much needed air as they surveyed the scene.

'We lost at least two ships,' Wulfstan commented. 'I saw them go under. Some of the shipmen managed to make their way to us, or to one of the other ships.'

The wind had fallen away as though there'd never been a storm and the passage back along the River Severn had been accomplished easily enough, the estuary being kind for once.

Warm blankets were thrust around their shoulders, by a concerned looking woman of middle-years, another followed on, offering beakers of warm pottage. Ælfgar ate eagerly, feeling the ache in his limbs as he relaxed. But, where were his other two cousins, and Olaf?

As though summoned by the thought, he saw a figure he recognised pushing his way through the crowd. Orkning, Olaf's brother. His eyes were frantic as he spied Ælfgar.

'My son? My brother?'

'I don't know,' Ælfgar admitted grudgingly, as the other man slumped as though felled by a blow. 'They'll be well, I'm sure of it,' he continued, but he wasn't as convinced as he sounded.

They'd been entirely outnumbered. That they had the victory was perhaps more down to the weather than any great skill.

'Did the king's reinforcements arrive?' Orkning queried.

'No, not as far as I know. The storm must have kept them at bay.'

'Eowa,' Orkning noticed the ship's commander, and bent before him, steady hands checking on his wounds.

'He needs tending to,' Orkning called over his shoulder, and the scurrying steps of someone rushing to do as Orkning demanded were obvious.

'There, another ship,' Wulfstan hurried forwards, but Ælfgar remained where he was, aware that Eowa leant against him still.

Quick calls from those who yet lived could be heard, and Ælfgar quickly saw Otryggr.

'There, Orkning, Otryggr is on that ship.' Orkning embraced his son quickly. The older man scampered away, relief evident in the way he quickly resumed control of the docking ship. Wounded were handed onto dry land. Those who were dead were left, for now.

Ælfgar watched with dull eyes. He wanted to cry for all they'd endured, but no tears would come. He felt hollowed by what he'd endured. Another ship limped along the quayside, and then another, but his cousin and uncle were still missing. Wulfstan stood with Orkning, the two of them taking command over the operation, as those ships commanders who'd survived, were helped or assisted their men.

Ælfgar didn't wish to count those ships that had reappeared. He could feel his hopes fading. Surely his father's second ship hadn't sunk. He thought of Lady Mildryth, Ælfwine's mother. And then he thought of Beorhtric, so newly come to his position as ship's commander.

He could sense the sun starting to set beneath the pale of thin, grey clouds. Eowa had long since been taken from his side, but still he stood. He felt useless, empty, broken.

Where was Ælfwine? Where was Olaf? And where was Beorhtric?

Braziers were lit on the quayside, and flaming brands as well, offering light to guide the ships home. And still, no other ship came.

The quayside quietened as the darkness increased. His hopes fled as the sky continued to darken.

This wasn't his fault, and yet he felt responsible. Why had the king not responded sooner to the request for more ships? Why hadn't his father prevailed upon the king? Anger stalked him as he strode to the ships that had returned. Not wishing to, but knowing he had to, all the same, he took a brand and began to search the grisly cargo of dead, white, lifeless bodies.

Men he knew, and boys he didn't, lay forever staring, their wounds gaping and horrifying. He gagged more than once.

'Leave it,' Orkning grabbed him from behind, his words not unkind. 'Leave it, Ælfgar. You don't need to do this now.'

'I do,' Ælfgar muttered. 'I had the nominal command. This is my fault.'

'It's not,' Orkning remained firm, as he hauled Ælfgar back onto the slick quayside. 'Anyway, they might have been forced ashore further south. It's not impossible that they're there, worrying about you, just as you worry about them now.' A spark of hope allowed Ælfgar to nod along with his uncle's brother.

'Yes, they might be further south. At Bristol?' he murmured.

'I've sent a fast rider there already,' Orkning confirmed. Again, Ælfgar nodded.

His desolation didn't quite fade, but it enabled him to stop his morbid search through the dead. Only then he heard it, a shushing sound through the night time air.

'Bloody hell,' and he heard Ælfwine's voice. 'You could have built a bigger bloody fire to help us see.' The complaint was petulant, filled with pain. Ælfgar rushed back to the quayside's edge. He was no longer alone in holding a brand, and now with the night lit by flames, he saw Olaf, a bloody bandage around his chest, Ælfwine, a gap-toothed smile on his lips, and then Beorhtric, commanding the men as they powered into view, only half the benches filled.

Men had died. Good men and Ælfgar would mourn them, but his family was still complete, and finally, he cried. Tears of relief, and sorrow and terror. And anger at the king. And at the Welsh king who'd brought this about, and at Sweyn, who's damn fault this was. His legacy as an earl had been terrible.

41

LEOMINSTER, LADY GODGIFU

'My lady,' Abbess Eadgifu smiled on meeting her at the door to her private room, and Lady Godgifu returned the smile. Better to share some joy now than when she's imparted her message to her. She could easily here the chuckles of small boys and no doubt, the other nuns, as they played with them. It was rare to hear such joy in a nunnery, but Lady Godgifu found comfort in it, rather that offense.

'It's been some time since we last met. Your boys thrive?' she asked the other woman. Abbess Eadgifu was two decades younger than Godgifu, and wore her youth lightly. Not that Godgifu felt any jealousy. No, as with the queen, she felt some pity for her plight, and yet was also in awe of all that Eadgifu had accomplished.

'Hakon and Tostig are very well, thank you.' A faint blush was all Abbess Eadgifu offered to mask the trauma she'd been through when Sweyn Godwinesson had abducted her, raped her, and then forced her to marry him, only to then cast her aside. 'But what brings you to Leominster? The king is well?' Eadgifu asked hastily. 'And your husband, sons and grandchildren?'

Godgifu nodded, taking the seat offered to her. There was no blaze in the hearth. It was a warm day, even the wind bringing no relief from the heat. It was unexpected for September, but welcome all the same.

'We are well, my dear, thank you for your concern.'

'I pray for your good husband, and the king,' Abbess Eadgifu murmured.

'And we thank you for such care. But no. I'm here for an altogether different reason.' Lady Godgifu had taken the burden upon herself. Now she worried that the unenviable task of informing the abbess that her husband had murdered his cousin shouldn't have fallen to her.

'What has he done now?' It seemed Eadgifu's thoughts weren't far from Godgifu's own.

Lady Godgifu paused, taking a moment to consider the best way of replying. It was nothing short of a miracle that Eadgifu didn't know about it already.

'It is regarding Sweyn Godwinesson, yes. This will be difficult to hear. I'll simply say the words bluntly, there's no softening to this. Sweyn Godwinesson has murdered his cousin, Earl Beorn Estridsson.' The gasp from the abbess was filled with horror, even as she slipped to her knees, hands clasped before her, soft prayers on her lips.

'He prevailed upon Beorn to speak to the king on his behalf, and then had him violently murdered, and abandoned in a shallow grave. The king has arranged for Beorn to be retrieved, and placed beside his uncle, King Cnut, in Winchester.'

Still, the soft prayers mumbled from Abbess Eadgifu's lips, and alongside them, tears slipped from her closed eyes. Lady Godgifu looked away. She didn't need to witness such grief for a man who deserved none at all. He should have been dead these last few years. The archbishop and bishop should have done more than just excommunicate him. The king should have done more than just outlaw him. Sweyn Godwinesson should never have been allowed to wreak such havoc on his family.

'The king has declared him *nithing*. He'll never be allowed to step foot on English soil again.'

Once more, the laughter-filled voices of two small boys could be heard inside the small room into which Lady Godgifu had been shown. She winced at the reminder of all the abbess had endured.

Only then, a claw-like hand was on her arm, and she met the beseeching eyes of Eadgifu.

'Tell me the king won't take my children. Tell me.'

'The king has no designs on your sons, for that's what they are—your sons. As with Lady Estrid, Beorn's mother, it is to you your sons will look for all guidance. And if they need another, it will be the king himself, or the queen. Your children are safe, provided there's no contact with Sweyn, ever again.'

'I wish to never see him. But, will I be safe here? Will he come for his children?'

'No, he won't. The king has determined he'll be executed should he be found in England again. All know of this. The churches will spread the news. The bishops. The earls. The king's thegns and the thegns. Any man or woman of consequence will face no recrimination should they encounter Sweyn and him be killed as a result of it. I know this is a place of God, prayer and now, children, but you must have this.' And Lady Godgifu slipped into Eadgifu's hand a seax, the blade sharp, the sheath conveying the holy symbol of the dove, and as the woman sobbed, Godgifu pressed the weapon into her hand, and then left her.

Abbess Eadgifu carried a heavy burden, but Lady Godgifu was as sure as she could be, that should Sweyn ever show his face here, he'd be dead before he could so much as demand entry to the nunnery.

That gave her small comfort.

42

AD1049, WINCHESTER, LEOFRIC

'My lord king,' Earl Godwine's voice was broken with grief, yet Leofric knew no sympathy for his plight. After all, he was alive. The same couldn't be said for his nephew. Leofric kept his eyes on the king.

'Earl Godwine, once more I assure you, I have no interest in speaking to you further about this matter. Your son is a *nithing*. He may never again set foot in England. He was not just your nephew, Earl Beorn was also my kin.'

Silence filled the hall. Nothing stirred other than the crackle of a fire, far back in the hall. Leofric felt as though everyone there breathed together, in unison. All apart from Lord Godwine who huffed and puffed, his vast belly, straining against his warriors belt, devoid now of all sharpened blades.

Leofric's view shifted slightly, to take in that of the queen. The queen was without child, as the king had always promised. She was also the brother of a traitor many times over. Sweyn had undertaken the most despicable of deeds. Perhaps, after all, there was more Danish in the damn bastard than there was English-man. Certainly, it would behove Earl Godwine, no matter the dishonour it would heap upon his wife, to cast aside Sweyn once and for all. But Leofric knew he wouldn't. Earl Godwine was a stubborn man. He wouldn't do that to his wife.

He was the biggest fool Leofric knew. Earl Godwine believed the king would forgive all. Leofric knew the king wouldn't. The king was furious. It had been bad enough when Sweyn had treated with the Welsh king and stolen the abbess and kept her against her will. The murder of Lord Beorn was another matter entirely. Leofric knew, because he'd been the one to tell the king what had happened. In this, the king wouldn't falter, as he might have done in the past.

'News of this calamity has been sent to Lady Estrid Sveinssdottir. She'll demand the wergild for her son. This will fall on you to pay, not once but twice over.' Leofric nodded. This wasn't an insubstantial sum, and yet it was obvious that Lord Godwine and his wealthy family would have no difficulty in paying the sum.

'My lord king,' and still Lord Godwine thought to complain. He sounded like a petulant child.

'My lord,' the king's words were colder now. Leofric was amazed that Godwine didn't hear the censure in them. 'You'll do well to remember who's king here. Be grateful I've not cast aside your daughter and outlawed your entire family.'

At last, that seemed to deprive Lord Godwine of all arguments, and Leofric felt the tension in the room ease as the business of the witan moved on to less controversial matters. All the same, he watched Lord Godwine, and couldn't fail to notice the grief that marred Earl Harold's face for the death of his cousin.

LEOFRIC STOOD UNCERTAINLY at the back of the Old Minster in Winchester. Ahead, he could make out the familiar but long-since absent figure of Lady Estrid, mother of Earl Beorn. He longed to pray with her as she visited her son's final resting place. But this was a matter for family, and he wasn't family and never had been.

Instead, he watched, seething quietly, as Earl Godwine, and his expansive waist and his wife, showing the ravages of her decades of childbearing, attended upon Lady Estrid. The king had even allowed his mother to attend this private ceremony of remembrance, even though she'd been all but banished from court. Not that he'd been excluded. And indeed, he'd already caught the king's eye, and knew that he was welcome here, even if it didn't feel as though he was.

Leofric thought sorrowfully of the events of last year when Sweyn Godwinesson had murdered Earl Beorn. Sweyn hadn't been seen since. Certainly, he'd made no attempt to take his children from their mother. But, in the intervening period, relations between the king and his wife's family had deteriorated. Not even Earl Harold was overly welcome in the king's court. Instead, it was to him and to Earl Siward that the king turned with increasing regularity for advice. Earl Siward stood close by, an old friend of Lady Estrid, his head bowed in sorrow to match the sombre family reunion.

Leofric closed his eyes, and murmured his own soft prayers in gratitude for the safe return of his son, nephews, and Olaf and his nephew. He'd heard about the dangers the ships army had endured fighting the Viking raider fleet to the west. Internally he seethed at that. If not for Sweyn and his antics, then Earl Godwine and Harold would have been there to assist the small Mercian force, led by his son. Not that he wasn't proud of Ælfgar. He was. All of his family. But the risks they'd been forced to take had been too great. The king, he knew was aware of it. Earl Godwine was oblivious. Earl Harold had arrived in time to ensure the enemy made no further attempts against the weakened force that had lost three ships, and near-enough a hundred ship-men to the enemy's blades, and the ferocious storm.

'My lord Leofric,' Lady Estrid was before him, her eyes hazed with pain, her back rigid with defiance. He gazed into the well-known but subtly altered face. The passage of time had been kind to her. He couldn't say the same for himself.

'My lady, my sympathies.' A brittle smile cracked her lips as she gripped his forearm. The others had moved aside. There was just the two of them, together, hallowed by the light of the candles, the ceiling stretching away far overhead. Lady Estrid inclined her head, no doubt searching his face as he did hers.

'That family are bastards,' she murmured, although her words were filled with blades. 'That family are bastards,' she repeated. 'They always have been, and they always will be. My brother was a damn fool. But there's time for your king. For Edward. Keep him away from them. Drive a wedge between them and the king. For if you don't, my living son will have every single last one of them murdered. And if that fails, then my lord, King Svein Estridsson of Denmark, will come for England, just as his uncle, and my father did. I warn you; these words are not ill-spoken. We will have our revenge.'

He gasped at the threat, her grip intensifying, and then he nodded. A slow smile spread across his lips.

He might not have looked for an ally in Denmark. But it seemed he had one, all the same. And this one was far from unwelcome.

Together, they emerged from the gloom of the Old Minster in Winchester. He didn't smile and neither did Lady Estrid.

The family of Godwine had broken both of them, but they would gain their vengeance. No matter what.

ANGLO-SAXON CHRONICLE ENTRY FOR 1049

'Here in this year the emperor gathered a countless army against Baldwin of Bruges, because he had broken down the palace at Nijmegen, and also caused him many other offences. The army which he had gathered was untold, there was: Leo, the pope from Rome, and numerous famous men from many nations. He also sent to King Edward, and asked him for support with ships so that he would now allow his escape by water. And then he [Edward] went to Sandwich, and there lay with a great raiding ship-army until the emperor had all that he wanted from Baldwin. There Earl Swein came back again to King Edward, and begged him for land so that he could maintain himself on it; but Harold his brother, and Earl Beorn, opposed it, in that they did not want to give him back anything of what the king had given to them. He came here with guile, said that he wanted to be his [the king's] man, and asked Earl Beorn that he should be of help to him, but the king refused him everything. Then Swein turned to Bosham to his ships, and Earl Godwine went from Sandwich with 42 ships to Pevensey, and Earl Beorn along with him. Then the king allowed all the Mercians to go home, and they did so. Then when the king was informed that Osgod [Osgot] lay in Wulpe with 29 ships, the king sent after the ships he could send for, which lay within the North Mouth. But Osgod set his wife in Bruges, and turned back again with 6 ships, and the others went to Eadulf's Ness in Essex and did harm there and turned back to the ships. Earl Godwine and Earl Beorn then lay at Pevensey with their ships. Then Earl Swein came with treachery and asked Earl Beorn that he should be his companion to Sandwich to the king – said that he wanted to swear him oaths and always be loyal to him. Then, because of their kinship, Beorn imagined that he would not betray him, then took 3 companions with him, and then rode (just as if they were to go to Sandwich) to Bosham, where Swein's ships lay. And he was immediately bound and led on ship, and then conveyed to Dartmouth, and there killed and buried deep. But Harold, his relative, fetched him from there and led [him] to Winchester, and there buried [him] with King Cnut, his uncle. And the king and all the raiding-army then declared Swein to be a 'nithing.' He had 8 ships before he murdered Beorn; afterwards all abandoned him except 2. And then he returned to Bruges, and lived there with Baldwin.' (C)

HISTORICAL NOTES

When I began writing The Earls of Mercia series, I did so with the idea of following the story of this period as reported in The Anglo-Saxon Chronicle, thinking it the most contemporary of all accounts. Since then, and particularly in the few years since writing the last book, my research has revealed to me that I'm somewhat mistaken in this belief. The nine extant recensions were not only written at different times but also not necessarily all at that period in time or by one hand. While elements of the 'A' version are the oldest, they are not believed to be 'the oldest' (please see Pauline Stafford's work, After Alfred, for a full explanation of the incredibly complex history of the writing of the chronicles – it is fascinating, I promise.)

That said, I could hardly abandon my ethos half way through the series, and so once more, this is based on what is known from the Anglo-Saxon Chronicles. Still, there are a number of disconnects in the surviving manuscripts of this period – entries that are out of sync with others, and this it seems, has created something of a discrepancy in the period being written about. Did Sweyn ally with the Welsh king in 1046 or 1047? Did the pirates attack in 1047 or 1048? Having true knowledge of this does impact how the entries can be interpreted. These issues seem to primarily affect the D and E version, where some entries are dated a year early, or a year too late – as far as can be determined. Many of the entries are also overly concerned with the affairs of the churchmen, with more secular matters only occasioning a brief mention. This perhaps speaks to the surviving versions being held at religious centres at that time. That said, the C version is associated with Abingdon and is dated to this time period. However, the association with Abingdon has been challenged and is based on the attribution in the sixteenth century by John Joscelyn. The D version is associated with Worcester, and is difficult to date, and the E version is associated with Peterborough. As such, the C and D are perceived to be more Mercian orientated, and E, perhaps more Godwineist, with its compilation dated to the early twelfth century, and so likely to have been tainted with the knowledge of later events.

'Work on C was in large part completed before 1066. Its making and its continuations can be fairly closely dated...Up to the annal for 1048, it is the work of two scribes, and of several scribes thereafter.' (p.191, After Alfred, Pauline Stafford) It is found in London BL, MS Cotton Tiberius B. i and with the other contents of that manuscript, 'the aim was...to produce a 'book of histories.' (p.191, After Alfred, Pauline Stafford). It can be securely dated to 1045 to 1048. 'His [the scribe] work on the annals 1045-1048 seems to have been undertaken on two or three separate occasions; although there is agreement that this is the same scribe, his work has a different appearance from annal 1045 onwards.' (p.192-3, After Alfred, Pauline Stafford) This raises the possibility that C was a copy of another chronicle (now lost) and that only in 1045-1048 were its entries contemporary or near-contemporary, the entries prior to these having been copied from another, lost version of the Anglo-Saxon Chronicle. As you can perceive from this brief look at Pauline Stafford's fabulous work, which has taken twenty years to complete, the precise nature of these entries, and the annals themselves, is complex and often defies a clearly defined explanation.

You can view the C version of the Anglo-Saxon Chronicle online.

https://www.bl.uk/manuscripts/FullDisplay.aspx?ref=Cotton_MS_Tiberius_B_I

All quotes in this book are taken from The Anglo-Saxon Chronicles by M Swanton.

The interaction between the king, his wife's family, and Leofric and his family continues to perplex me. Earl Godwine was powerful. Earl Leofric was powerful. The king was powerful. Why, then was one not able to overawe the other? Edward's father, King Æthelred II, is permanently tarnished as being too easily swayed by his ealdormen. Yet, this period seems a little different, and Edward has a much better reputation than his father – indeed, he has saintly status. He is Edward the Confessor, and his father is Æthelred the Unready, although the exact phrase is Æthelred Unræd, which means 'ill-counselled.' I'm keen to continue my research into the period and events and to draw my own conclusions on what might actually have been happening.

There are several extant law codes from the Saxon periods. More often than not, these were promulgated in the name of a king, and indeed, some kings issued more than one law code. These are usually given Roman Numerals to differentiate them, for instance, II Cnut. As with all surviving manuscripts from this period, it's as important to understand why these law codes have survived as it is what they contain. There is equally a discussion to be had about whether these law codes were enacted or whether these were the 'ideals' by which the Saxon kings thought to provide good law and order.

While we have a specific belief in 'right' and 'wrong' in our laws, it is thought that the laws of the Saxons were often applied with the thought of causing the least amount of trouble. Often, a compromise was sought. (See Crime and Punishment in Anglo-Saxon England by Andrew Rabin for a fascinating look at, well, crime and punishment.)

In the discussion about what crime Lord Sweyn should be charged with after abducting the Abbess of Leominster, I have made use of translations by Dorothy Whitelock, in English Historical

Documents Vol 1, of Extracts from the Laws of Cnut (1020-1023), Concerning the Betrothal of a Woman and also The law of the Northumbrian Priests (dated to 1020-23) in which the law about a nun lying with a man and both of them needing to pay wergild was found. It interests me that Sweyn was able to 'get away' with abducting the abbess but fell foul of the church by claiming their lands, and only then was outlawed – again, this might have more to do with the belief that in the case of justice, causing the least amount of trouble was preferable. Undoubtedly, the king didn't wish to outlaw his brother by marriage. It was storing trouble for later in his reign. And poor Earl Beorn was the first victim of that.

Affairs with the Welsh kings are complicated. One current interpretation shows Edward encouraging Sweyn to ally with Gruffydd ap Llewelyn; another has Sweyn acting without the king's knowledge. The truth may lie somewhere in between.

My initial intention with this book was to follow events to 1051, but I have yet to make it that far. As I wrote the story, I realised that it was essential to add more depth. I do hope you welcome the arrival of Lady Godgifu and her own part to play in this series. I have, so far, underused her, and it was time to correct that.

ACKNOWLEDGMENTS

I must thank you, my loyal readers, for waiting for this next book in the series. It has been a long time coming, and I must apologise for this. I have every intention of finishing this series, but it may take some time with my other writing commitments.

CAST OF CHARACTERS

THE HOUSE OF LEOFWINE

Leofric, born 998

m. **Lady Godgifu** in 1018

Ælfgar, son, born in 1018

m.**Lady Elgiva**, the daughter of Morcar (a thegn murdered by Eadric Streona) and Ealdgyth, the niece of Ealdorman Ælfhelm (murdered on Æthelred II's orders).

Burgheard – b. 1038

Eadwine – b. 1039

Ealdgyth – b. 1041

Morcar – b. 1042

Ealdgyth, Leofric's sister born 1000

m. **Olaf** son of **Horic** (fictional, but so is Ealdorman Leofwine's daughter – the vague understanding that he had five children, one of whom is unnamed.) Two children

Brother Leofric of Peterborough (historically accurate, although perhaps not at this time)

Æthelflæd (fictional)

Godwine, his younger brother born 1002,

Eadwine, his younger brother born 1006, Sheriff of Shropshire, dies in 1039 at the hands of the Welsh king

Leofwine, father of Leofric and his brothers and sister, Ealdorman of the Hwicce/Earl of Mercia under Cnut, although difficult to pinpoint where his power was based (dies 1023). Son of **Ælfwine,** who dies at the Battle of Maldon in 991.

m. **Æthelflæd**

Northman, Leofwine's oldest son, born in 996, was executed 1017 on the orders of Cnut.

m. **Mildryth** in 1011(fictional)

Wulfstan born1012 (fictional)

Ælfwine born 1014(fictional)

LEOFRIC'S HOUSEHOLD

Orkning (son of Horic, one of Leofwine's household troop)

Otryggr – his son

Olaf (son of Horic) married Ealdgyth, Leofric's sister (not historically attested)

Godwulf, Winhus, Scirwold, Cena, Osric and Æthelheard, some of Leofric's warriors

Edmund, Æthelred, Wulfhere, some of Ælfgar's warriors

KING OF NORWAY

Magnus, the illegitimate son of King Olaf Haraldsson of Norway, becomes King of Norway in 1035, following Swein Cnutsson's exile, and with the support of two regents and his father's wife, Astrid, who was not his mother but was the sister of the king of the Svear

(Sweden) Anund Jakob.

KINGS OF ENGLAND AND THEIR FAMILIES

Æthelred II of England (dies April 1016),

m. 1) **Ælfgifu of York**

He has nine children – six sons and three daughters, of which the below are mentioned.

Edmund Ironside (d.1016) marries the widow of Sigeforth before his death, Ealdgyth, has 2 sons,

Edward the Exile m. **Agatha** has 3 children, **Edgar, Christina, Margaret**

Edmund Ætheling

m. 2) **Emma of Normandy**

Lord Edward, now king of England m. Edith, daughter of Godwine

Lord Alfred (dies 1037 in England)

Countess Godgifu, Dowager Countess of Vexin

m.1 Drogo, Count of Vexin (dies 1035)

Walter

Ralph, becomes an earl in England

Fulk

m.2. Eustace of Boulogne

KINGS OF DENMARK AND THEIR FAMILIES

Swein Forkbeard of Denmark (dies 1014)

Cnut (son) of England (from 1016 with Edmund/1017 sole ruler of England) and Denmark (from 1018, after the death of his brother, Harald).

m.1.**Lady Ælfgifu**

Swein, King of Norway (1030-35)

Harald, Regent/King of England (1035-1040)

Secretly marries **Alfifa,** one son, **Ælfwine** (he is mentioned in the historical record)

m.2.**Lady Emma**

Harthacnut, King of Denmark AD1035-1042, King of England 1040-1042

Gunnhilda, married to **Henry**, son of **Conrad II**, Holy Roman Emperor, died in 1038 but had a daughter, **Beatrix**, before her death.

Harald of Denmark (from 1014 when his father, Swein, dies in England until 1018 when he dies).

Lady Estrid, daughter of Swein Forkbeard, wife of Earl Ulfr, with whom she has two children

Svein Estridsson (take their mother's name, not their father's.)

Beorn Estridsson

Asbjorn is thought to be a son of her husband, but not her son.

WELSH KINGS

Gruffydd ap Llewelyn – King of Powys and later Gwynedd

Gruffydd ap Rhydderch – King of Gwent

CNUT'S WIVES

Lady Emma, Queen Dowager (King Æthelred's second wife – mother of Edward, Alfred and Godgifu) (King Cnut's wife from Summer 1017 – mother of Harthacnut (son) and Gunnhilda (daughter))

Lady Ælfgifu (King Cnut's first wife, even though also married to Emma – sons Harald and Swein.)

EARLS, NOBLEMEN/WOMEN AND OTHER COURT NOTABLES

Earl Hrani (Herefordshire) died in 1042

Earl Godwine (of Kent and later Wessex)

Married to **Lady Gytha**, sister of Earls Ulfr and Eilifr

Sweyn, Earl of Hereford from AD1043

With Abbess Eadgifu two sons**, Hakon and Tostig**

Harold, Earl of the East Angles

Tostig

Edith married King Edward in 1045

Gyth

Leofwine

Wulfnoth

Elgiva

Gunnhilda

Earl Siward of Northumbria married Ealdred of Bamburgh's daughter, Eadwulf of Bamburgh's niece.

His son, **Osbjorn** – his son, with first wife, not the Earl of Bamburgh's daughter/niece

Earl Leofric of Mercia (see above)

Earl Sweyn Godwinesson of Hereford – takes over Earl Hrani's vacant earldom

Osgot Clapa, not an earl but a prominent thegn, outlawed from England

Gunnhild, niece of King Cnut, outlawed in 1044 by King Edward

m.**1) Earl Hakon**

m. **2) Lord Harald** (son of Thorkell the Tall).

Hemming

Thurkill

HOLY MEN

Archbishop Eadsige – Archbishop of Canterbury, resigns in AD1044 due to infirmity; Siward replaces him as Bishop of Canterbury. Eadsige remains the figurehead. But then Siward resigns, and Eadsige retakes his position.

Brother Leofric (Leofric's nephew – historical, although perhaps not at this time.)

Bishop Ælfweard – Bishop of London until his death

Bishop Robert of Jumieges – Bishop of London

Bishop Æthelstan – Bishop of Hereford

Tremerig – aid to Bishop Æthelstan

Bishop Lyfing - of Worcester until his death

Bishop Aldred – of Worcester, after Lyfing's death

MISC (MOSTLY FICTIONAL)

Oswald – Leofric's horse

Commander Eowa – Leofric's ships commander

Brihtric – sailor

Hunter – Leofric's new hound

Ælfwold – the king's messenger

Edwin Haroldsson – one of Earl Beorn's allies

Osbeorn – one of Earl Beorn's allies

Ælfwold – the king's messenger

Lothen and Yrling – pirates – mentioned in the Anglo-Saxon Chronicle

Beorhtric – shipman

Hering – port reeve of Thanet

Æthelwald – the leader of the king's huscarls

PLACES MENTIONED

St Peter's Church, London – would become Westminster Abbey

Deerhurst – the ancestral home of House of Leofwine (this is my assertion), from about now onwards, it is associated with Odda of Deerhurst

Oxford –House of Leofwine holds land there (according to Domesday Book).

Shropshire – on the border with the Welsh kingdoms, its capital is **Shrewsbury.**

Gloucester – the River Severn flows through Gloucester

Hereford – on the border with the Welsh kingdoms

The Foss, Ermine Street, Icknield Way, Watling Street – the oldest roads in England

Sandwich – busy harbour, where Harthacnut claimed the English crown

Coventry – part of Mercia. According to Domesday Book, Leofric held land there, and Lady Godgifu is heavily associated with Coventry

Ditton Priors, Wellington, Ford, Ellesmere, Emstry, High Ercall, Crudington, Doddington, Much Hadham, Mathan – all places named as belonging to the family of the House of Leofwine in Shropshire in Domesday Book

The River Severn and the Severn Estuary – flows through Gloucester and Shrewsbury

The River Wye – flows through Hereford

ABOUT THE AUTHOR

I'm an author of fantasy (Viking-age/dragon-themed) and historical fiction (Early English, Vikings and the British Isles as a whole before the Norman Conquest), born in the old Mercian kingdom at some point since the end of Anglo-Saxon England. I write A LOT. You've been warned! Find me at https://mjporterauthor.com mjporter-author.blog and @coloursofunison on twitter.

BOOKS BY M J PORTER (IN SERIES READING ORDER)

Gods and Kings Series (seventh century Britain)

Pagan Warrior

Pagan King

Warrior King

The Eagle of Mercia Chronicles

Son of Mercia

Wolf of Mercia

Warrior of Mercia

Enemy of Mercia

Protector of Mercia

The Ninth Century

Coelwulf's Company, Tales from Before The Last King

The Last King

The Last Warrior

The Last Horse

The Last Enemy

The Last Sword

The Last Shield

The Last Seven

The Tenth Century

The Lady of Mercia's Daughter

A Conspiracy of Kings

Kingmaker

The King's Daughters

The Brunanburh Series

King of Kings

Kings of War

The Mercian Brexit (can be read as a prequel to The First Queen of England)

The First Queen of England (can be read as a prequel to The Earls of Mercia)

The First Queen of England Part 2

The First Queen of England Part 3

The King's Mother (can be read as a sequel to The First Queen, or a prequel to The Earls of Mercia)

The Queen Dowager

Once A Queen

The Earls of Mercia

The Earl of Mercia's Father

The Danish King's Enemy

Swein: The Danish King

Northman Part 1

Northman Part 2

Cnut: The Conqueror

Wulfstan: An Anglo-Saxon Thegn

The King's Earl

The Earl of Mercia

The English Earl

The Earl's King

Viking King

The English King

The King's Brother

Lady Estrid: A novel of Eleventh-Century Denmark (related to the Earls of Mercia series)

Fantasy

The Dragon of Unison (fantasy based on Viking Age Iceland)

Hidden Dragon

Dragon Gone

Dragon Alone

Dragon Ally

Dragon Lost

Dragon Bond

As JE Porter

The Innkeeper

20th Century murder-mystery

Cragside – a 1930s mystery

The Erdington Mysteries

The Custard Corpses

The Automobile Assassination

Printed in Great Britain
by Amazon